IN THE HUSH OF THE NIGHT

ALSO BY THE AUTHOR

Novels

Evil Hours
Face Blind
Sweetie's Diamonds
A Hard Day's Death
Dark Side of the Morgue
Artifact of Evil
Torment—A Love Story
The Secrets on Chicory Lane

The Black Stiletto Saga

The Black Stiletto
The Black Stiletto: Black & White
The Black Stiletto: Stars & Stripes
The Black Stiletto: Secrets & Lies
The Black Stiletto: Endings & Beginnings
The Black Stiletto: The Complete Saga (anthology)

James Bond Novels

Zero Minus Ten
Tomorrow Never Dies (based on the screenplay)
The Facts of Death
High Time to Kill
The World is Not Enough (based on the screenplay)
DoubleShot
Never Dream of Dying
The Man with the Red Tattoo
Die Another Day (based on the screenplay)
The Union Trilogy (anthology)
Choice of Weapons (anthology)

Tie-In Novels

Tom Clancy's Splinter Cell (as "David Michaels")
Tom Clancy's Splinter Cell—Operation Barracuda (as "David Michaels")
Metal Gear Solid (based on the videogame)
Metal Gear Solid 2—Sons of Liberty (based on the videogame)
Hunt Through Napoleon's Web (as "Gabriel Hunt")
Homefront—the Voice of Freedom (co-written with John Milius)
Hitman: Damnation (based on the videogame series)
Dying Light—Nightmare Row (based on the videogame series)

Non-Fiction and Miscellany

The James Bond Bedside Companion
Jethro Tull—Pocket Essential
Thrillers—100 Must-Reads (contributor)
Tied-In: The Business, History, and Craft of Media Tie-In Writing (contributor)
Mystery Writers of America presents Ice Cold—Tales of Intrigue from the Cold War (co-editor, contributor)
12+1: Twelve Thrillers and a Play (anthology)

IN THE HUSH OF THE NIGHT

A NOVEL

RAYMOND BENSON

Skyhorse Publishing
A Herman Graf Book

Skyhorse Publishing books may be purchased in bulk at special discounts for sales promotion, corporate gifts, fund-raising, or educational purposes. Special editions can also be created to specifications. For details, contact the Special Sales Department, Skyhorse Publishing, 307 West 36th Street, 11th Floor, New York, NY 10018 or info@skyhorsepublishing.com.

Visit our website at www.skyhorsepublishing.com.

10 9 8 7 6 5 4 3 2 1

Library of Congress Cataloging-in-Publication Data is available on file.

Cover design by Brian Peterson
Cover photo credit: iStockphoto

Print ISBN: 978-1-5107-2987-2
Ebook ISBN: 978-1-5107-2989-6

Printed in the United States of America

FOR MY FAMILY

ACKNOWLEDGMENTS

The author wishes to thank the following individuals for their help: Michael A. Black, Susanna Calkins, Herman Graf, Will Graham, Iryna Iakusheva, Kim Lim, Cynthia Manson, and, as always, my wife Randi Frank. Finally, I send a very big "thank you" to the folks at FBI Chicago.

AUTHOR'S NOTE

While most of the locations featured in this story exist, Lakeway, Michigan, is fictional. The organization Safe Haven is inspired by the many real not-for-profits that provide help for victims.

1

Early May

So, you want to go to America?

The man had a pleasant voice. Rich and deep, with a solid timbre. He reminded her of a nicer version of her father.

"Yes," she replied.

After all, it's what she'd dreamed of doing someday. At last she had a chance.

It is an important decision, one you should carefully consider. It will change your life.

"I know."

Yana, what is your family name?

"Kravec."

Oh, that's right, Borya told me. Forgive me.

He was dressed sharply. A suit. He was in his forties, perhaps? Fifties? He vaguely resembled the American actor George Clooney. It was easy to talk to him.

"Borya said you could get me a job."

The man nodded. Nikolai was his name. Yana liked him.

That's right. A girl like you, yes, I can get you a job in America. Beauty goes a long way in America. You'll do just fine, believe me.

They sat in the back of the club, near the rear employee entrance. Yana had only a few minutes left before she had to dance again.

"What do I have to do?"

We need to get a photo of you so we can get a passport made and prepare your visa. Everything legal.

"How long will it take?"

He shrugged. *A week. No more than two.*

Yana wasn't stupid. She knew gold didn't grow on trees. She may have been from a small village, but she was pretty sure she could distinguish the swindlers from the honest businessmen. This was a pretty sweet deal. Could she trust him? *Should* she trust him? He exhibited an appearance that seemed to say he had a lot of money. Many of the Bratva types she had met—the Russian organized crime members—also wore designer clothing and smelled of wealth. Nikolai, however, possessed a softer demeanor. He was different from the toughs who occasionally visited the club.

"Tell me again about the job. Who will I be working for?"

At first you'll be a waitress or a house cleaner in New Jersey, maybe New York. Everyone starts there. But then you're free to pursue whatever you want. Some of the girls travel west to Chicago or Los Angeles. If you marry a wealthy American man, well, you will be set for life.

"I'd like to be a fashion model."

You certainly have the qualifications, Yana. I say that with respect. You are a very beautiful girl. Our people in America know how to get you seen by members of that industry. It happens all the time.

Yana was well aware that she was attractive to men. Twenty years old, tall, slender, brunette, and quite pretty. By the time she had gone through puberty, she knew how to use her looks to get what she wanted. Unfortunately, in the tiny village of Chudovo, there weren't many opportunities in life other than getting married to a rustic, uneducated laborer and working on a farm for the rest of her years. Yana couldn't stomach the selection of eligible bachelors in Chudovo. She wasn't about to throw away her dreams for one of them. As soon as she summoned the courage, Yana left home, went to the big city of St. Petersburg, and found a room in a boardinghouse on the southern side of the dark Neva River, complete with a view of the stately dome of St. Isaac's Cathedral. The most Westernized city in Russia was a vast onslaught of culture, art, fashion, and excitement, a metropolis that, for centuries, had yearned to be a part of the West.

The fight with her parents had been the prime motivator. They couldn't understand that she had ambitions beyond the dead end of her rural village. Her mother had argued nonstop when Yana announced she was leaving. Her father had said nothing. He was drunk. She hadn't bothered to contact them since arriving in St. Petersburg. They could stew in their juices. Father with his daily vodka, Mother with her constant criticism. Just because Yana had been the firstborn of four children didn't mean she always had to play surrogate parent. Would they even miss her? No. She believed her parents would only regret the loss of a servant who waited on them hand and foot.

Wouldn't they be surprised when they received a letter from America?

Nikolai Babikov opened a folder containing illustrated brochures and an American women's magazine, which he removed. He turned to a marked page and revealed photos of a gorgeous model in an advertisement.

This is Tania. She is from Kiev. I go to Ukraine and help girls there, too. Tania got a job with the Ford Model Agency. I helped her cross the Atlantic just fourteen months ago. I told you, I've arranged for many girls to move to the United States. You're not the only one who wants to leave Russia. I don't blame you. There are no prospects for young people here.

Yana had met Borya not long after her arrival in St. Petersburg. He was a handsome, burly bouncer at the cigarette smoke–filled Spy Bar, the trendy nightclub on Nevsky Prospect, just west of the Moyka River. As it was on the city's main drag, not far from the Dumskaya Ulitsa area that was populated by students, the place attracted a young crowd that liked to dance. Bikini-clad girls employed by the club served as incentives for the customers by gyrating on tables in the style of 1960s Western spy movies. Go-go girls. The design of the Spy Bar was very retro, to match. More important, the booze was cheap.

She had secured a position as a go-go girl within minutes. She was tempted to phone her parents and rub it in. Yana was working on the most cosmopolitan boulevard in all of St. Petersburg, where the road was lined with more chic American shops than any other street in Russia. Sadly, it was also populated by a higher number of homeless people.

Frankly, the job paid rather poorly, but the earnings were consistent, and Yana did get to keep her own tips. It was all right. After a month on the job, though, she had mentioned to Borya that she wished she could run away to America. He told her about his friend Nikolai and the service he did for people who wanted to inexpensively emigrate to the US. Borya had said Nikolai was very good and had a one hundred percent success rate. Yana told him to set up the meeting.

And here they were.

"When do you want to take my picture?"

How about right now? He removed a cell phone from his inside jacket pocket. *Stand up, your back against the wall.*

"Is there enough light?"

Yes.

He took several shots.

What nights do you work here?

"Every night but Sunday."

I will return when I have the papers. You can leave at the drop of a hat? It's not like making a reservation on United Airlines. The exit window is tiny. Big Port is a busy place. It's the busiest port in the country. You have to be in the right place at the right time. You'll be saving a lot of money by doing this. If you tried to leave the country the normal way, there would be all kinds of problems. This way, you'll have a work visa. It's called H-2B. You can look it up on the Internet.

Her break was over. Yana stood and held out a hand. "All right. Let's do it."

Nikolai grasped her hand. *I will be in touch. Remember—*

He held a finger to his lips.

—don't talk about it to anyone. We could get in trouble.

"I won't."

The man nodded, smiled, and bowed slightly. Then he said *Do svidaniya* and left.

Yana, her insides tingling with a sudden nervousness, went back to the club floor, climbed on her table, and began to dance to the Beatles' recording of "Twist and Shout."

The world was about to change for Yana Kravec. Everything would be better in America.

2

Late May

There goes the free weekend, Annie thought as the phone on the desk rang at six, the Friday before Memorial Day. It happened just as she had risen from her cluttered desk at the FBI Chicago field office, ready to shut down her computer, call it a day, and enjoy a full, long weekend ahead with no cases to work. A vacation of sorts.

The caller ID indicated it was the SSA.

"Hey, John," she answered.

"Is this Special Agent Annie Marino?"

She smiled. "No, she's left for the day. She's going to be gone all weekend. Completely out of touch. She's shutting off her cell phone and won't look at it again until Tuesday morning. But if you want to leave a message, I'll see that she gets it."

Supervisory Special Agent John Gladden replied, "She's *gone*? Why, it's only six o'clock! Special Agents work until at least ten on Fridays before a three-day weekend. I guess I'll just have to demote her. Make sure she never has a tap dance class ever again. Have her shuffle paper for a week or something."

"Ha. That's what I've been doing for two full days. And I'll quit the FBI before I stop going to tap class. What do you want, John?"

"No big deal. At least I don't think so. Maybe. You need to get in touch with Police Chief Bill Daniel in Lakeway, Michigan."

"Michigan?"

"Yeah, Newaygo County. I know it's not our territory, being *Chicago* and all, but I think they've got something there that will interest you."

"What's that?"

"A body. White female, unidentified as of yet, early twenties. Not sure of the details, but the chief alerted the Bureau when he came to the conclusion that she was probably trafficked."

"Why doesn't Detroit handle it?"

"They are. A Special Agent Harris Caruthers in VC-2 in the Detroit office is advising on the case." Violent Crime-2 was the same unit Annie was in. Her squad, Civil Rights, fell under VC-2. "Turns out the vic has one of your tattoos."

That got her attention. "The bear claws?"

"Yep. On the neck, below the right ear. Just like before."

"Huh. I was wondering when we'd see another one. What do you want me to do?"

"Call Caruthers." The SSA gave her the agent's cell number. "See if this is related to those other cases you were working on."

"I will. Thanks."

"It's probably not pressing enough that it'll ruin your weekend."

"That remains to be seen. I'll call him. *You* have a good weekend."

"Thanks, you too." He hung up.

Annie stared at the number she'd scrawled on the notepad. Should she call now or wait until Tuesday morning?

The vic has one of your tattoos.

Nope. It couldn't wait. She dialed the number.

"Agent Caruthers."

"Hi, this is SA Annie Marino in the Chicago FO. I'm in the Civil Rights Squad. I understand you have a human trafficking case there in Michigan?"

"Yeah, thanks for calling. I know Rick Perrin, he's in your squad, isn't he?"

"No, Rick's in VC-1, but I know him." Violent Crime-1 was the most populous unit in the Bureau. Those folks handled serial murder, rape, theft, kidnapping, and other examples of the "hard stuff." VC-2 often worked with VC-1, as well as with the three Residential Agencies in the north, south, and west suburbs of Chicago.

"I was talking to Rick earlier today, and he suggested I get in touch with you. He and I have worked together a lot on cases that cross the state line."

"How can I help you?"

"I'm here in the police station in Lakeway, Michigan. Rick told me about that thing you're—I saw your request in the database to contact you if we ever came across someone with a tattoo of bear claws."

"That's right. You've got something?"

"The Bureau was called in by the chief of police to help the locals with what looks like a kidnapping and murder here, and I was the guy who drew the lucky number. A white female who appears to have been kidnapped and held against her will was subsequently killed in a car crash. She may have been already dead when the accident happened, because she was in the *trunk* of the car."

"Jesus, when was this?"

"Two days ago. The body's still in the morgue. She had no identification. About nineteen or twenty years old."

"Who was driving the car?"

"A guy named Vladimir Markov, with a Chicago address. He was killed in the accident, too."

"What happened?"

"It was the middle of the night and it was raining hard. Markov was driving a 2010 Chrysler Sebring on Highway 82, not too far from Lakeway, but outside the city limits. It's a county case, but it was caught by the police in Lakeway. It seems the car was headed for Chicago, but from where we don't know. A bakery truck barreled toward them, and Markov skidded on the wet road. The truck plowed into the sedan. It was Markov's fault, though, he was straddling the center line. Had a high blood alcohol level. The driver of the truck is all right."

"So the fact that she was in the trunk—"

"—led the chief to believe she'd been kidnapped. I happen to think she was a victim of human trafficking. Chicago PD checked out Markov's address. His ex lives there but claims not to have seen Markov in two years. I called Rick about it, and he told me I should talk to you, that it's your squad. Anyway, she's got the tattoo on her neck, just like you described."

Annie noted the time and said, "I'd like to see the body. You say she's in the morgue in Lakeway?"

"Actually the morgue's in another town, but it's close. I was planning to go back to Detroit on Sunday. Can you drive up tomorrow? It's about three and a half hours from Chicago. I realize it's Memorial Day weekend."

As she'd figured. It was the nature of the job, not relegated to Monday through Friday, nine to five. Sometimes she worked impossible hours. Luckily, the endless office paperwork contrasted with the field work, which was terribly interesting and, for Annie, something that had become a personal cause. Since this had something to do with the tattoo, the vision of a three-day vacation vanished with no remorse.

"All right," she said. "I'll drive up in the morning. I can be there by, what, eleven, is that okay?"

"Sure. I'll meet you at the police station. I have your email, I'll send you the details and the case file right now, and you can have a look at it this evening."

"Thanks." They exchanged cell numbers and her inbox on the computer dinged. An email from harris.caruthers, with the subject line, *Bear Claws*. "Looks like I got your message. Okay, see you tomorrow. Thanks for calling."

"You bet. Have a good evening."

Annie sat back at her desk. She opened the attachments and found typically lacking crime scene reports by the local police chief and a captain, as well as photographs and autopsy results.

No, she wouldn't be leaving the office just yet, even though it had been a long day in her cubicle. Annie had spent it reading analyst reports, going over new case files, and catching up on bureaucratic paperwork. She was way behind and grateful for what had been two whole days of relative quiet on the tenth floor. That was rare. Most of her time was spent at any number of locations in and around Chicago, interviewing victims and suspects and interacting with the not-for-profits.

The tattoo had become something of a fixation for Annie. After studying two previous trafficking/murder cases—one in Minneapolis and one in Chicago—she was convinced there was a large white slavery network operating between the United States and Russia. The victims in those two cases—and possibly this new one—had been subjected to trafficking violations prior to being murdered. Each one bore the tattoo of a bear's paw, claws outstretched, on the neck behind the right ear.

The Minneapolis case had occurred in 2009, the year Annie first became interested in the FBI as a career choice. She'd been twenty-four, having just received her MS in forensic psychology, and she simply applied. The acceptance came as a surprise, and then it all became a whirlwind of activity—five months of training that fall at Quantico, and then moving to New York from her Chicago home to work as an intelligence analyst in Manhattan. In 2014, she was granted the request to transfer back to Chicago, where she was promoted to Special Agent.

One of her first assignments that year after joining the Civil Rights Unit was the investigation of a different human trafficking incident—also a murder—in the western suburbs. While working the case, Annie discovered similarities to the 2009 murder. Besides sharing the same tattoo, both victims were illegal Russian immigrants in their early twenties. While the 2009 woman's body was found in a hotel room in Minneapolis, the 2014 corpse was discovered in a dumpster on the Chicago south side. Neither case was solved. The 2014 case was such a disturbing crime that from then on, Annie kept an eye out for information regarding the "tattooed girls."

The Michigan accident scene reports outlined what Chief Bill Daniel and Captain Mike Baines gleaned from the evidence at hand. The collision was just as Caruthers described. The woman had been locked in the trunk of the Sebring. The autopsy showed that she had been restrained, beaten, and raped prior to her death. Obviously, the driver, who was drunk, had been transporting her from one crime scene to possibly another. The sedan's registration was bogus. It was in a name other than the driver's and, according to Agent Caruthers, didn't exist.

Annie transferred the files to a flash drive and shut down her computer. She would study the rest of the material at home over the leftovers of a Chinese take-out meal she'd had the night before and a glass of red wine. Her original plan of stopping for a half hour at the studio to practice the latest tap routines went out the window. So much for her misguided idea to take a dance class in her spare time!

She drove the Bureau car—the Bucar—a blue 2008 Ford Fusion, out of Chicago's FBI field office lot on Roosevelt and headed north on Damen. The expressway on an early Friday evening was going to be madness, so Annie took the alternate route she preferred during rush hour to get home. It was a diagonal northeast slice across the near west side via Ogden and Larrabee Streets. She lowered the driver's side window and allowed the breeze to ventilate the hot car as she turned on the A/C. At a stop light, she undid her ponytail and let her shoulder-length brown hair fall freely. In the rearview mirror, she noted that her dark Italian eyes were bloodshot from a full day of staring at a computer monitor.

Ugh. I need that glass of wine. But if I'm going to study a case file, I might need a tad bit of CAFFEINE.

At Fullerton, she headed east toward Lincoln Park and the assigned lot for her building, the oddly named Cakewell Apartments on West Fullerton Parkway. Although the complex was populated by what seemed to be a large assortment of much younger adults—well, younger than her thirty-one years, anyway—Annie liked the location *and* the price. It had been the first choice on the realtor's list when she was transferred back to Chicago. Her salary as a Special Agent allowed her to just barely afford the rent in such a trendy area, so why not? If she was going to do potentially dangerous work, she deserved to enjoy where she lived. Jogs through the park to the shore of Lake Michigan were welcome diversions and tension-releasers. Former Broadway hoofer Derek McGrath's dance studio, where she attempted to take a weekly tap class, was two blocks away. The nightlife around her home was vibrant, and there were plenty of outstanding restaurants. Its access to public transportation was good, too. When she didn't want to use either the company car or her personal one, a 2011 Honda Civic, the Red and Brown lines of the El were just a stone's throw away at Clark and Fullerton. Most anything she needed was within walking distance except a grocery store. For that, she had to drive.

And there was a Starbucks on the corner across the street from the parking lot.

As she entered the coffee shop, she heard a familiar voice from one of the tables. "Oh, hey, Annie."

She turned and smiled. It was a familiar sight—him sitting with his laptop and a cup of java.

"Hi, how are you, Jason?"

They often ran into each other; he lived in a building nearby with the help of a trust fund that a grandparent had left him. Although Jason Ward was a student five or six years younger than she, they had become friendly since she moved into the neighborhood. Frequent sightings on the street—and especially in Starbucks—had developed into a sociable relationship. Jason was the type of guy who exuded intelligence and sensitivity, which, to Annie, was counter to the macho Italian wannabe tough guys so prevalent in her adolescence. He wanted to be a writer and had already completed one novel, which was still unsold.

"Great," said Jason. "And you? Long day fighting bad guys?"

She laughed. "Long day, yes. Fighting bad guys, not today. Just paperwork." She ordered a beverage (half decaf—she didn't want to be up *all* night) and stood in front of his table as she sipped the hot drink.

"Well, that doesn't sound like fun," he said. "Actually, paperwork is probably the only thing I could *do* at the FBI. You ready for the long weekend at least?"

"Are you kidding? I have to work tomorrow. After that—we'll see."

"Ugh, sorry."

"So I haven't seen you recently—did you graduate?"

"I did. Master of Arts. Now I can look forward to the rest of my life with a totally useless degree." He nodded at the laptop. "And write my book."

"That's terrific, Jason. Congratulations. And it's not useless."

He rolled his eyes. "Thanks. I hope you're right."

"What do you have planned for the weekend?"

"Nat's parents are throwing a big graduation party for us tomorrow up in Highland Park. She got her master's in psychology."

"Oh yeah? My bachelor's is in psychology. Are you still looking at a fall wedding?"

"Yep. Next October."

"Well, congratulations on both. Am I ever going to meet your fiancée?" Annie wondered what Nat was like. With his dark hair, blue eyes, trim build, and a nice smile, Jason was good-looking—and sharp as well.

"You haven't met? I'm sorry. She's over at my place a lot, I figured you'd seen each other."

"Well, I do live in a different building, and it also seems like I'm never home. Listen, you can't marry her unless she meets my approval, you know."

Jason said, "Whoa, that's a lot of pressure. I'll get her to make an appointment."

"You do that. Okay, I have to run. Have a good evening."

"See ya later, Annie."

She walked the half-block to her building, grabbed her mail from the box in the lobby, and rode the elevator to the third floor. As she unlocked her door and turned on the lights of her one-bedroom apartment, Annie grinned at herself. She could tell he found her attractive. There was always a hint of flirtation between them, despite their five- or six-year difference. It was flattering, in a way.

"Forget it, Annie," she said aloud. "He's taken already, and he's too young for you." She locked the door behind her, the cue for Aloysius to wander in from his kingly spot on the bed in the other room and meow a greeting. "Hello, and you're too young for me, too. Are you really fourteen now?"

The cat meowed again.

"Okay, dinner's coming up in a sec."

Before kicking off her wedge heels, Annie performed a quick succession of tap moves, reciting them in her head—

Right paradiddle, Left paradiddle
Right para para, Right paradiddle
Left paradiddle, Right paradiddle
Left para para, Left paradiddle

—and then she put down her coffee, purse, and keys and went through the night's tasks. First, feed the cat. Second, take the leftovers from the fridge and start them in the microwave. Third, remove the Glock 27 and take off her ankle holster. Fourth, turn on the iPad that still pumped music through two speakers she'd had since college. The choice? Bonnie Raitt. *Nick of Time*. Her mother had been a huge fan of '70s, '80s, and '90s female singer-songwriter artists, and the appreciation had soaked into Annie's blood by osmosis. Fifth, get out of the business attire and put on a robe. She could study the case files while she ate, and, a little later, in bed. She figured she'd have to get an early start in the morning.

As she poured dry food into Aloysius's bowl and set it on the floor, Annie reflected on the last six months without Eric. It had been difficult in the beginning, but now she was used to flying solo. She didn't miss him anymore. Weekends alone weren't so bad.

Which was why, she supposed, she delighted in occasionally and inadvertently flirting with younger guys who lived nearby. She told herself it was harmless. And therapeutic.

As she went to the bedroom to undress, she forgot all about both Eric *and* Jason. She had a case file to study.

3

Jason Ward had been to his fiancée's family home on Lyster Road in the Chicago suburb Highland Park several times, and it never failed to fill him with awe. It wasn't among the fanciest houses on the affluent North Shore by any means, but it was still a mansion by his standards. The English Tudor-style structure was less than ten years old, and it sat on an acre of land not far from Lake Michigan. It had at least 7,000 square feet of living space on the first and second floors, and the classic two-story foyer was dominated by a grand, sweeping staircase. A basement level held an additional 3,000 square feet, plus a gym, home theater, wine cellar, and a bar. The Paleys had more bedrooms than they needed. The pool, bar, and expansive lawn in the back were a bonus.

The imported wool business must really be swell.

Jason only knew a mere 10 percent of the attendees at the graduation party—and they were all fellow students from Roosevelt. The event had begun at 11 a.m. and would last until 5. Outdoor grilling, swimming, volleyball, and heavy drinking would be the main attractions for the next six hours or so.

Natalia was dressed in a breezy summer dress with a bikini underneath for quick-change aquatics. She looked marvelous, as usual.

Note to self: pinch yourself again.

That he could land such a beautiful, brainy woman—and a wealthy one at that—was nothing short of a miracle. She was the same age as he, medium height, blonde, and into literature. That's what he had really found attractive. She liked to *read*, and to a writer, that meant a lot.

Nat already had a job lined up in Chicago at a mental health facility. Jason, on the other hand, was hoping to finish his second unpublished novel, and perhaps substitute-teach to help make ends meet. Nat had temporarily moved back in with her parents for the summer, and after the wedding she and Jason would live together in his apartment in the city. That was another thing, too—Nat didn't care what her family may have thought about her intentions to "live like a Bohemian."

They were out by the pool where Trey, Nat's brother, was about to throw burgers and hot dogs on a grill the size of a ping pong table.

Nat held out an empty glass. "Honey, could you go inside and bring me a refresher? The sangria is in the fridge. You might as well bring out the pitcher."

Jason took the glass. "You lush, it's not even noon yet!"

"Hey, I'm celebrating my graduation. You should, too, Mr. I-love-mimosas-on-Sunday-mornings."

"I'm kidding, Nat." He shrugged. "I'm going to pace myself since it's so early."

Trey had overheard. "Oh, woopsy-doo, Mr. Ar*tiste*," he said. "Or should I say Mr. Wuss . . ." In a high-pitched voice and with prissy gestures, Trey whined, "I'm going to pace myself since it's so early; I don't want to get shit-faced before noon."

Trey's friend Mack, who was often joined to his buddy at the hip, guffawed. He handed Trey the meat for the grill in an assembly-line fashion.

"Hush, Trey," Nat said. "Pay no attention to my jerky brother, Jason."

"It's okay, Nat," Jason replied, getting up off the lawn chair. "Trey's a war hero. He can say whatever he wants, can't he?"

"Damn right, I can."

Jason stepped up to Trey. "And just so you know, I got over letting playground taunts bother me when I was in third grade." He walked away, crossing the patio and into the house as Trey and Mack glared at him.

Jason didn't like his future brother-in-law. The guy had a big mouth and was something of a bully. Trey Paley never had anything nice to say. He was also a bit of a weird character. Today, Trey was dressed in an odd hybrid of summer beach wear and army fatigue cut-offs. Older than Nat by two years, Trey had spent some time in the army. He had the kind of he-man physique Jason could never imagine displaying, as well as several tattoos. Jason wasn't impressed by the ink; he had always found too many tattoos a little distasteful, even though Nat had one on her left ankle.

Yeah, I'm a wuss, but at least I can diagram a sentence.

Mack was strange, too. He was from Russia or Ukraine, something like that. Never said much, just grinned at everything Trey blurted out. He was older, probably thirty or so, and was just as buff and illustrated as Trey, with bright blue eyes. Girls liked Mack even though he was short—only five and a half feet tall. His bulk made up for stature.

Angela Paley, Nat's mother, was in the kitchen with a couple of servants she had hired for the day. They were busy preparing a gigantic salad and other side dishes, such as stuffed mushrooms, roasted root vegetables with curry and cilantro, and "pigs in a blanket" for those who didn't want to go too chichi.

"Hello, Jason, how is it out there? Hot?" she asked.

"Not too bad." He found the pitcher in the fridge. "Nat wants the sangria."

"When are your parents arriving?"

"They said they'd be here by noon. Dad's assistant manager wasn't able to take over for him, so they had to be open for a little while this morning and close early."

"Oh, I'm sorry to hear that. They're closing early just to come to the party?"

"That's right."

Jason couldn't tell what Mrs. Paley's reaction was to that. Impressed? Surprised? It was no secret the woman had qualms about her daughter marrying a guy who wanted to be a writer. Not only that, his family ran an independent *hardware* store and was most certainly in a tax bracket far below that of the Paleys. Nevertheless, Jason liked her. While both of Nat's parents were striking, his fiancée mostly got her good looks from her mom. Angela Paley had a popular blog covering high society news and events in the Chicago area. Jason thought it was actually well written and sometimes humorous. He believed that although Nat's mother may have been concerned about his choice of career and financial prospects, she liked him, too. He preferred to think she did so *because* he wanted to be a writer; after all, she was one, too.

In fact, Nat had let slip that Mrs. Paley had once even posed nude in a men's magazine in the early eighties. He was not to mention it to anyone. A trophy wife for Mr. Paley, perhaps?

He took the sangria back outside to the patio, where Nat was now helping one of the servants with the buns and condiments.

"Jason!"

It was Nat's father at the back door.

"Hi, Mr. Paley."

"What did I tell you before? You're supposed to call me Greg."

"Sorry, it's a habit to always address my future fathers-in-law that way."

"Well, stop it. I think your parents are here."

Jason followed his future father-in-law back inside and through the house to the foyer. Greg Paley was a tall, formidable guy who might have frightened Jason a great deal if he'd had the personality of his son Trey. Instead, he was one of the nicest fathers-of-girlfriends Jason had ever met. Fifty-eight or so, the man was in excellent health. He, too, had been in the military when he was younger. The shock of white hair over rugged, Slavic features made him strikingly handsome. His grandparents had apparently somehow managed to emigrate from the newly formed Soviet Union back in the 1920s, which placed Nat in the third generation of her Russian American family.

"I'm looking forward to seeing them again," Greg said, gently slapping Jason on the back. "Oh—here they are!"

Charlie and Tricia Ward, along with Jason's older sister, Miranda, were just coming through the large double front door, held open by Dudley, the Paleys' butler.

"Hey Mom, hey Dad, hey Sis," Jason said, giving them hugs all around. "You remember Mr. Paley?" He gestured back to the host, who had his hand out.

"Glad to see you again, Charlie." Mr. Paley shook Charlie Ward's hand. "How was the drive?"

"Not too bad from Mount Prospect, since it's Saturday."

He turned to Jason's mother and kissed her on the cheek. "Nice to see you, Tricia, how are you?"

"Fine, thank you, we're happy to be here."

He indicated Miranda. "And who is this gorgeous young lady?"

"Mr. Paley, this is my sister Miranda. She's here visiting from Indiana."

The man shook her hand. "Nice to have you here, Miranda."

"Thank you, I wouldn't have missed the party."

Jason appreciated the fact that Greg Paley, unlike his wife, didn't seem to have a negative opinion of his daughter's choice of husband and his family. Mr. Paley also seemed to respect Charlie Ward's independence in business. At any rate, Jason thought, by most standards his family had always lived comfortably in an upper-middle-class slot. They weren't poor. They did quite well with that little hardware store. Jason had grown up in it, worked there, and could have taken it over. He couldn't tell if his father was genuinely disappointed by his son's decision not to carry on the family business, but if he was, Charlie Ward didn't show it. Both of his parents supported whatever Jason wanted to do. Miranda worked for a not-for-profit organization in Indianapolis, where she was also seeing someone.

Miranda leaned in to Jason and spoke softly. "I thought you said they lived in a mansion. This place isn't so big."

He looked at her sideways. "Is that sarcasm, big sister?"

She elbowed him. "Duh. This is pretty impressive."

As the group moved through the foyer toward the back of the house, Jason glanced upward to the second-floor landing above the staircase. Nat's grandfather, Maxim Paley, sat in his wheelchair, gazing down at them, his wrinkled face typically deadpan and silent.

Over a hundred guests came and went throughout the day. They all seemed to be a part of the Paleys' country club social network, except for the twenty or so students who were friends of both Jason and Natalia. Even the mayor of Highland Park stopped by to give his regards to the couple. Live music was provided by a popular local band that played classic rock and recent pop songs. Angela Paley's eighty-one-year-old mother got on the dance floor and gyrated with the younger men to Joan Jett's

"I Love Rock 'n' Roll." The food and drink kept coming. It was quite the soiree. Everyone was drunk by mid-afternoon, when a large group photo was organized and shot by many cell phone cameras.

Jason paced himself so he wouldn't get too sloshed. Nat, on the other hand, was passed out on a lawn chair in the sun at three o'clock. Jason laid a towel over her so she wouldn't get sunburned.

As things were winding down, Jason's father, struck by all the opulence, pulled him aside to join him and Miranda and asked, "How much do you think Greg Paley makes a year?"

"I have no idea, Dad," Jason answered. "They have a nice home, don't they? Palit Wool does pretty well, I guess."

"I'd never heard of it until you started dating Nat."

"Me neither."

"I had," Miranda said. "I've seen some of the shawls. Very pretty. You should get Mom one for her birthday."

"That's a good idea, Sis. Thanks for the suggestion." Jason looked over at Greg, who was holding his liquor quite well. The man spotted his future in-laws, gave them a wave, and sauntered over with a beer in hand.

"Enjoying yourselves?"

"Sure are, Greg, thank you," Charlie said. "Tricia and I will have to be going soon, though. We've had a great time."

"And I have a million things to do before I head back to Indianapolis tomorrow," Miranda added.

"Well, I hope you've had some fun. But you know you're welcome to stay past the end of the party and have supper with us."

"Supper? I couldn't eat another thing!" Charlie said.

Mr. Paley smiled broadly and turned to survey the pool and yard, where the band continued to play. There were still a few lively guests jumping in and out of the pool or playing volleyball, but much of the energy of the first couple of hours had diminished.

"Jason, have you ever been hunting?" Greg asked.

The question took him by surprise. "Hunting? Uh, no."

"You want to go?"

Jason looked at his dad, who made an expression—*say yes!* Miranda, on the other hand, appeared to be horrified.

"I don't know, I've never done it. What kind of hunting? Where?"

"Up in Michigan where we have our cabin, it's a forested area with a lot of deer, even black bear."

"I'm not sure I could shoot Bambi's mother," Jason said.

Greg laughed and put a hand on Jason's back. "If you're going to be my son-in-law, you're going to have to learn how to hunt. You don't have a choice." He laughed some more, indicating he was only kidding. Jason and Charlie laughed, too, but Miranda remained silent.

"I don't know," Jason said. "Maybe I will sometime. When do you go?"

"Oh, usually at the beginning of the fall. September. Trey goes up there a lot more often than I do. He goes hunting all the time." Paley leaned in, conspiratorially. "He probably does it when it's out of season, too." He shook his head. "That boy can be a handful."

"Would Trey be going with us?"

"Of course! I can't go hunting without Trey, he wouldn't let me."

Jason's brief interest was dashed. The last thing he wanted to do was be cooped up in a cabin in the woods with Trey Paley.

"When I get back from my business trip, I'll take you to the range, let you practice firing a gun."

"What's your business trip?" Charlie asked.

"I leave tomorrow to go overseas. I fly back and forth over the Atlantic four or five times a year. It's part of the job. Have to check on Palit Wool's manufacturing plant." Greg shrugged. "I'm used to it. Sometimes Trey goes with me, keeps me company."

"How long will you be gone?" Jason asked.

"Three weeks, probably. No more than a month, I hope."

"Where is the plant?" said Miranda.

A loud *crack* in the yard startled everyone. A few of the women, including Miranda, screamed.

"What the—?" Greg did a double take.

Trey Paley had a pistol in his hand and had fired it into the sky. He was drunk, laughing, and stumbling like a fool. Mack was on the ground, also drunk and laughing.

"Trey!" Greg shouted.

"Sorry!" Trey called back, but he kept laughing and swinging the gun around.

"Excuse me a moment." Greg strode across the patio and onto the yard. He approached his son, grabbed Trey's forearm with lightning speed, and took the pistol with his other hand. Jason and Charlie watched Greg exchange low, harsh words with Trey. His son wouldn't wipe the grin from his face, so his father gave him a little shove. Trey lost his balance and fell on his ass. That did the trick. Trey stopped laughing, jerked up straight, and grimaced, turning beet red.

Greg said something else to him and walked back to the patio and inside the house with the handgun, ignoring everyone's looks, as Trey stared him down. Mack got up, said something to his friend, and together they turned and swaggered off to another side of the property.

"How lovely," Miranda said quietly.

"Reckless ass," Jason muttered.

"You don't like Nat's brother, do you?" his father asked.

"Not at all."

"Well, I suggest you start trying to like him. You're going to be married to his sister."

"You saw what he just did."

"I know. It's one of the hazards of matrimony, son. I couldn't stand your mother's Aunt Hilda, but I did my best to get along with her."

"Aunt Hilda scared the crap out of me when I was little," Miranda added.

That made Jason laugh. Aunt Hilda had long been the butt of many family jokes.

"Was Greg in the military?" Charlie asked, after Miranda excused herself to find a restroom.

"Yeah, I think so."

From the corner of his eye, Jason watched Nat, who was in her bikini, as she approached them with a frown on her face.

"Did that nasty bang wake you up, my dear?" Jason asked.

She cuddled him and put her head on his shoulder. "Ugh, I feel awful."

"Should have paced yourself."

"I know." She looked up at Charlie and Tricia, who had just joined them, both wearing expectant looks on their faces that signaled the end of their stay. "Are you guys leaving already?"

"Yes, we have to go. I just said goodbye to your mother," Tricia said. "We'll see you soon, okay? You two come over to our house for dinner real soon."

"Okay."

"I'm going to go see them out," Jason said to Nat, who nodded and embraced them.

"Thank you for coming!" Then she added to Jason, "I'm going to go lie down."

Jason followed his parents through the house to the front, where Miranda was waiting for them in the foyer. He noticed the look on her face. "Didn't you have a good time?"

"Sure," she answered, "if you like hobnobbing with royalty when they think you're the peasants."

"Oh, come on."

She shrugged. "I'm sorry. It's just not my scene." She furrowed her brow. "You like your girlfriend's family?"

Jason lifted his hands. "Sure. What does it matter? I like Nat."

"Her brother's a real jerk."

"That, he is."

"Be careful around him."

"I will."

"I heard him putting you down. Don't stand for it."

It was true. Throughout the afternoon, Trey had never let an opportunity to insult Jason go by. He always did it in an *I'm-just-kidding* way, but Jason knew better.

"He's bigger than me."

"Just don't let him run over you."

"When Nat and I are married, we won't see him much."

"Her mom is a character."

"Angela's funny. She's like this vintage glamour queen who doesn't believe she's pushing sixty."

"And her dad is nice enough; I like him. You like Mr. Paley?"

"Yeah, I do. With all his money and stuff, he could be a real dick, but he's not."

"He inherited his business, right?"

"From his father, who inherited it from *his* father. I guess Trey is supposed to inherit it, but I'm not sure that's going to happen." He raised his eyebrows and rolled his eyes at that. "Thanks for coming."

"Sure. I can't believe my baby brother has a master's degree." They hugged and said goodbye, promising to stay in touch more often.

Jason watched them drive away and went back inside. Glancing up to the second-floor landing, he wasn't surprised to see Maxim Paley again, still sitting there in his wheelchair. Why hadn't they brought him down to the party? Jason knew there was an elaborate staircase lift for the chair, and he had seen Nat's grandfather downstairs in the past.

Jason waved at the old man. Though Maxim was in his eighties, he looked as if he was ten years older. A stroke he'd suffered in his sixties had left him partially paralyzed and without speech, but Jason wasn't sure if the man could hear or not. He could move his arms, as well as propel the wheelchair by himself.

Maxim Paley nodded at Jason.

Jason decided to say hello. He ascended the grand staircase and approached the old man. "Hello, Mr. Paley. I'm sorry I haven't come up earlier to say hi. How are you doing?"

Maxim Paley just looked at him.

Jason saw that he kept in his lap a little notepad of Palit Wool stationery and a marker attached to it with Velcro. He squatted next to the wheelchair.

"Why didn't you come join us? You didn't want to come to the party?"

No response.

"Can you hear me, sir?" Jason nodded at the notepad. "You can write messages?"

No movement.

Jason reached over and clasped the patriarch's right hand. "Well, if it means anything to you, sir, I love your granddaughter, and I'll do everything I can to keep her happy."

Maxim Paley squeezed Jason's hand.

Oh my God, he can *hear me!*

"I don't know Mr. Paley very well yet, but I like your son, too. My future father-in-law."

Another hand squeeze, a little harder.

Was that approval or disapproval?

"I have to be honest, though, I don't think your grandson, Trey, likes me much. I'm doing my best with him, but he's making it very difficult."

The hand squeezed again, this time even harder.

4

Saturday for Annie began by feeding Aloysius, having a bite of breakfast, practicing for five minutes the most recent tap routine she'd learned, and then leaving Chicago at 7:30 in the morning. As she drove the Ford around the southern tip of Lake Michigan toward Grand Rapids, she listened to the eclectic music and news selection on the PBS station until she could no longer receive it. After that, the radio had slim pickings; there was no CD player or digital audio input in the Bucar. Lakeway was located another three hours north, at the bottom of the Manistee National Forest. The scenery grew more attractive the farther into rural Michigan she went. The trees that dotted the landscape at first multiplied in number, size, and girth. When she eventually reached her destination, she found Lakeway to look pretty much like what she expected. A town of about 2,000 people, mostly white, the community had a reputation for being the staging area for various types of wilderness adventures—camping, kayaking, and hunting. Hence, there were a lot of motels, lodges, and "country cabins" in town and on the road leading to it. The setting for these adventures—the forest—surrounded the village and grew denser toward the north.

Annie had never been much of an outdoors person. Having grown up in Chicago with two older brothers and a younger sister, her sensibilities were strictly urban. Her life had always been about the pavements, the streets, noisy traffic, and the melting pot of diverse people of all races and ages. She craved the pulse of a metropolis; it energized her. It was in her blood. Living in New York during her analyst years only intensified her love for big cities. While she found the surroundings in Lakeway, Michigan, beautiful and even breathtaking at times, she still felt like a fish out of water. It was so incredibly quiet. She thought if she had to spend too much time in the wilderness, the silence would drive her mad. If there wasn't Wi-Fi or a Starbucks within a stone's throw, forget it.

For the journey, she dispensed with the business attire and wore jeans, a polo shirt, and sneakers. Her second weapon, a Glock 22, was in the holster at her waist. She constantly switched between the 22 and the 27 because the latter was smaller, although they were both .40 caliber. The 22 held sixteen rounds, whereas the 27 held only nine. She usually carried the Glock 27 at work and the 22 out on arrests, surveillance, searches, and other operations. As was the case with all female FBI agents, carrying a gun also sometimes presented wardrobe challenges. Wearing a gun with a business suit—skirt and jacket—at the office could be awkward. Usually, she preferred slacks and a blouse, which allowed her to carry one of her Glocks in the ankle holster.

She arrived on time at the police station, which was located across from a city courthouse in "downtown" Lakeway. The reception area was small, consisting of a few chairs. Across from her was a door marked EMPLOYEES ONLY, and next to it a man in uniform sat at a desk behind a window. He had a mop of curly hair and looked to be in his early thirties. Annie registered the name tag. "Captain Baines?"

"Yes, ma'am. How can I help you?"

"I'm supposed to meet FBI agent Harris Caruthers here. I'm Special Agent Anne Marino." She flashed her credentials at him.

The captain raised his eyebrows and stood. "Oh, yeah, I've—we've been expecting you. Agent Caruthers is in our conference room. I'll take you back." He opened the security door and let her inside. She noted how his eyes went up and down her body, a familiar visual assault she, as well as every other woman, experienced regularly. It was no longer a surprise to Annie, but it never failed to annoy her when law enforcement "colleagues" ogled her.

When his eyes got to her legs and feet, Baines creased his forehead.

"You'll have to remove the gun, ma'am. Regulations. You can lock it in one of the cubbies over here."

It was standard operating procedure for visitors to stow their weapons inside a prison or a police department building. She nodded at him, squatted, undid the holster, and drew the handgun. She proceeded to place the gun inside one of the designated safes, locked the door, and pocketed the key.

Baines smiled. "There we go. Safe and sound." He led her through another door and held out a hand. "I'm Captain Mike Baines. Call me Mike. Or Captain Mike. That's what everyone else does."

"Thanks, Captain Mike, I'm Annie."

He showed her into a small conference room where a man, also in his early thirties, sat at a table with the contents of a case file spread out in front of him. He was dressed in a plaid shirt and jeans. The telltale holster—empty, for he, too, had to stow his weapon—was on his waist. Across from him was a much older man in uniform—the chief.

"Guys, this here's Agent Marino," Captain Mike said.

They both stood. The younger one spoke first. "Glad you could make it. I'm Harris Caruthers."

"And I'm Chief of Police Bill Daniel."

Hands were shaken all around.

"Can I get you anything?" the captain asked. "Coffee? Water?"

"Coffee sounds great, thanks. Cream, no sugar."

Captain Mike went off to fetch the beverage and the remaining three sat.

"How was the drive?" Caruthers asked.

"Fine. Very pretty, in fact, once I got out of the Chicago sprawl."

"Have you had lunch?"

"Um, no."

"We'll go across the street to the diner in a bit, is that all right?"

"Sure."

The captain returned with the coffee as she liked it. When he joined them at the table, Caruthers nodded at the chief. "Go ahead."

Daniel cleared his throat and spoke. "Captain Mike here was on patrol on Wednesday night. Technically, early Thursday morning. Mike, tell her what you encountered."

"Yes, sir. Well, ma'am, I was driving down on 82, heading west toward Highway 37." He pointed at the road on a map that lay flat on the table. Annie noted that Highway 82 was a straight east-west line not too far south of Lakeway.

"Isn't that out of Lakeway city limits?" she asked.

"Yes, ma'am, but we often patrol on the back roads in the vicinity. The county sheriff is in White Cloud, so we do it. He asked us to do the preliminary investigation 'cause they're swamped, and we're kind of quiet right now. Anyway, it was raining pretty hard. Just after midnight, here, about two miles west of the intersection with Garden Road, I came upon an accident. The Sebring appeared to be going west, and the bakery truck was headed east on 82 toward Howard City. We're pretty sure we know how the collision occurred. The truck driver said the Sebring suddenly swerved into his lane, maybe skidded somehow, and the impact was practically head on. The driver of the truck, name of Samuel Zielinski, was just calling it in to 9-1-1 on his cell phone as I approached the scene. I'd just missed the accident by less than a minute, if you can believe that."

He explained how he checked on the man behind the wheel of the Chrysler after seeing that the other driver was all right. "He was dead. No question about it. At that point I didn't think there were any other passengers. The car was totaled, so I called it in. Now this happened pretty much out in the middle of nowhere; the forest is all around, there weren't any witnesses."

"Where does Garden Road go?"

"It goes north toward the Muskegon River and into the forest where there are some private homes tucked away in the woods. Chief Daniel and I know the people who live there; they're all good folks. Everyone vouches for everybody else."

"There are lots of rural roads that intersect with 82," Daniel added. "Both vehicles were towed into Lakeway, and that's when the driver discovered the body in the trunk. He called us back immediately." The man sighed and shook his head. "She was in there with her hands tied behind her back and ankles tied together with zip cords." Daniel slid eight-by-ten-inch color photographs across the table. "These were taken in the tow yard."

Annie studied the gruesome images of a badly mangled woman trapped in the clutches of twisted metal. Lots of blood. The limbs were clearly immobilized, as the chief had described.

"Looks like she's wearing, what, blue jeans and a T-shirt?" she asked.

"Yeah."

"And she's barefoot."

There were also photos taken at the scene of the collision. The driver's head had smashed through the windshield and he lay on the bowed hood.

"I understand the car's registration was bogus," Annie said.

"That's right," Caruthers answered. "It's a counterfeit registration. The VIN number was reported stolen three years ago."

"But . . ." She looked for the driver's name. ". . . this Vladimir Markov, that's his real name?"

"We think so. The phone at the address on his driver's license belongs to Markov's ex-wife, whose name is also Markov. We got Chicago PD to go by the house and talk to her, and he hasn't lived there for two years."

The chief continued the story. "We had an autopsy done on the driver and it showed a blood alcohol level of .19 percent. He was drunk. That's how the accident happened."

"Yeah, I read that."

"Anyway, we got her out of the car and to the medical examiner over in Big Rapids. I guess you've seen her autopsy results, too."

"I studied them last night. There was evidence of brutal sexual assault by more than one perpetrator. She was beaten, had an orbital rim fracture, a broken collarbone—seems to *me* it's clear all this occurred before the crash—you know, many contusions on her body *under* her clothes that were created earlier. From the ligatures on her wrists and ankles, it was obvious she had been restrained by cords that cut into her skin. She was in bad shape before the accident. Your pathologist wasn't sure if she was even alive when the collision occurred. She wouldn't have bruised after death. I think the crash was just the last straw."

"That's right. We're thinking that if she was still alive, she might have died within hours anyway," Caruthers said. "Her body was being transported somewhere."

"And you think Chicago?"

"It's a guess. The fake registration was Illinois. The driver's license address is Chicago; like I said, it's his ex's place, but we don't know where he actually lived. They were headed west on 82. Sure, they could've been going anywhere—Grand Rapids, Kalamazoo, one of the dozens of small towns along the way—but I'd bet money they were going to Highway 37 to head down to Chicago."

The chief cleared his throat again. "Once I saw that this girl had maybe been kidnapped and held against her will, I called the FBI. That's a federal crime."

Captain Mike said, "I kind of thought we could solve it ourselves, you know, but the chief insisted on calling in you guys before the county boys stepped in."

Annie wasn't sure what he meant by that, but it was probably a case of small town resentment of the feds "taking over" an investigation, which in reality almost never happened.

"Captain Mike, I hope you *will* solve this yourselves," she said. "As I'm sure Agent Caruthers told you, the FBI is here only to assist and advise. As for me, personally, I'm really here just to observe and gather information as it might pertain to some cases I've been working in Chicago. I'm sure Agent Caruthers will offer you any assistance you need on solving the kidnapping and—I'm going to say it, because I believe it's what you have—the crime of murder. But don't worry, you'll be doing all the heavy lifting."

The chief addressed that. "We're a two-man shop, Agent Marino. I have two other officers who work on a part-time basis. But we'll certainly do what we can. As Captain Mike said, we're turning the whole thing over to the Newaygo County Sheriff. It's their jurisdiction, technically, but they asked us to do the preliminary investigation since it happened this close to Lakeway."

They went over more details in the reports until Caruthers looked at his watch and said, "Lunchtime." The chief and captain bowed out to stay at the office. Annie retrieved her weapon from the cubby and left the building with Caruthers. They crossed the street to Barbara's Diner.

She found his company to be similar to that of her colleagues in Chicago. He was a clean-cut example of the all-American boy, properly groomed, physically fit. He seemed nice enough. At least he didn't run his eyes up and down her body like the small-town captain had done.

"How long you been with the Bureau?" she asked.

"Three months."

"What?"

"Yeah." He blushed. "I'm a newbie. I'm still learning the ropes. I got assigned to VC-2 right after I got out of Quantico. I'm originally from New Mexico."

"I thought I detected a different kind of accent. I was going to say Texas. What were you doing before training?"

"I did four years in the army."

"Oh, my. Did you go overseas?"

"I did. Two years in Iraq. When I got back, I decided to try for the FBI. I didn't have a master's degree, but they took me."

After more small talk, their discussion went back to the case.

"I think I'd like to take a look at the car," she said over a BLT that wasn't half bad. "They still have it somewhere?"

"Yes, I was looking at it yesterday."

"It had to have been driving from *somewhere*. Where it came from is more important than where it was going. How many places are we talking about in this region?"

"Plenty. A lot of the forest is federal land and a lot is state land, but you'd be surprised how many cabins the woods can hide."

"Agent Caruthers, I—"

"Call me Harris. Please."

"All right, Harris, I also want to interview the ex-wife of the driver in Chicago. I might do that tomorrow. You talked to the truck driver? Zielinski?"

"We have his contact info. Daniel and Baines let him go. He lives in Howard City, where the bakery's located. His truck was messed up, so he stayed in Lakeway that night. His wife picked him up sometime on Thursday. He was just delivering goods to a grocery store in Fremont and was heading back home."

"So how is this going to work?" she asked. "I handle wherever the case takes us in Illinois, and you take on the Michigan end?"

"That's how my SSA saw it, and I think yours, too?"

"Yeah, I guess. Great, we just ate," she said, wiggling her eyebrows. "Just in time to see the victim's body!"

Captain Mike drove Annie and Harris to the county morgue, which was a half hour away in the township of Big Rapids in Mecosta County, just east of Lakeway. The facility was shared by the two counties. Along the way, Mike pointed out landmarks, including where "Old Man Jameson" bagged a black bear the size of a Buick. "That thing was a monster," he said. "I never would have believed it if I hadn't seen it with my own eyes. He was king of the forest, I'll bet. Well, until Old Man Jameson got him."

Annie pegged the captain as an honest-to-God country boy, probably having grown up in a nearby part of the state.

The morgue was located in the basement of the small administrative building. Mike led them through and explained to the pathologist on duty what they wanted. They signed in, and the pathologist opened the cold chamber door.

"We're keeping her in the fridge until we get some kind of ID," Mike explained as the pathologist pulled out the drawer containing the corpse.

Annie put on rubber gloves and stood close to the victim's head and shoulders. She gently turned the head to the left, pulled back the thick, dark hair, and exposed the right ear. Sure enough, there it was. A bear's paw, baring its long, sharp claws that dripped with a few small globules of red blood. Even though she had already seen the case file photos, Annie took a few pictures with her cell phone.

"The autopsy said the tattoo was recently applied," she said. "Looks new."

She turned to look at Mike. "You ever seen this?"

"No, ma'am."

"It's come up before. It probably means she was the 'property' of someone." Annie held up her hands and ripped off the gloves. "Allegedly. I think whoever that someone is, he's Russian, and he's probably overseas. I think. I'm betting our Jane Doe here is Russian, probably an illegal immigrant."

"She looks Eastern European," Harris noted.

The captain scratched his head. "Wait, you think there's some kind of prostitution ring here in Michigan that's run out of Russia?"

"I don't know if it's prostitution. Obviously, she was restrained. Kidnapped? Forced labor? This was a pretty woman. Could be she was being trafficked for sex work."

Mike almost laughed. "We don't have that kind of thing here in this part of the state. Really? I don't believe it. Maybe in Detroit or Grand Rapids or Kalamazoo, but not here."

"You do now," said Annie.

Harris said, "Like I said before, I think Mr. Markov was taking her to Chicago."

Captain Mike nodded. "That's probably right. Chief Daniel and me, we don't think anyone around here has anything to do with this. They could have just been passing through the state."

"But from where?" Annie asked. "We're north of Detroit and Grand Rapids and Kalamazoo and all the other sizable cities in Michigan. If you go straight east you run into Lake Huron. No,

I think whatever happened to her before the accident occurred somewhere up here in rural Michigan."

"Seeing that most of Michigan *is* rural . . ." Harris added.

". . . then that could be anywhere," Annie finished.

Back in Lakeway, Captain Mike took the agents to the garage where wrecks were stored. In the front, the Chrysler Sebring resembled an accordion. The back end, where the victim had been shut away, was relatively unharmed.

"She would have been knocked around in the trunk by the accident, but do you think it killed her?" Annie asked.

"I'm beginning to lean toward the idea that she was already dead," Harris replied.

Annie stooped to examine the tires, which were caked with dried mud. "You've had some rain, huh," she said to the captain.

"Uh, yeah, as a matter of fact, we did. Last Tuesday and Wednesday."

"The car was on a dirt road for some time, I think. Look at those treads."

She stood and looked in the open trunk. Dried blood stained the upholstery. Annie imagined the woman's body squeezed into the claustrophobic space. If she hadn't already been dead, then the terror the victim must have felt would have been insuperable. "Was anything else in here with her?"

"No, ma'am."

What a horrible death, she thought.

Annie left Lakeway at three o'clock, figuring she'd make it back to Chicago around seven. There was food in the apartment, so she wouldn't have to stop. Along the way, she reflected on what she'd seen. Had she learned anything? Not really. The trip was probably unnecessary, but she was glad to have seen the tattoo herself. She had serious doubts that the chief and his captain would solve the case; they didn't have the manpower to visit every residence in the Michigan forests. Hopefully the county sheriff would put more men on it. There was, however, something bugging her about the visit to Lakeway, but she couldn't put her finger on what it was.

The only thing she could do was follow up in Chicago with Markov's ex-wife. Maybe, with the right questions asked, she would pick up a few more bread crumbs.

5

Annie had an unexpectedly leisurely Sunday morning. At first Aloysius refused to leave her lap, but she eventually pushed him off, dressed in workout clothes, and practiced tap. She'd missed the last three classes and was terribly behind. Derek was going to chastise her in his lovingly sassy way the next time she showed up, if she ever did.

He's a good-looking man; too bad he's gay, she thought as she pictured Derek with his hands on his hips, lecturing her for not being "disciplined."

Ha.

It was her discipline that had wrecked her relationship with Eric—the devotion to her job, the fact that being a Special Agent in the FBI was more important to her than having a boyfriend. It was the cliché of the week, of the month, of the year—she was the law enforcement woman who was too much of a workaholic.

She wasn't supposed to miss the romance after it had failed.

Ha.

Annie changed into jeans and a T-shirt, affixed her gun to her waist, and left her apartment around two. She'd found that interviewing subjects could be more productive if you appeared when they least expected you. A Sunday afternoon knock on the door by an FBI agent? Most people who were guilty of something usually revealed it.

As she got in the Ford, her cell rang.

"Anne Marino."

"Annie, it's Harris. Agent Caruthers."

"Hi, Harris."

"I see you made it home okay."

"I did, thanks. What's up?"

"I'm in Chicago."

"You are?"

"Yeah. I decided I wanted to interview the truck driver's ex-wife, Mrs. Markov. I find that Sunday afternoons are a good time to surprise someone. You want to come along?"

Annie laughed. "I was just getting in the car to do the same thing. Sure, we can back each other up. I'm twenty minutes away from the house."

"I'll see you there. Park across the street. I'll wait for you there."

Mrs. Markov lived on the south side, near Chinatown. As Annie headed for Lake Shore Drive, she reflected that it was best to have a partner whenever dealing with the public. She'd gone solo numerous times to interviews—one-on-one, usually with women—and that was all right. Still, one couldn't be too careful. Most of the time, her partner from the FO was an agent named Ed Barnley; however, Barnley had been placed on a special task force that was going to take up most of his time over the summer. Annie was on her own for a while.

Harris was parallel parked across the street, two doors down from Mrs. Markov's house, which was a wreck of a place with a dilapidated 2002 Toyota parked in the drive. Annie got out of the car and greeted him.

"You have a game plan?" he asked.

"Not really. I just want to hear what she has to say."

They knocked. After a moment, a thin woman with tired eyes answered. She wore an apron and looked to be in her thirties.

"Yes? What is it?" Her accent was thick.

Annie and Harris showed their credentials. Annie spoke. "FBI, ma'am, we'd like to ask you some questions. May we come in?"

The woman's eyes grew wide. "Oh. Is this about Vlad? I already talked to police. I have nothing to do with him anymore."

"May we come in, ma'am?"

She grudgingly let them inside. The house was hot—no A/C. The woman led them into a living room where two small girls were watching television. Annie's first impression was that this was a family just getting by. They'd sacrificed the A/C to save money.

The woman sat on a sofa while the agents remained standing. Harris held up a photo of Markov's driver's license. "Is this your husband, ma'am?"

"My ex-husband," she replied. "We divorced two years ago; the creep walked out on me. I haven't seen him since. I told police that already."

"You haven't seen him in two years?" Annie asked.

"That's right. He's still in Chicago, though."

"You know that?"

She shrugged. "I hear things from my friends, from the neighborhood. He's been spotted spying on the girls. He's not supposed to come around, but he does."

"Do you know where he lives now?" Harris asked.

She shook her head. "I have no idea. I don't care. I don't want to know. He can rot in hell, the bastard. He left me with no money. Look around you. I can barely keep our house. I work two jobs." Then she stopped and looked at both of them. "Why? What's he done? The other police would not tell me."

"Ma'am," Annie said, "I'm sorry to say that he's dead. He was in an automobile accident last Wednesday night in Michigan."

"Oh." She didn't flinch. "Good riddance. I hope no one else was hurt. Was he drunk? I bet he was drunk."

Annie and Harris exchanged glances. "Ma'am, do you have any idea why he would be in Michigan? Did he have business there?"

"How should I know? I have no idea what he did. He was a crook. He associated with undesirable men."

"What undesirable men?"

"That run the strip club." She made a face in disgust.

"What strip club?" Annie asked.

"That one on Cicero, near the airport."

Annie thought a moment. She knew all the strip clubs in the Chicago area. "Midway Airport?"

The woman nodded.

"The Cat's Lounge?"

"That's it. He had friends there. I imagine he worked there. I don't know. When he started associating with those people five years ago, that's when he started ignoring his family."

Annie and Harris looked at each other.

"What time does the Cat's Lounge open?" Harris asked when they reached their cars.

"On a Sunday? Not until five. Let's get a cup of coffee and then we can go."

Annie and her squad kept records on all the strip clubs in Chicagoland. They knew who the owners and managers were, and periodically someone from the squad would stop in the establishments and "check on things." Some strip clubs were notorious for trafficking violations, although the ones in the city had kept their noses clean. Did a criminal element operate behind the scenes for a lot of these places? Certainly. The Italian mob—the so-called Outfit—still existed in Chicago. In fact, every community had its own organized crime group, just like in New York. It came with the territory of big cities.

They stopped at a Starbucks and took seats in a corner.

"The Cat's Lounge is owned and run by a Russian immigrant name Fyodor Utkin," Annie told Harris. "He's been around for twenty-five years or so, ever since the fall of the Soviet Union and we started getting an influx of immigrants from that part of the world. I know him. He runs several of the clubs in and around Chicago. I understand he has interests in Milwaukee and other spots in Wisconsin, and up in Minnesota, too. I wasn't aware of anything in Michigan, but maybe he does now. He's a wealthy slimeball. But so far he's kept his nose clean and by all accounts runs a legitimate business. I don't like the business, but he's not breaking any laws that we know of."

"His name has come up," Harris said. "But I've only been on the job three months, as you know."

"Well, hopefully, if he's in town, you'll get to meet him."

There were four cars besides theirs in the Cat's Lounge parking lot. Annie knew there was a back entrance and noted six cars parked in the rear, which most likely belonged to dancers, security, and wait staff.

There were three types of strip clubs, in Annie's experience. The A-list "classy" ones were pricier, allegedly had the most beautiful women, and served a full menu. These were the places least likely to have legal problems. Below that was a category Annie called the "B-clubs," which usually only served snack food. Sometimes they were raunchier, and they mostly appealed to a working-class clientele. Clubs that served booze couldn't display full nudity and were topless only, but the dry joints left nothing to the imagination. The bottom rung of clubs were sleazier, cheaper, and often transient; this category included the so-called massage parlors—dives that came and went, often acting as fronts for illegal activities such as prostitution. Those were the ones the squad had to be on top of.

The Cat's Lounge was definitely a B-club. It sold booze and was thus only a topless joint. The food available consisted of typical bar fare. Operating costs were low.

A tough-looking man in his forties was at the door, sitting on a stool. He wore black trousers and a short-sleeved black T-shirt to emphasize his muscles. He eyed the guns and immediately said, "You can't bring those in."

Credentials flashed, and Annie said, "Is Fyodor here?"

"Uh, yeah, he's in the office."

"Can you tell him we'd like to see him?" She and Harris handed over business cards.

The bouncer got up and said, "Wait here."

After he'd gone into the club, Annie jerked her head at Harris, and they went inside anyway. The lights were low, except for two stage areas, one of which was occupied by a short blonde woman dancing in a "police" costume. She was grinding and slowly unbuttoning her clothing to the strains of "Money for Nothing." There were four customers, all men, sitting separately, staring at the dancer as if she were a goddess.

The bouncer appeared from behind the bar. He noticed them and frowned, annoyed that they had come in, but he waved them onward. The agents moved around the bar and into a back hallway. Dressing rooms were to the right, a storage and supply room was in front, and the manager's office was to the left. There wasn't much to the real estate. All the money had gone into the bar and main floor.

The bouncer gestured them inside the office, where Fyodor Utkin sat at a desk. There were two other chairs in the room. On the desk were stacks of correspondence—bills, statements, and the like—and a thick pile of US currency.

"Special Agent Annie Marino and a colleague," Utkin said with a Russian accent. "Always a pleasure to see you."

She shook his hand when he stood. "Hello, Fyodor. How are you doing?"

He gestured to the money. "Just fine, can't you see? I was just going through last night's take."

Utkin was a man in his mid-fifties with graying dark hair. His physique indicated that he was obviously someone who worked out.

"And what do I owe for this unexpected visit from the FBI?" he asked, returning to his seat.

She opened a folder and removed a photo of Vladimir Markov. "Do you know him?"

Utkin frowned and shook his head. "No. No, I don't know him. Who is he?"

"You sure you don't know him? He hasn't worked for you at some point?"

"What? No, I would remember if he worked for me. I don't know who this is. Who is he?"

Annie took back the photo. "His name is Vladimir Markov. His ex-wife says he used to hang out here a lot."

"Never heard of him."

"So if I ask any of your employees or your dancers if they know him, they'll tell me no, too?"

"I don't know! You asked if *I* knew him, and I don't. I don't know everyone who comes in here. I have other clubs, and I'm not always here. I travel a lot."

Annie pulled out photos of the victim and a close-up of the tattoo. "Do you know her?"

Utkin recoiled at the brutality of the picture. She had purposefully shown him the one taken of the Jane Doe in the trunk, and one of her face. "Jesus Christ, that's horrible! Why you show me this?"

"Sorry, she turned up dead a few days ago, and I just want to know if you recognize her."

"No, I don't! God." He gave the pictures back.

"Wait. See that tattoo?"

"Yeah?"

"Have you ever seen it before?"

He shrugged. "I don't know. Lots of girls—and men, too—have tattoos. I pay no attention." Annie studied his face. "What? I run legitimate business here, you know that."

She returned the photos to the folder. "I'd like to show these pictures to your staff. Is that all right?"

"Go ahead."

She turned to the bouncer, who was still standing at the door. "You want to look? What's your name, anyway?"

"This is Boris," Utkin said. "He's new."

"What do you say, Boris?" she asked. "Know this man or this woman?"

He looked quickly, shook his head, and said, "No."

"What a surprise," Annie muttered.

She led the way out of the office and down the hall. She knocked on a dressing room door.

"Come in!"

Annie made sure the occupant was decent, and then she and Harris entered. She knew the woman who sat in front of a mirror applying makeup. The woman looked up. "Oh, hi, you're that FBI agent, ain't you!"

"Special Agent Annie Marino. This is Special Agent Harris Caruthers. How are you, uh, Tina, right?"

"That's right, you got a good memory."

"You've been working here a while, haven't you?"

"A little over a year."

"A year's a long time in this business. Everything good? No complaints?"

"Nope. I like to dance, and I make good money. No complaints."

Annie looked at Harris, who nodded—he was letting her handle the interview. Annie handed over the picture of Markov. "Do you know him?"

She didn't look long. "Yeah, I've seen him around."

"Around?"

Tina gestured toward the bar. "Customer. He's a regular."

"You ever see him back here, with Fyodor or other staff?"

Tina shook her head. "Mm, no, I don't think so."

"But you've definitely seen him here?"

"Uh huh."

"You ever talk to him?"

She shrugged. "Yeah. If they tip, if they want a lap dance, you know, sure, you talk to them."

"He ever say anything beyond what you'd normally hear?"

"No. He's not one I tend to remember, if you know what I mean. He's pretty quiet when he's here. Not like some of the noisy ones, you know, the ones that say vulgar shit about your ass or tits. Why, what's he done?"

Annie didn't answer her. She thought she'd spare Tina the graphic photo of the victim and instead pulled out the close-up of the tattoo. "Ever seen ink like this?"

Tina creased her brow. "Mm, no. I don't think so. Wait. Yeah, maybe. A girl that passed through here a couple months ago had ink like that. She'd just come into the country, I think. Didn't stay long. Worked two days at most."

"Just come into the country? From where?"

"Russia, or Eastern Europe, somewhere like that."

That answer prompted Annie to go ahead and show her Jane Doe's trunk shot. "Is this her?"

"Oh my God!" Tina turned away.

"I'm sorry, Tina." She said, more gently, "This girl was trafficked and murdered. We're trying to identify her. I'd appreciate it if you looked."

Tina peered through fingers. "Ew. No, I don't think that's her. Wait. No, well, it could be, but I don't . . . no . . . I don't think it is."

"So are you saying it's improbable that this is the girl who was here for a couple of days, but not impossible?"

"I guess so."

After a few more questions, it was clear they weren't going to get much else from Tina. They interviewed the sole waitress and the bartender, both of whom confirmed that Vladimir Markov was indeed a Cat's Lounge customer at times, but no one knew anything else about him. No one copped to the tattoo or the pictures of Jane Doe, either. Annie and Harris went back to Utkin's office.

"Apparently Mr. Markov was a regular customer," Annie told Utkin.

"Like I said, I don't know everyone who comes in. You're lucky you caught me here today. I'm leaving town tomorrow."

"Who runs the place when you're gone?"

"Ivan or Ludwig comes over from the Den. Or bartender Sandy; she's very capable."

Annie knew Ivan Polzin as well. He had immigrated to the US in the early nineties and worked in Utkin's organization.

"Guess I'll have to talk to Ivan. Oh, by the way, I heard the woman in this photo *may have* worked here a couple of days. You sure you don't recognize her?"

She watched his body language, especially the way his eyes darted around the room instead of looking at the photo. "If she did, I didn't know her. And I see every girl who works here, so that means I don't know her. Sorry to disappoint you. Who of my employees told you this?"

She ignored the question. "Thank you for your time, Fyodor. Do me a favor—if you happen to see anyone with that tattoo, let me know, would you?"

When they got outside to their cars, Harris asked, "Do you think he's lying?"

Annie looked back at the building as it vibrated from the heavy bass notes pounding inside.

"Yeah, I do."

6

Early June

The ship rocked with the waves, sending one of her roommates to the toilet again.

Yana Kravec clutched the edge of her cot and sat up. It was better than lying down—that was what made her seasick. Fortunately, she hadn't continued to vomit like Christina. Sofia, her other roommate, seemed to be doing all right.

"Is it going to be like this the whole way?" Sofia asked, her face a little green.

"I hope not," Yana replied.

"It's only the fourth day at sea. We have eight more days of this torture."

"The second day was calm, remember? We will get out of the rough waters. It won't be like this all the way to America."

At least Yana hoped not.

It had been two weeks since her last meeting with Nikolai Babikov before he came through with her passport and visa to the United States. She paid him the small fee, which she thought was an incredible bargain. Yana knew of people who had turned over their life savings to emigrate. She was getting transport essentially for free.

Nikolai told her to meet him near the Big Port of St. Petersburg on the designated day. They met at a coffee shop. She carried a single suitcase, a shoulder bag, and a purse. He had told her to pack as lightly as possible. Once again, he asked her if she had told her parents—or anyone—about the arrangements. She hadn't. He then handed over the lovely passport and visa. Her picture wasn't the best, but it would do. The visa said that she would be working as "domestic help" for the Caviar Nanny Agency, based in New Jersey.

Sofia and Christina also showed up at the coffee shop. They were around the same age as Yana, both very pretty. Christina was from St. Petersburg. Sofia was from a small town called Kirishi, which was still larger than Yana's little village of Chudovo. They were expecting to become models or actresses as well. Yana joked that she hoped they wouldn't become competitors. Over the meal Nikolai bought them, they quickly became fast friends. They were going on a wonderful adventure together!

Nikolai had explained that they would be ushered through the port authorities with the crew of a large shipping container. He assured them there wouldn't be any problems with their passports or visas. There might be a few days in which they'd be inside their quarters before the ship actually left port. The trip at sea would take twelve days, but the entire journey, from boarding the boat to disembarking, could be between fourteen and twenty days.

You are not to leave your quarters during the journey.

"Why not?" Sofia asked.

Those are the rules. We are getting around certain procedures. You cannot call attention to yourselves. Not everyone aboard the ship will know you are there. Only a select few. You will be brought food and water on a daily basis. You will have your own private toilet.

He gave them a deck of playing cards. *This might occupy some of your time. I understand there are Russian books and magazines in your quarters, as well as American ones. I know you can all speak English, but you might use the time to practice. Everyone speaks English in America.*

That had been five days ago. Nikolai had taken them into the port later that night, after midnight. An official who looked as if he'd been awakened met them at the terminal. He stamped their passports without really looking at them. Nikolai handed him an envelope, and a crew member of the *Okulovka* escorted the three young women aboard.

Their room was a box. Fifteen feet by fifteen feet. No windows. There were four folded cots on the floor when they arrived, so one was removed. It was a good thing, because when the three cots were fully opened, there was already barely enough room to pass between them. A toilet the size of a kitchen pantry was attached, but there was no shower or bath. A small empty shelf was attached to the wall. A box of paperback books and old magazines sat in the corner.

When the crew member shut the door, he locked it.

The three of them were in a bit of shock. How could this be their accommodations? Did they have to be stuck in this little room with each other for three weeks?

The women calmed down and discussed it, and it was Sofia who convinced them all that this was the way it was going to be because what they were doing *was* illegal—but it was the only way to get them to America for free. They had to suck it up and make it work.

That made them feel better, and when dinner was brought to them, the crew member—Von was his name—was kind. He spoke pleasantly and explained a little about the voyage across the sea. It would not always be smooth sailing. Sometimes the ocean was rough. He told them a few things they could do to combat sea sickness and gave them pills to help prevent it. Von also emphasized that they were not to leave the room—*because they weren't supposed to be there*. He and a couple others were the only ones who knew there were "passengers" aboard. Von asked them to make an adventure out of it. Look at it as the sacrifice they had to make in order to go to America. Enjoy it—it would be something to remember for the rest of their lives.

So they had made the best of it.

Now, five days later, four days of which were at sea, the girls were ready to strangle each other. Christina, in particular, had been upset about the conditions the entire time. While she was willing to put up with it, it didn't mean she couldn't complain—and she did. Yana, however, kept a positive attitude. She knew this was the hardest part of the journey. Besides, she was *happy* to leave Russia. She wasn't sorry at all to say goodbye.

Everything was going to be better when they reached America.

7

On the first Sunday of the month, Annie ran into Jason Ward at Starbucks again. That morning, she had planned to go for a brisk walk through Lincoln Park, and caffeine helped to get the heart rate and sweat going. Seeing him at the table with his laptop early on a Sunday morning, plugging away on his book and dedicated to his craft, was inspiring.

"How you doing, Jason?"

"Just fine, Annie. Have a seat."

"I'm about to head to the park—it's a beautiful day—but I'll sit for a minute."

"Please honor me with your company," he said as she sat across from him.

"How's the writing going? Don't you work in your apartment?"

"That's two different questions. The writing is going—*eh*. And yes, I do work in my apartment, but I like the vibe here. And it sometimes provides me with the opportunity to meet jet-setting FBI agents who live in my neighborhood."

"Ha, you're seeing me at my Sunday-morning-no-makeup worst," she said. She gestured at the sweatpants, T-shirt, and tennis shoes.

"Well, I haven't shaved or showered, so we're even."

She appreciated the company, as it had been a frustrating week with not much progress in the case of the tattooed woman. Agent Caruthers had returned to Detroit, and she had continued to look into the Cat's Lounge on her own. She had stopped by again and met Ludwig Vasiliev, who was managing the joint while Utkin was away. Once again, she had pressed the employees about the Jane Doe. She questioned Tina again, who had since gained a bruise on her left cheek. She explained that she had tripped during a dance and fallen on her face. This time, she was adamant that she hadn't seen the woman in the photos at the club, and that it was all a mistake. However, she maintained that she had seen the tattoo before, but she couldn't recall where.

As for the Jane Doe, her body couldn't be kept in the morgue forever. The US Attorney's Office got involved and a judge eventually ordered that the unidentified corpse be properly buried. That wouldn't stop Annie from continuing to work on the case. There was nothing more the victim's remains could tell them. They had plenty of photographs and DNA samples.

"Working on anything juicy?" Jason asked as he pushed the laptop aside and took a sip from his own coffee cup.

"I'm working on lots of things, but you know"—she made a face—"human trafficking is not juicy."

He winced. "You're right, I'm sorry. I shouldn't have said that."

"It's all right." She shook her head. "To tell you the truth, I had no idea how awful it was until I joined the Civil Rights Unit. It really is one of the cruelest crimes someone can inflict on a human being."

"Yeah, I know. I didn't mean—"

"It's okay. But to answer your question, yes, I've got ongoing cases, which of course I can't discuss. How about you? Didn't you have a big graduation party or something?"

"I did! That was Memorial Day weekend. Big to-do over at Nat's parents' house up in Highland Park. Maybe you saw my pictures on Facebook?"

Annie hadn't looked at Facebook in a while. She had a very discreet personal page with not a lot of friends, intentionally kept that way. Jason was one of them.

"Sorry, I didn't, but I'd like to see them!"

Jason brought up the site and turned the laptop so they could both see the monitor.

"That's their house."

"Wow."

"And that's their backyard."

"Nice."

"There's Nat and me."

"Aw."

"Those are my parents and my sister Miranda."

"I remember meeting them; they're very nice. I forgot—where does Miranda live?"

"Indianapolis."

"I enjoyed talking to her that one time we met. She still works for the not-for-profit?"

"Safe Haven. And guess what."

"What?"

"Well, you know Safe Haven is an organization that helps women in lower income situations and at the poverty level. Mainly they provide shelter and items for battered women and their children, too. Domestic violence stuff."

"I remember that."

"So, they've got this new initiative on human trafficking."

"Really?"

"Yeah, it's a new part of their agenda, and Miranda might be overseeing it."

"That's great! We'll have to talk when she comes to visit you next."

"She actually wants to speak to you. Can she call you?"

"Sure. Feel free to give her my office number." Annie dug into her fanny pack and pulled out a business card. "Nine times out of ten you get my voice mail, but I'll return the call."

"Thanks." He put the card in his pocket and continued to flip through the photos. "Oh. That's Trey, Nat's brother. I've told you about him."

"You said he's a bully."

"Yeah."

"Let me see." She turned the computer to get a better look. "He looks like one. I would tag him from the get-go as a bully."

"He's mostly a jerk."

The picture showed Trey clowning around at the barbecue grill, gesturing with a spatula.

Annie turned her attention to the other man in the picture. "Who's the guy with the blue eyes?"

"That's a friend of Trey's. A Russian guy named, uh, Mack. He really is Russian—he speaks with an accent—although I believe he came to this country when he was like six or seven. I don't like him either. I do like Nat's mom and dad. They're as American as apple pie—typical white, upper-class North Shore we've-got-money people." He scrolled to the next photo, a group shot of about twenty-five people, all party guests.

"There's Nat's dad. I have to say I really like him. He's genuinely nice and seems to like me all right. And there's Nat's mom."

"She's pretty."

"Yeah, she was some kind of glamour model."

"What are their names?"

"Paley. Nat's dad is Greg Paley. Her mom is Angela. Nat told me her grandfather Maxim was the first of the family to be born in the US. His parents had emigrated from Russia in the 1920s. He still lives there at the house, but he's in a wheelchair."

"Fascinating. What do they do?"

"Have you ever heard of Palit Wool?"

"I don't think so."

"They import wool made from some kind of exotic goat in Russia. They make all kinds of wool products but are mostly known for those nice shawls and scarves that are so Russian. Look, I have a picture of one here . . . I was going to give it to my mother for her birthday." He found a shot that revealed a beautiful white shawl made up of an intricate pattern of fine threads.

"Oh, I've seen those. I've heard them being called wedding ring shawls."

"The goats breed only in a particular place, and they have a very fine wool on them."

"It's so big, but it looks like it's light and soft."

"It is."

"So, your future in-laws import the wool?" she asked.

"The wool, the shawls, scarves, ties, pajamas—you name it. It's kind of a big deal, I guess. The company is based in Chicago but their main operation is over in Russia. St. Petersburg, I think."

"Is their manufacturing plant here?"

"No, it's in St. Petersburg. The US side is mostly retail."

They had scrolled to the end of the photos so Jason turned the laptop back to face him. "Oh, I've been meaning to ask you—do you know a good range or something where I can learn to shoot a hunting rifle?"

"A hunting rifle?"

"Yeah, Mr. Paley invited me to go hunting with him at their cabin in Michigan. He's a real macho type that does outdoor sports and stuff. He was in the military, a real discipline-oriented guy. You should see him yell at Trey when he's mad at him. He's like a drill sergeant. But he's nice to me. He's probably a pretty good hunter. The thing is, I've never hunted."

Annie laughed. "And you don't want to look like a complete idiot when you go."

"Right."

"Let me think about that." She was reminded of her Memorial Day weekend investigation. "Where in Michigan is it?"

"I'm not sure. Sort of in the middle of the state, where there's a lot of forest."

"Huh. I was just up there on a case. The Paleys have property there?"

"Yeah. A cabin and a big spread, apparently. Nat said her grandfather Maxim bought the land originally. So you think you can help me out?"

"I know some good instructors. You gave me your email; I'll send you a couple of names."

"Cool. Thanks."

"You don't sound very enthusiastic."

"Well, to tell the truth, I don't think I really like the idea of hunting. I don't want to kill a deer or a bear. I worked in my parents' hardware store, and we *sell* guns. Hunting rifles and shells. But I've never in my life fired one."

"Well, then don't go hunting. You don't *have* to, do you?"

"Uh, I kind of think I do. I mean, if I didn't want to go I probably wouldn't have to, but he might think I'm a wuss. I don't want my father-in-law to think that."

"You're probably right. I'll get you those names. In the meantime, get yourself a book on hunting." She sighed. "And I guess I'd better get going or this fine day will pass me by."

"Have a good walk, then!"

She swung out her legs and stood. "Write a masterpiece! See you later."

8

Annie spent the next week juggling various assignments. There were always a number of cases on her plate. While most were relatively minor, a handful of them were significant. Even so, in her mind, nothing related to human trafficking was ever "minor."

She was usually the go-to agent in the squad for human trafficking incidents, but Annie also spent time on other categories that the Civil Rights Squad investigated—"color of law" violations, in which law enforcement or judicial personnel allegedly violated a victim's civil rights; hate crimes; and Freedom of Access to Clinic Entrances (FACE) offenses, such as when patients are blocked from entering a facility that legally performs abortions. A separate unit in VC-2 was the Crimes Against Children Squad, which included child pornography (called "Innocent Images" at the FBI), illegal child labor, and the like. Annie preferred to be where she was. She wasn't sure that she could emotionally handle a crime-against-children case, but she would rise to the challenge if asked. Although she was childless herself, she loved children, and perhaps *someday* she might have one of her own.

Ha! I guess I'd need a partner for that.

These days, that was practically impossible. Her work came first, and that left little time to socialize and meet men. Her coffee chats with Jason were her only non-business interactions with a male person since the breakup with Eric. Derek at the studio didn't count—he was her tap dance instructor, and he was gay. Jason was also more like a little brother than anything remotely like a possible romantic interest. Plus, he was engaged.

Has it really been almost seven months since I've had a date?

She didn't miss *him*, but she missed the companionship. Even though she and Eric had rarely seen each other when they were together, it had been nice to occasionally come home and slip into bed with another warm body.

So I like human contact. What the hell is wrong with that? Can't I be a kick-ass FBI agent and *still like sex every once in a while, too?*

There was a time when she had thought Eric was the One.

More like just another in a long line of men who are threatened by a strong, independent woman.

It hadn't helped that he was needy and jealous of her time, and that wasn't going to work.

To hell with him.

At least she could honestly say that she loved her job more than any man in her life so far. She hadn't asked to be on the Civil Rights Squad—she'd been assigned to it. At first, she wasn't sure it was for her. She'd had her eyes set on VC-1, particularly the organized crime section of the Criminal Enterprise Branch, or perhaps the Behavioral Science Unit. Human trafficking was close, though, since trafficking crimes were often instigated by organized, hierarchy activity. After six months in the squad, Annie developed a passion for her specific vocation. When she saw firsthand the horror of what victims went through, she dedicated herself to the mission. She liked to think of herself as a crusader for the sufferers.

The investigation into the tattooed girls was moving slowly, but she was amassing helpful information. Annie spent a day in her office studying the 2009 Minneapolis case again. The victim there had been identified as an illegal Russian immigrant who had been in the country for at least three months. A suspected prostitute, her body had been found by a maid in a motel room on the outskirts of the city. An unknown white male in his fifties had paid for the room in cash. The killer was never found. The victim had been deliberately strangled after the sex act had been completed, so essentially the perp had paid for the privilege of murdering someone. Since no cash was found at the scene, the guy most likely took it back before leaving the motel.

Minneapolis police traced the victim's prior movements and learned she had worked at a strip club called the Hot Spot, which closed down a year later.

There wasn't much else in the file. No mention of family.

Annie noted the name and phone number of the homicide detective in charge of the case, picked up the phone, and dialed.

"Brinkley," the man answered.

"Detective Bud Brinkley? This is Special Agent Anne Marino at the FBI Chicago field office. Do you have a moment?"

"FBI? What's this about?"

"I'm calling about an old case, a cold one from 2009."

"Jesus, I can't remember that far back. What case? What do you want to know? I'm pretty busy here; we had a double homicide this morning and it ain't pretty."

Why did men always think they're busier than anyone else? "I can call back later if you want."

"No, no, go ahead. I love talking to the feebs."

The sarcasm in his voice wasn't lost on Annie. She explained the case she was calling about.

"Okay, I do remember that. Never caught the killer."

"I know. Do you recall who the manager or owner of the Hot Spot strip club was? That information is not in the case file, at least not in what I have, which isn't very much."

"Not off the top of my head. I'll have to dig out the file to find that out. How is it you have the file?"

"Back in 2014 I worked a human trafficking case that involved a homicide in Chicago. The victim in that case also had the same tattoo of bear claws as your vic did."

"No shit? I remember that tattoo."

"A ViCAP search told me about your victim's tattoo."

"Give me your name again and your number, and I'll get back to you as soon as I can. Is that okay?"

"Sure, I appreciate it." She gave him the information and hung up.

Annie also spent time looking into what the Bureau had on Fyodor Utkin. The man had a rap sheet that included a few arrests, including one for procuring, but that case was dismissed. Utkin had entered the United States in 1990 through Newark, New Jersey. His first activity on the books was logged in 1994 in Chicago when he applied for a liquor license for a strip club he wanted to open. The license was denied then, but he successfully received it in 1996 for a now-defunct establishment called Zebra. The pimping charge came in 2003 when a brothel in the suburbs was busted. Unfortunately, the local police botched the evidence, and Utkin went free. Notes by investigating officers indicated that Utkin was suspected of working with Russian organized crime members in Chicago, but no proof was ever collected. He had owned and operated several strip clubs in the area over the past twenty years. Three in Chicago—the Cat's Lounge, the Den, and Paradise—were still in business today. He also had interests over the years in clubs in Wisconsin, Minnesota, and Michigan, all legitimate. Annie took a hard look at his Michigan activity. Utkin's businesses in Detroit and Ann Arbor were closed, and it didn't appear that he currently held any assets in that state. His holdings in Minnesota did include clubs in Minneapolis, but there was nothing to indicate he had anything to do with the old Hot Spot. That didn't mean he hadn't at one time.

She made some calls to contacts she knew in Chicago and the suburbs where Utkin's clubs were located. By asking the right questions, she learned that Utkin technically didn't own the establishments. A company called Eyepatch, LLC was listed as the owner.

The next call was placed to a colleague in the Financial Crimes Section. SA Sally Bertram was an ally when it came to discreetly looking into a suspect's finances. Annie and Sally had worked together twice on trafficking cases in which the criminals' money trail needed to be tracked.

"Hey, Annie, what's up?"

"The usual, Sally. I heard you got married?"

"I did! I've had two months of wedded bliss. Unfortunately, I've spent most of that time here."

"I hear you. I think that's why I'm still single."

"Oh? What happened to . . . weren't you with someone?"

"Yeah, but that's not a headline anymore. We broke up seven months ago."

"Sorry to hear that."

"Don't be, I'm better off. But congratulations. Seriously."

"Thank you. So, what's up?"

"Can you look into a company for me? I'd like to find out who the owners are, where it's based, anything you can. Could be relevant to a case I'm working on." Annie told her about Eyepatch, LLC.

"Let me get back to you. I'll see what I can dig up."

"Thanks, I owe you a wedding present. Or at least a drink."

"A drink sounds great, thanks. Talk to you later!"

Annie hung up. Again, she had to wait on a call-back. That was one of the few frustrating aspects of the job. Some things simply took time. There were some instances in which she had waited months to receive a returned call. In this case, however, Sally phoned back an hour later.

"Okay, Eyepatch, LLC appears to be a shell company, and its listed address is in Belize."

"That's not surprising."

"But there are no red flags from the IRS. They must pay their taxes."

"No idea who the principals are?"

"Nope. It was incorporated in a jurisdiction that does not require owner, shareholder, or director's details to be filed publicly, and there is no TIEA with the US." Annie knew Sally was referring to a Tax Information Exchange Agreement. The financial and management information of Eyepatch, LLC was very private indeed.

"Okay, thanks. I appreciate it."

"Sure thing. I'm waiting on that drink."

"This week. I promise." Another call was coming in. "My SSA is calling, got to run." She switched lines. "Hi, John."

"Annie, we have a situation."

The main command post on the ground floor was occupied by seven people—SSA John Gladden, SAC Michael Tilden, ASAC Sharon Feliz, two SAs from VC-1, and two from VC-2, including Annie. Everyone had a laptop open in front of them on the conference table.

Feliz spoke. "At 12:07 today, the FO received this call from Mrs. Angelique Washington in Memphis, Tennessee. After the initial screening, she was transferred to an agent who took the call." She pressed a key on her laptop and the recording filled the room.

FBI, can I help you?

"Uh, hello?"

This is the FBI, how may help you?

"My daughter just called me, she's been missing for two months, she says she's a prisoner of some men in Chicago! Please, you need to find her! They have guns! Please hurry!"

Ma'am, please slow down, can you tell me your name?

"Angelique Washington."

You're calling from Memphis?

"Yes! I told the first person who answered all this. They transferred me to you. Karen's in danger! Please, you've got to hurry! She's being held prisoner she says, they s-s-sexually assaulted her, she's afraid they're going to make her do . . . oh God in heaven, please, my poor baby, my darling girl . . . !"

Mrs. Washington, please slow down, take a deep breath.

The woman did so audibly.

Now, please tell me your daughter's name and age.

"Karen Washington. She's seventeen."

And you say you haven't seen her in two months?

"She . . . she ran away. Well, I mean, she left. I knew she was going. I couldn't stop her. She went to Chicago, and I didn't hear from her. I reported her missing."

Feliz stopped the recording. "The Memphis police contacted the Chicago PD when they were unsuccessful in tracking Karen's movements. We've asked their Missing Persons Division to get us any information they have, but I don't think there's much. We now have the missing persons report that was forwarded from Memphis." She pressed a key and the victim's school photo appeared on the overhead screen. A pretty, bright-eyed African American girl. Feliz punched another key to continue the recording.

"Karen called me out of the blue this morning. She said she stole the man's phone and made the call without him knowing it. She says she took a big risk doing it, that he'd kill her if he found out. He has a gun."

How long was your conversation, Mrs. Washington?

"About a minute. She was afraid to talk longer. She was whispering."

Did she give you any clues as to where *in Chicago she is?*

"Yes, I . . . I wrote some of it down. She said she's being held in an apartment building in Chicago. She didn't really know where she'd been taken, but she's near the train tracks. She said a train rumbles by outside every so often."

Did she say if it was a commuter train or an El train?

"No. What's an El train?"

Never mind. Did she say anything else?

"She said the windows are covered with cardboard. She snuck a peek outside through a small hole she'd made with a pen in one in her bedrooms. She said she could see a sliver of the street and part of the building on the other side. There was a road sign in her view, it had a number on it—'forty-three.'"

Highway 43?

Annie looked at Gladden. "That's Harlem Avenue."

Another agent added, "It's also Waukegan Road in the north."

Ma'am, are you sure she meant Highway 43?

"I don't know, she just said there was a square sign with a white circle in the middle and the number forty-three in black in the circle. Oh, and she said she could see part of the name of the building across the street. It's a store, and the name has big letters. She saw R, N, I, T, U."

Let me repeat that. R, N, I, T, U.

"Yes. That's all she said. Then she had to hang up. She thought they'd heard her."

Feliz stopped the recording. "The rest is just getting details about the girl. We have an agent in Memphis interviewing Mrs. Washington, and we'll get an update after that's occurred. Now we just have to figure out where on Harlem Avenue."

"Harlem Avenue runs the entire length of Chicago, up and down, through all the suburbs," one of the SAs said.

Annie added, "But she said her daughter could hear a train. Like the agent on the phone said, it could be a Metra or it could be the El. Or both."

"Right. It shouldn't be too hard." Feliz flicked a switch and a map of Chicagoland appeared on the big screen behind them. With more manipulation, Highway 43 was highlighted. It ran north-south from Park City in the north down through several suburbs, into Chicago city limits, and then south all the way to Tinley Park.

Annie stood to examine the map closer. "Okay, let's count all the instances where the Metra lines intersect with or run alongside 43. Up in Northbrook, 43 is Waukegan Road. This Metra line runs alongside it for a bit. What line is that?"

Someone said, "Uh, that's the Fox Lake train."

"Milwaukee District North," another person added. "I'll write these down."

Annie continued tracing 43 down. "Here it turns into Harlem Avenue. And here's another line it crosses in Park Ridge."

"That's the Union Pacific Northwest to Harvard," Gladden said. "I took that every day when I was just out of college working at the US Attorney's Office."

The highway crossed several different lines as she named the suburbs. "Then Elmwood Park. Forest Park. Riverside. Forest View. Worth. Tinley Park. Hey, that's really not a lot. We should be able to find this."

SAC Tilden picked up the phone on the desk. "I'll get satellite images of every intersection."

As the Special Agent in Charge phoned the surveillance section, Annie moved next to Feliz. "Please pull up Google Maps, Sharon." The screen was projected so the room could see. Now search for 'furniture store.'"

Tilden heard her and put a hand over the mouthpiece. "Furniture store? She didn't say anything about a furniture store."

Annie nodded. "I'm guessing the letters R, N, I, T, and U belong in the word 'furniture.'"

SSA Gladden stifled a laugh. "How did you figure that out so quickly, Annie?"

"I was a *Wheel of Fortune* addict when I was a kid. I'm a nerd."

Feliz entered the words in the search box. Icons dotted the entire Chicagoland map. Annie started pointing to furniture stores that could be possibilities on Highway 43. There were a few along that long stretch of city thoroughfare.

Annie said, "That little yellow guy, the street view fellow, he can really be your friend."

"I know how to use Google Maps, Marino, but be my guest."

Annie took over and pulled the icon to the top furniture store on 43 that was near a train line. "We won't bother with the ones not near train tracks." The display switched to street view, standing in the middle of the intersection. Annie turned the POV a full circle. "I don't see anything that looks like an apartment building, and the furniture store is a Crate and Barrel. No good." She moved to the next one, further south, and repeated the process. "Nothing here, and no furniture store with those big letters." She kept going.

"Marino, our surveillance drones will get us these images in a second," Feliz said.

"Look, I've got it," she said. The street view scene revealed an apartment building that looked like it was built in the eighties. "Tinley Park. Harlem Avenue and 175th Street. There's an apartment building there. And right across the street is MS Furniture. Big letters. And look, there's the highway sign."

"What was this, a race?" Feliz asked.

SAC Tilden ended his call and hung up the phone. "John, liaison with the county and let's get a task force together ASAP. Marino, you're in charge. We're going to rescue Karen Washington."

9

It took two hours to assemble the task force. Nine officers—seven men and two women—from the Cook County Sheriff's Department made up the SWAT team, the use of which was justified by Mrs. Washington's indication that the men inside the apartment were armed. Lieutenant Carl England was in charge of the team, while Annie would act in a supervisory role, participating in the raid but not in the first wave to breach the apartment. One man from the Southern Residential Agency (RA) was on hand to assist her; otherwise she was the only FBI presence at the scene. Another member of the task force was the operator of a thermographic camera. A warrant had been quickly issued by the United States Attorney's Office so that the police could use the device to determine how many souls were currently occupying the apartment. Annie's role would be to talk to the victims and take them under her wing while the police took care of the pimps.

It didn't take long for the reconnaissance of the twenty-four-unit building to locate the target, a two-bedroom apartment. Four windows on the second floor were covered from the inside by sides of cardboard boxes. Two of them—one a smaller bathroom window—faced Harlem Avenue. The blocked-out windows were not visually suspicious, mainly because they were in keeping with the overall feel of the complex. The place was run down and only half occupied by tenants. Other residents had unusual decorations in their windows. Tattered drapes, cracked glass, and even a torn American flag acted as blinds. No one would think twice if they spotted the cardboard-covered windows.

The building's parking lot contained ten cars. A walkway balcony ran in front of the second-floor apartment doors, motel-style. The SWAT team was positioned on the staircase between floors, just out of sight of the target apartment's front door.

It was a quiet, hot, and sunny weekday afternoon. Not much traffic. A great time for a surprise visit from the police.

Annie and the lieutenant watched the structure from an unmarked van parked across the street—right in front of the Highway 43 sign.

"Thermal images still reveal only four people," the tech at the controls said. "Nothing has changed. I'm confident that the two in the bedroom are women. The other two are men. They're in the living room, sitting on a sofa and watching TV."

"Right," England said. He spoke into the mouthpiece of his helmet. "Now listen up. Everyone is in place. First wave goes in strong, neutralize the two men in the living room. They will most likely be armed. Remember—try not to let any harm come to the women in the apartment. Naturally we'd like to arrest the men without any violence, but deadly force is authorized if there is a threat to your own—or the women's—safety."

Annie was dressed in a Kevlar vest over a polo shirt and jeans, the back of the vest plainly reading "FBI." The Glock 22 was in a holster at her waist. She felt ready. The potential for violence always came with the job.

"There's our man," said the lieutenant, nodding at the building. Annie saw an undercover cop approach the apartment door.

He held a pizza box. "We went through the garbage for the apartment. They seem to get a lot of pizzas delivered."

The cop knocked on the door. He spoke to someone on the inside.

"Ready . . ." England said.

The door opened.

"Go!"

The pizza delivery man backed away and dropped back against the balcony as four SWATs stormed the walkway from the staircase. The man who reached the door first kicked it open hard before the man inside could shut it. The leader charged inside, his Heckler & Koch MP5 raised and pointed in front of him. His comrades followed as shouts of "Police! Hands in the air! Hands! Let's see your hands! Police!" were suddenly overcome by gunfire.

The lieutenant drew a sharp breath and exchanged looks with Annie.

One, two, three, four . . . and five shots. Then it was quiet. The lieutenant, listening to the progress in his helmet earpiece, caught Annie's eye and nodded. "They found the girls."

"I'm going in," Annie said.

"I'll come with you," the RA man added.

As England gave orders to bring up the support personnel, ambulances, investigators, and technicians, Annie and her colleague left the van and ran across the street to the building. They went up the stairs, down the walkway, and into the apartment.

"Clear!" someone shouted. The operation had lasted less than a minute.

A Cook County cop was lying on the worn carpet, badly wounded. He'd been hit in the neck where the helmet couldn't protect him. The two pimps were dead. One lay near the cop in a rapidly expanding pool of blood. The other still sat on the couch, lying back with his shirt open, hit in the chest.

"Bastards shot at us," the SWAT leader said. "What else could we do?"

The TV was on, blaring a baseball game. Annie, her hands covered in rubber gloves, turned it off. She then moved past the carnage and into a dark bedroom illuminated only by a night stand lamp. Two cops guarded the women, who lay face down on the bed, holding each other, sobbing and trembling. Annie sat on the edge of the mattress.

"Hey, it's okay, you're safe now."

The victims looked up. One was Asian and the other African American. Annie addressed the black girl. "Are you Karen?"

Tears ran down the girl's face as she nodded. They were both terribly frightened, thin, and pale. The Asian girl had a bruise on her face and appeared to be in worse shape than Karen.

"Come on, let's get you both out of here."

The women moved toward Annie and embraced her, sobbing into her vest. Annie held them and stroked their hair.

Then she saw the bear claws tattoo below the Asian girl's right ear.

It was nearing eight that evening and Annie had not eaten dinner. She was at Palos Primary Care Center, a small hospital in Palos Heights, not far from the crime scene. The two victims had been taken there for examinations while the county police processed the apartment and gathered evidence. Seventeen-year-old Karen Washington had been properly identified. The other girl claimed to be twenty-one-year-old Teresa Wang, from Ukraine. It was quickly determined that she was in the country illegally. Her passport and work visa were found in the apartment, along with $50,000 in cash, weapons, and drugs, all locked in a strongbox that the police opened.

The girls were in pretty good shape, considering. They were malnourished and had been roughed up. Both claimed to have been raped several times. Wang had suffered a beating. But they were alive and had no serious injuries other than the psychological trauma they would live with for the remainder of their years. For the next day or so they would remain sedated.

The wounded officer was still in surgery. He was expected to survive, but he would most likely be in intensive care for at least a couple of days.

Annie had given the girls some time to settle in for an overnight stay in their hospital rooms. She finally got a chance to grab a snack at the cafeteria and settle her own nerves. The raid had gone well enough, although she wished they'd been able to interrogate the pimps. So far the police had found nothing that indicated who was behind the crime.

It wasn't a brothel, as was first suspected. Preliminary interviews with the victims indicated that the apartment was simply a place where they were being held, waiting to be moved at a later time to yet another secret location. Annie was anxious to document the women's stories.

After she finished her meal, Annie went upstairs to Karen's room, where she lay in bed. A nurse was taking her vitals.

"Karen, I spoke to your mother an hour ago," she said. "She'll be here first thing tomorrow."

Karen just nodded. She had a wide-eyed, deer-in-the-headlights look. She was obviously in a bit of shock.

"Do you feel like talking?"

The teenager looked at her. She sighed heavily and said, "All right."

Karen Washington told Annie a familiar story. She met a boy—older, charismatic, and kind. He paid attention to her, made her feel pretty and wanted. Karen grew up in a family that consisted of a single working mother and three siblings.

She'd been lonely and at odds with her mother, and was a bit of a rebel. The boy, "Harold"—the name was probably fake—wooed and seduced her and eventually talked her into going to Chicago with him. Against her mother's wishes, Karen left with her knight, who turned out to be a very dark one. As soon as they got to Chicago, Harold introduced Karen to harder drugs and a group of men who wanted to "help" her. Before she knew it, she had been taken to a house and locked up. There, she was gang-raped, including by Harold. She was kept in the house for nearly two weeks and then moved to the current apartment in Tinley Park. Her captors' names were Vasil and Auric. She was denied a phone, a computer, or access to the outdoors. Karen claimed that the men told her she would remain there until she was "sold." One morning, while Auric was still sleeping and Vasil got in the shower in the one bathroom, Karen managed to sneak into the men's bedroom, take Vasil's cell phone, go back to her own bedroom, and call her mother. The conversation wasn't long, and it ended once she heard Vasil turn off the shower. She quickly hung up, deleted the call record, and rushed to the men's bedroom to replace the phone before Vasil emerged.

Annie assured Karen that she was safe now. There were lots of services available that could help her readjust. Therapy was a must, and she could utilize it at her own pace.

"Thank you."

"You're quite welcome. I'm going to want to talk again in much more detail, but now you should rest. And if there's a special meal you'd like tomorrow for lunch, I'd be happy to bring it to you."

That brought a smile to Karen's lips. "Barbecue pulled pork sandwich like we get in Memphis?"

Annie laughed. "I can probably find you a pulled pork sandwich, but I'm not so sure it will be like Memphis. I'll do what I can, though."

Teresa Wang had a far more disturbing tale. In broken English, she described how she had met a man in Kiev. He told her she was pretty enough to be an American model. She, too, was a runaway, a young woman who had found no prospects for a good life in her hometown, a rural village. She was promised free transportation to America, a passport, and a work visa. Teresa described how she'd ridden on a ship with three other girls from Eastern Europe and Russia and how they'd been kept inside a cabin and unable to leave for the entire voyage "for security purposes." The craft was a container ship, and she never knew its name. When they reached the port in Newark, the girls disembarked with a couple of crew members. The documents proved valid, for they were ushered through Customs and Immigration.

Then they were met by a man named Abram and a woman named Nadine. They took the women to a house, where Abram and another man named Bobby raped and beat them. Their passports and visas were taken for "safe keeping." Then, they were transported across the country in a van. When they reached Chicago, the girls were separated. Teresa was taken to a house, much like Karen was, where she was held prisoner and occasionally raped.

One day, a man came and took her on a road trip. The only problem was that Teresa was locked in the trunk of the car for the duration of the ride, about four hours. When the car stopped, she was let out and brought to a log cabin in a densely wooded area. The driver and a man at the cabin took her into a shed at the back of the cabin and chained her to a bed. A day or so later, a new man arrived and tattooed her neck with the bear claws.

"He told me, 'Now you're the property of The Bear.'"

"The Bear?" Annie asked.

"That's what he said," Teresa answered. "The Bear is the boss in Russia."

"He's in *Russia*?"

"Yes, I think so. That's what I understood. Probably in St. Petersburg. That was the port we left from."

"What did this tattoo artist look like?"

"Tall. Bald. Fifty-something."

"Russian?"

"No. American."

One night, some men came to the cabin to "party." She was the object of their fun. One of the men was very rough and liked to hurt her. She was afraid he would kill her. The next day, weak and vulnerable, Teresa was taken by the same driver in the trunk of his car back to Chicago. She ended up in the apartment in Tinley Park and had been there a week before the police showed up.

"I am so grateful to Karen," she said as her eyelids drooped. "She was brave enough to steal that phone and call her mother."

Seeing that Teresa was starting to fade from the sedatives, Annie ended the interview. The women were exhausted and needed rest and recovery. Annie would refer them to a not-for-profit organization that worked with victims and survivors of trafficking crimes. Karen and Teresa had a long road of healing ahead of them. Annie would talk to them again soon.

At least now she had something to work with. If The Bear was in St. Petersburg, Russia, then he had to have a second-in-command in the US—someone to manage what appeared to be a significant operation that spanned continents.

10

It was after midnight. Jason and his fiancée strolled arm in arm from his assigned parking space toward his apartment building on Clark Street. There was still a little life left on the block, but streets like Fullerton were quiet. Jason considered himself lucky that he'd found the one-bedroom basement dwelling for a song. So what if it had bad plumbing and bugs? The rent was affordable for a starving student. It was paid for with a teeny-weeny trust fund that his grandparents had stipulated could be used only for housing and expenses while attending college.

"I love Ravinia," Nat said with a satisfied sigh as they approached their townhouse.

"It's my favorite venue for a concert," Jason agreed.

"You know we could have stayed the night back at my house. Ravinia is *in* Highland Park. We didn't have to drive all the way back into the city."

"We're by ourselves here, no one from your family around. Oh—hey, that's Annie!"

Jason recognized the figure walking toward the Cakewell Apartments on Fullerton.

"Who?" Nat asked.

"My friend I told you about," he said. "Annie!" he called from across the street.

Annie turned, recognized him, and waved. The couple crossed the street to say hi, both noticing that she wore her gun at her waist. "Hello! You're out late," said Annie.

"So are you. Nat, this is Annie Marino, my friend who lives around the corner. Annie, meet Nat."

The women shook hands. "Congratulations on the upcoming wedding!" said Annie. "I bet you're excited."

"Thank you, we are!" Nat answered.

"Been out on the town?"

"We went to Ravinia to see Emmylou Harris," Jason replied.

"Oh, I love her! She was one of my mother's favorites. I would have thought most people our age these days wouldn't know who she is."

"Well, *we* do. You look like you've been working," Jason said, nodding at the gun.

"Yeah, I'm just getting home. It's been a hell of a day. My cat is going to be very annoyed with me. He doesn't like it when dinner is served after midnight. He'll be up, dancing on my face for the rest of the night, just to punish me. But at this point, I'm so tired it won't bother me. I'll be out like that." She snapped her fingers.

"Well, it was a pleasure to meet you," said Nat.

"Pleasure to finally meet you, too. Have a good night."

"G'night, Annie," Jason said.

"She seems nice," Nat said once they were inside his apartment. "Did you say she works for the police? She had a gun."

"FBI agent!"

"Oh, right."

"Don't spread it around, though." He went to the kitchen. "Want something to drink?"

"Glass of red wine?"

"Coming up." He worked on preparing their nightcaps.

"Why can't I spread it around?" Nat asked as she sat on the sofa and kicked off her shoes.

"Annie likes to be discreet about it."

"It's not very discreet when you wear a gun on your belt."

"Touché."

"How come *you* know she's an FBI agent?"

"She told me. We've been neighbors forever, it seems. Well, she moved into her building a couple of years ago, I guess. I see her at Starbucks all the time. Her friends and family know about her job; it's not a big secret. It's just that she doesn't go around introducing herself with, 'Hi, my name is Annie, and I'm in the FBI.'"

"What does she tell new people when they ask what she does?"

"I think she usually says she's in 'law enforcement,' or that she 'works for the US Attorney's Office.'"

"Interesting."

Jason brought the glasses around and sat next to her. They clinked glasses. "Cheers," Nat said as they took sips. "So you think she's attractive?"

"What? Come on, we're just friends."

"You do, don't you."

"Well, sure, you saw her, she looks good. She tap dances, too."

"*Tap dances?*"

"Well, she takes lessons."

"A tap-dancing FBI agent? You *do* like her." Nat poked him and laughed. "How long have you been getting it on with your sexy FBI agent neighbor?"

"Oh, stop." He leaned over and kissed her. She warmly accepted the embrace and pulled him on top of her.

When Jason came out of the shower to slip on his boxers, Nat was already in bed, wearing just a long sleep shirt. After the lovemaking, she had showered, removed her makeup, and found the garment she always kept at Jason's apartment.

"Hey, I forgot to tell you," he said from the bathroom.

"What?"

"Annie fixed me up with a firearms instructor. I'm going to learn how to shoot a hunting rifle."

She turned her head to look at him. "Are you seriously considering going on that hunting trip with my father and brother?"

"Yeah. I want to show them I can be just as manly-man as them."

"Jason, honey, you are *not* as manly-man as them, and that's okay. I love you *because* you're not that way."

He turned out the light and slipped into bed beside her.

"Yeah, yeah, I know, I'm a sexy nerd," he said, "but I think your dad will respect me more if I do this."

"Jason, you don't have to do it."

"I know, but I want to. I should at least *try*, don't you think? The worst that can happen is that I'll make a fool of myself and then Trey will make fun of me even more. Big deal."

"Hm, that's not the worst that can happen."

"What do you mean?"

Nat was quiet for a few seconds.

"Nat?"

"I had an uncle. Uncle David. My dad's younger brother by a couple of years. He was killed in an accident on a hunting trip in Michigan with my dad and some of his friends. He was shot."

"Shot? How?"

"A gun fell and went off or something like that. Freak accident. Nobody's fault."

"Geez. Really?"

"I don't know a lot about it. It happened the year I was born. I never got to know my Uncle David."

"Was he married? You have cousins?"

"Yes and sort of. You haven't met my Aunt Carol. She remarried a few years after that and has children with her second husband. So they're not really related to me. My uncle was the blood relation. The rest of the family doesn't see Carol much ever since she remarried, but I do occasionally. She was around when I was real little. I think she took a liking to me when I was a kid. Then we sort of bonded when I was a teenager. I've always known her as Aunt Carol."

"When did she remarry?"

"Gosh, I think I was five. They live in Naperville. We get together every three or four years. I think we're about due to do so soon, and besides, she needs to meet you!"

"She's not in touch with your parents?"

"My parents don't have anything to do with her now, I'm sorry to say. I think there may have been some bad blood after my uncle was shot. She has her own family now. Can't blame her, really."

There was silence for a while. Jason put his arm around Nat and closed his eyes.

"Are you still going to take the shooting lessons?" she asked.

Jason mumbled, "Yeah, why not."

"Okay, whatever you think."

"I want to show Trey I'm as good as he is."

"Ha. Trey is Super Soldier. Or at least he thinks he is."

"I know."

After a pause, she softly said, "I think he already had psychological problems *before* going to Iraq. When he came back, he was so much worse."

Jason gave up trying to go to sleep. He propped up his head on his hand. "What happened to him over there? You've never really told me."

"I don't know. He won't talk about it."

"Do your parents know?"

"I don't know. Dad knows, maybe. He tends to protect Trey, and at the same time he's really strict with him. It's like Trey is still a child. Dad gets frustrated and yells at him a lot, but he . . . *protects* him. That's the best word I can think of to describe it. I mean, look, Trey's living with my parents and has been since he got back. It has to do with all the violence Trey saw. He was discharged with PTSD. It's been six years, and I don't think he's improved. He's still as nuts as he was when he got home. He kind of scares me. Oh, I know he wouldn't hurt me or anyone else, really, but he does have a temper. He can get pretty violent. He and my dad really go at it every now and then."

"I bet your dad usually wins."

"He does. My dad can be formidable when he wants. But he knows Trey is sick, too."

"He must have killed people in Iraq," Jason said.

"I'm pretty sure he did."

"I'm sorry to hear that."

Silence. Now Jason was wide awake. He waited for her to respond. "Are you sleepy?" he asked.

Her breathing was slow and regular.

"I guess from your answer that means we aren't having sex again."

She started. "What?"

"Nothing. Go back to sleep."

11

Annie spent the next two days interviewing Karen and Teresa. She took it easy on them, speaking for only an hour or two at a time. Their shock was starting to wear off by the third day in the hospital, which was when the doctors in charge recommended that the women could be released. Karen was ready to go back to Tennessee with her mother, who had driven to Chicago to pick her up. Teresa, on the other hand, had nowhere to go. She was an illegal immigrant. Annie was instrumental in guiding her to STOP-IT, a division of the Salvation Army. They were going to help Teresa deal with the citizenship issue and find a place for her to live. Many trafficked illegal immigrants chose to stay in America, either too ashamed or too afraid to return to their home country.

Before leaving town, Karen provided more details about "Harold" and other men she had encountered beyond Vasil and Auric. Annie also learned that the men had told Karen she was going to get the bear claws tattoo. She, too, would be branded as a product, and they had in store for her what had happened to Teresa. Annie wished Karen luck and promised to keep in touch. The teenager might be needed as a witness if and when the bad guys were brought to justice.

That left Teresa, who had one more night before she would return to society. Annie visited her, and they had a productive conversation. She asked Teresa to elaborate in more detail what her captors had threatened her with.

"At first they told me I could work off my 'debt' to them in a strip club," Teresa answered. "Or by working in a 'party house.'"

"A brothel."

"Yes. They say I owed them thousands of dollars for my trip to America and getting me in the country. I was about ready to give up and go strip or work in the brothel, but then there was another possibility I became aware of."

"What was that?"

"I could be sold to someone, and be like a slave."

Annie nodded. "How did that work, exactly? Do you know? Do you know any other women who were sold?"

"I'm sure all of them I encountered were eventually sold if they did not work in the strip clubs or brothels. Some were probably picked only to be slaves. The girls on the boat and in the van coming to Chicago—where did they all go? We were separated; I never saw them again. They were probably taken to different houses or apartments to await their fates."

The network is large and well-funded, Annie thought. *To have that many temporary holding houses where the women are kept takes a lot of money.*

"The Bear specializes in selling slaves to wealthy men. To *keep*. Or do whatever they want with them. I heard stories. One of the girls in the first house where I was said that many times the buyers are sadists who just want to torture and eventually murder their new 'possession.' They pay a lot of money—several thousand dollars—for a girl they can kill in the privacy of their own home."

Annie was horrified. She had heard of ugly human trafficking violations, but to be in the business of selling slaves was

the most repulsive thing she could imagine. She was reminded of the repugnant case in Cleveland, Ohio, in which a man had abducted three different young women and kept them captive as slaves in his house for over a decade. One of them was forced to have his child. Was The Bear trying to capitalize on that idea? Make a *business* out of slavery in the twenty-first century? Had the Jane Doe in Michigan been to that same cabin in the woods as Teresa had to receive her bear claws tattoo? Was she in line to be sold as a slave? Was that what all this was about?

"And you've seen other women with the tattoo, the same one as yours?"

"Yes, one other. I told you about her. Katrina. She was already there in the house when I arrived in Chicago. She was gone after a week."

"Teresa, I want to show you a photo of a dead woman. It's graphic. I don't want to upset you, but I would like to know if you might recognize her. We've been trying to identify her. She had the tattoo as well."

Teresa pursed her lips. "You can show me."

Annie had delayed this moment, waiting for a time when Teresa wasn't so shell-shocked. She opened the file and showed her the photo of the Jane Doe in Michigan.

Teresa squinted in revulsion, but then her eyes widened as she studied the image. "My God, I know her. That's not Katrina, but I know her."

"You do?"

"She was on the boat with me."

"Really! What's her name?"

"Irina. Irina Semenov. She was from Gorelovo, a suburb of St. Petersburg. Oh, Irina. What happened to her?"

"She was in the trunk of a car, like you were. The car was in an accident." Annie took the photo back and put it in the folder. "We believe she had just received the tattoo twenty-four

to forty-eight hours prior to the accident, so perhaps she was at your same cabin in the woods. It happened in Michigan, in a wooded area."

"We got to know each other well on that boat," Teresa said. "She told me all about her life, just as I told her all about mine."

Annie felt a tremendous surge of satisfaction at finally identifying the victim in Michigan. Irina Semenov. Now she had some ammunition to give to her colleagues at ICE—Immigration and Customs Enforcement. They would work to trace Irina's movements backward from the moment she entered the country.

"Your voyage was late April to early May?"

"Yes."

The timing sounded about right. The traffickers were systematically tattooing their victims within a month or so after the women arrived in the US, before they proceeded to turn them out to strip, prostitute themselves, or be sold as chattel.

"Teresa, you've already given us very good descriptions of all the men you encountered, including this 'Nikolai' that you met in Kiev. We really want to find out who's in charge of the criminals who did this to you here in this country. I'm especially interested in the Caucasian man you said was at the cabin, the one who beat you. You're certain he was not a Russian?"

"No, he spoke like an American. He was American."

"And you say he's in his late twenties or early thirties?"

"I think so."

"And the men stayed in a different cabin nearby."

"Yes. I was all alone. I could sometimes hear them laughing and drinking in the other cabin when they weren't visiting *me*."

Annie nodded. That was a lot to go on.

"If there is ever anything else you can remember or tell me about any of these men or The Bear, you will call me?"

"Yes."

"Thank you, Teresa. You're a brave, strong woman. You're a survivor."

"Oh, one thing I remember."

"What's that?"

"The American. He acted like the cabin was his."

"Did he say it was his?"

"Not really. It was just the way he acted. Possessive. I remember he told one of the other men to 'chop some of *his* wood in the back.' For the fireplace. 'Chop some of my wood there in the back,' he said."

"That's good, Teresa. You have a very good memory." Annie took her hand. "You've given us a lot of good information. We're going to track these men down and arrest them. We're going to make sure they never do to anyone else what they did to you."

It was the last thing Annie ever said to Teresa. When Annie went home after the interview that night, Teresa Wang hung herself with a bed sheet, prior to being released into what she must have thought was a harsh, cruel world.

12

It was time to expand the investigation across the Atlantic.

Annie had worked with one of the ALATs in Russia before. Colin Clark was a good man, if somewhat overworked. After all, there were only a few Assistant Legal Attachés for all of Russia, and they were based in Moscow. The Legats and ALATs had a certain mystique at the Bureau. They were men and women of the FBI stationed in foreign countries, usually at US embassies, acting as liaisons to local law enforcement and security.

She worked on an email to Clark, attached the growing case file, and sent it. Annie laid out her suspicions about the international trafficking network and asked if he could get any information about The Bear and focus an initial probe in the St. Petersburg area.

The Russian embassy in Washington, DC, had already communicated the identities of the two dead tattooed women to their families. Irina and Teresa. At this point, the existence of the criminal operation was known by both countries. Whether Russia would do anything about it was anyone's guess.

Teresa's death had hit Annie hard. It was possible that the FBI agent had been the last person the victim had spoken to. Annie couldn't imagine the torture that had been going on inside that woman's head and heart. It wasn't the first time a victim had committed suicide after being rescued, and it wouldn't be the last. The psychological damage that trafficking inflicted on a victim was, in a way, often worse than the physical torment. Survivors' roads to recovery were personal, diverse, and always difficult.

The phone at her desk rang and brought Annie out of her funk. "Marino," she answered.

"This is Detective Bud Brinkley in Minneapolis."

"Yes, detective, how are you?"

"Fine. Listen, I'm emailing you the rest of the material on that case with the tattooed girl. I'm pretty sure it's all we have. That case went cold real fast. But you also wanted to know who the manager of the Hot Spot was back then?"

"Yes?"

"A Russian guy by the name of Fyodor Utkin."

What a surprise, Annie thought.

"He's still around," she said. "Here in Chicago."

"We couldn't prove that he or anyone at the strip club pimped out the victim to the motel. She didn't work at the club at the time of the murder. The report's in the file I just sent you."

"Even though you couldn't prove it, what did you personally think?"

"Well, those people are sleazy scum of the earth. I wouldn't put it past them at all if they were sending their strippers out as call girls, but we couldn't catch them at it. No, the place was clean, despite the bottom-feeders that ran the place."

"Did you interview Utkin?" Annie asked.

"Yeah. He was legit, we definitely checked him out. But you know, he wasn't the owner of the club."

"Would it by chance have been a shell company in Belize called Eyepatch, LLC?"

"As a matter of fact, it was!"

"Thank you, detective. I appreciate your help."

"You're welcome, and hey, keep me in the loop, will you?"

"I will, detective."

She hung up and brought up Fyodor Utkin's file on her computer. Was he working for The Bear? Was *he* the US manager of operations? The problem with that scenario was that he had been known to the FBI for years. They'd kept an eye on him. As far as the law was concerned, he ran his businesses without blemishes.

Near the end of the afternoon, her cell phone rang. The ID said CARUTHERS.

"Harris?" she answered.

"Annie, hi, how are you?"

"Good, and you?"

"Great. Listen, I'm in Chicago again. Just got here, thought I'd call. I wanted to thank you for your good work. Getting Irina identified was pretty incredible."

"Thanks. I appreciate it. Still . . . it's a sad thing to have to do."

"I know. Anyway, I've been reading your updates, and I want to help you. The locals in Lakeway are getting nowhere in their investigation. Chief Daniel is old and about to retire, and Captain Mike Baines is not the brightest bulb in the building, nor is he too concerned. He seems to think it's low priority and that the county sheriff should do all the work since it's a county case anyway. Part of the problem is that the sheriff doesn't want the case until it's near solving."

"Harris, it's possible that the cabin in the woods Teresa Wang mentioned might be in the area. You think?"

"That's why I want to work together. I mean, it's my case, too."

"Sure." Annie checked the time. "You want to go check out some strip clubs again?"

The Den was out near O'Hare airport, located in Des Plaines. This time Annie drove the Bucar with Harris in the passenger seat. On a weekday the traffic wasn't bad, but the heat index had shot through the roof. The A/C in the Fusion was adequate, but Annie was about ready to request a newer model car.

"Nothing like a surprise visit from the FBI to keep the strip clubs on their toes," she said as they approached the building.

"Toes? That's all we're going to see?"

She elbowed Harris. "Watch it."

A young man in his late twenties or early thirties served as the bouncer and money-taker at the cash register. At first Annie thought she knew him, but she wasn't sure.

The agents displayed their credentials. "Agents Marino and Caruthers, FBI. We'd like to see the manager on duty."

The man looked surprised. "FBI? Why?"

"Just get your manager," Harris said. "What's your name, anyway?"

"Makar Utkin."

"Utkin?" Annie asked. "Are you related to Fyodor Utkin?"

"He's my father." He had a light Russian accent. There was more of an American inflection in his speech since he'd probably lived in the US most—but perhaps not all—of his life.

"Is he here?"

"No, he's out of town."

"Who's in charge then?" Annie pressed.

"Ivan."

"I know Ivan. Please fetch him."

The younger Utkin went into the club. As before, Annie and Harris went inside behind him. The decor was very similar to the Cat's Lounge—dark, tacky, and furnished with thirty-year-old tables and chairs. A young woman was on stage displaying her wares, gyrating to the music of Prince. The agents positioned themselves by the bar, where a female bartender asked them if they wanted anything to drink. Annie didn't know her, but she hadn't visited the Den in a few months. The woman appeared to be in her late thirties, with tattoos up and down her arms. Her hair was as black as coal.

"No, thanks," Annie answered, "we're on duty."

The bartender noticed the guns at their belts. "Oh, I see."

"What's your name?"

"I'm Tiffany."

"Tiffany what?"

"Tiffany Vombrack. And it's my real name."

"Do you just bartend or do you dance, too?"

"Oh, I just bartend, help out with the management, you know, oversee the girls."

Annie opened the folder she carried and pulled out some photos, starting with the one of Vladimir Markov. "Ever see this man?"

"Yeah. He's a customer."

"When's the last time you saw him?"

She appeared to ponder this. "Gee, I don't know. It's been a few weeks, I'm sure."

"Does Ivan know him?"

"I don't know."

The manager appeared at that point, led from the back rooms by Makar Utkin. As the younger man walked past Annie, she gave him another scrutinizing look. His blue eyes stood out. Certain she'd seen him in the past, Annie spoke up. "Excuse me?"

He stopped. "Yeah?"

"Have we met before?"

Makar shook his head. "No, I don't think so." He winked at her. "I'd remember you if I had. Ladies with guns turn me on." He returned to his post at the front of the club.

Annie rolled her eyes at Harris and murmured, "Can't *wait* to give you my number, buddy," which forced her partner to suppress a laugh. She turned to the manager. "Hello, Ivan, how are you?"

"Fine, Agent Marino." Ivan Polzin was a thick-necked Russian immigrant in his forties. "To what do I owe the pleasure?" Unlike Makar, his speech was very thick with an accent.

"I was just showing Tiffany here some photos. I'd like you to take a look, too. Do you know him?"

Ivan took Markov's picture and frowned. "I think I've seen him. I don't *know* him. He's a customer."

"Well, he must get around, because he was a customer at the Cat's Lounge, too."

Ivan shrugged. "We're all the same business."

"I know. Fyodor is out of town, huh?"

"Yeah."

"When will he be back?"

"I don't know. He never tells me these things. He just says, 'I'm going to be gone for a while.' Sometimes he's gone for a few days, sometimes a month. Is possible he went to Russia. In the meantime, I'm in charge of the clubs, I have to make sure all three have managers in place and the girls' schedules are set, and I find a replacement if one of them doesn't show up, you name it." He wiped sweat from his forehead.

Next, Annie showed Ivan and Tiffany the photo of Irina Semenov. "How about her?"

Tiffany recoiled. "Ew!"

Ivan winced but didn't say anything.

"Her name was Irina Semenov," Annie said. "She had a tattoo of bear claws on her neck. Look, like this." She showed them the photo of the tat.

Ivan rubbed his chin and shook his head. "Nah, I don't think I've ever seen her before. I've never seen that tattoo."

Annie looked at Tiffany. "What about you?"

The woman had a crease in her brow, but she slowly shook her head. "No." But then she glanced at Annie and Annie noticed her eyes widen ever so subtly.

Was she trying to tell her something?

The next two photos Annie revealed were of Karen Washington and Teresa Wang. "How about them? Ever seen them before?"

Again, negative answers.

They were done. Annie and Harris pulled out business cards and handed them to Ivan and Tiffany. Annie said, "If something strikes you, if you remember something, or if you ever see someone with that tattoo, please give me a call, would you?"

"Sure thing," said Tiffany. She stuck the cards in the back pocket of her jeans.

"So, Ivan, I trust I don't need to have a look around?" Annie asked. "All your dancers are legally entitled to work in the United States and all that?"

"What, you think I would risk the wrath of ICE? Are you kidding me? We run a legitimate business here."

"That's what Fyodor insisted, too. Okay, have a nice evening."

On the way out, they stopped to talk to Makar Utkin again. "I might as well show these pictures to you," Annie said. "Do you know any of these women?" She revealed Irina's picture first, which elicited no visceral reaction like it did with everyone else who saw it. He simply shook his head. She then displayed Karen's and Teresa's pictures. Again, another shake of the head.

"No, I've never seen them before. Should I have? Did they dance here sometime?"

She put away the pictures. "Say hello to your father for me."

"I will. What's your name?"

She handed him a business card. "He knows me. I must have seen you around at one of the clubs before; you look very familiar."

He shrugged. "I've been working for my dad ever since I was old enough to walk inside."

"Okay. Stay out of trouble."

Annie and Harris visited the third club that Fyodor Utkin managed, Paradise, located farther south, near I-80. The manager on duty there, Sasha Treblinka, couldn't identify Markov at all. Annie figured the club's location might have been too far of a drive for the guy to regularly visit. Treblinka said nothing about Irina's photo or the tattoo photos as well. However, when he saw the pictures of Karen Washington and Teresa Wang, he blinked.

"You know them?" Annie asked.

The man shook his head. "No. I thought this one"—he tapped Teresa's picture—"looks like another Asian girl who worked here, but it's not her. Sorry."

As they left the parking lot, Harris asked, "Now what?"

"I'm calling it a day. Let's head back to the city. Where are you staying?"

"The Marriott at Ashland and Harrison, close to the FBI building. My car's there at the field office."

"I'll drive you back to the FO."

"So did we strike out on those visits?"

"Probably. Not too sure, though. That bartender, Tiffany. She knew something. I might need to have another talk with her away from the club." She looked at Harris. "I bet you a lunch that she calls me."

He shrugged. "Okay."

As she drove up I-294, Annie pictured an abstract representation of the trafficking network. It was right there, probably in front of her eyes, but it was covered by curtains. Hidden in plain sight, so to speak. These things always were.

She just had to find a way to pull back the curtains.

13

End of June

When the container ship arrived at the Port of Newark, Yana Kravec was hungry, thirsty, and had probably lost ten pounds. Christina and Sofia were also malnourished. It had been nearly three weeks since they'd first boarded the boat, but now, finally, it was time to disembark.

Everything would be better in America.

Von came and addressed the three women. He told them to get their bags and have their passports and work visas ready. They were happy to leave the little berth that had become extremely claustrophobic during the journey. Even though he had been kind during the voyage, now he was as gruff as he'd been when they first met, when Nikolai had handed them over to him in St. Petersburg. Von barked at them to hurry along as he accompanied them through a series of hatchways. It seemed as if they were going deeper into the bowels of the ship instead of up to the deck. There was no sign of other crew. Finally, they emerged into the open air and onto a gang plank that stretched to the pier.

It was night.

Von escorted them to the Customs and Immigration booths, where a single agent was working.

Yana looked at the clock on the wall. Two in the morning. What was a Customs agent doing working at that hour?

She watched as Von handed over a wad of bills to the man, who then gestured for each woman to come forward. Yana went first. The agent swiped her passport and stamped her visa. Yana had read on the Internet that she would be fingerprinted and have her photo taken when she arrived in the US, but for some reason the Customs man didn't do that. Once he was finished with her, he jerked his head to indicate for her to move on. She waited beside Von as Christina and Sofia went through the same procedure.

They were brought out to the pier where the huge steel containers were stacked. Even though bright floodlights illuminated the area, the dark night sky dominated the setting. A red van with blacked-out windows sat waiting for them, its engine running. The passenger door opened, and a woman appeared. In the dim light, Yana thought she might be in her forties. The woman held out a hand. Yana and her bunkmates each shook it.

"I'm Nadine. Welcome to the United States." She said it without cheer. Yana thought perhaps the woman didn't enjoy doing this job in the middle of the night; she must be merely grumpy.

"I'm Yana. It's so good to be here finally!"

Nadine grunted an acknowledgment and opened the side door, gesturing for the women to climb inside. Nadine closed the door and got in the passenger seat of the van.

"This is Abram," she said, introducing the driver. He was huge, built like a professional athlete. Each woman said hello, but he didn't return the greeting.

Then they were away. Yana turned to the window to say goodbye to Von, but he had already disappeared.

Something was very odd about all of this.

"Where are we going? To a hotel?" Yana asked.

Nadine turned and answered, "To a place where you'll be staying temporarily."

What was her accent? It wasn't American. She wasn't Russian. The woman looked European.

"Where are you from, Nadine?" Yana asked.

Without looking at her, the woman replied, "Budapest."

Yana exchanged glances with Christina and Sofia, who were just as mystified as she was.

Nevertheless, it was all very exciting. They were in America! The port was gigantic, and the skyline of tall buildings that made up Newark was impressive.

"Look, there's Manhattan!" Sofia said, pointing.

Yana gazed across the Hudson at an even more remarkable array of buildings, dotted with lights from windows. She recognized the Empire State Building among the other skyscrapers.

Wow . . .

The van drove out of the port and onto a highway. Even at that hour there was traffic, not much different from St. Petersburg.

An uncomfortable silence fell upon the three women. Their arrival didn't feel right. Weren't they supposed to be filled with joy? Why weren't Nadine and Abram happy to see them?

They drove for a half hour until the van pulled into a residential street somewhere deep in the city. Yana had no idea where they were. The van entered a garage. Nadine got out as Abram shut off the engine. The woman slid open the van's side door.

"Get out."

The three women took their bags and entered the house, where another man stood waiting for them. Unlike the others, he was African American. His size was intimidating, and his milky right eye immediately gave Yana the creeps.

The place was a dump. It looked as if it hadn't been cleaned in weeks. There was a rancid odor that reminded Yana of the nursing home where her grandmother had lived the last year of her life.

When they were inside, Nadine said, "Give me your passports and cell phones."

The three women looked at each other. Cell phones?

"Now!"

Her snap made them jump. Silently, they handed the items over and watched as Nadine put them in her own handbag. Abram came in, shut the door, and locked it.

"My name is Bobby," the black man said. "What are your names?"

"I'm . . . Yana."

"Christina."

"Sofia."

Bobby nodded. He spoke with an American accent. "From now on, you are property of The Bear. You will obey orders. You will do whatever we say. If you try to escape, we will kill you."

An icy chill ran down Yana's spine. *What?*

"What are you talking about?" Christina asked.

After he slapped her across the face, Bobby said, "That's what I'm talking about. Nadine, show the girls their rooms." He grinned, revealing a black tooth in front. "I'll be there soon to tuck you ladies in."

No. Yana had been very wrong.

Things were definitely not going to be better in America.

14

Mid-July

Carrying a hunting rifle in a padded case, Jason walked into the den of the Paley home as Trey followed behind him.

"Honey, I'm home!" he announced with exaggerated cheeriness.

Nat looked up from the television. She was lying on a leather couch, barefoot, dressed in jeans and a T-shirt. "How'd it go?"

"Great!"

"I have to admit he shoots pretty good. For a twerp," Trey said. He took the rifle out of Jason's hands. "I'll put these away before you hurt yourself. You know, you might not be such a terrible brother-in-law after all."

"Well, thank you, Trey," Jason said with sarcasm. "I know, coming from you, that's a real compliment."

"Don't be a jerk."

Nat said, "Trey, there's no need to insult Jason all the time. We're getting a little tired of it. *I'm* getting a little tired of it."

Trey shot her a look. "Shut up, Natalia. Jesus. You can be such a . . ."

"What? What, Trey?" Nat folded her arms.

Trey looked as if his anger might get the best of him, and Jason could actually see a vein appear in Trey's left temple, which accentuated and pulsed whenever he was agitated. But then he backed down, and the sudden tension dissipated almost as quickly as it had appeared. *The guy really needs anger management*, Jason thought. Nat had been coaching him on how to deal with her brother. "He flies off the handle at the drop of a penny," she had said. "You just have to realize that it disappears in the same amount of time. If he's mad, he'll calm down in a minute. It's weird."

"I'll put the rifles away," Trey said, and he left the room.

Jason and Nat looked at each other. "Whoa . . ." said Jason.

"Seriously, how did it go? To tell you the truth, I was a little concerned when you said you and Trey were going to the range to fire guns."

"It was fine. I think he was in his element, so he was in a good mood the whole time. And those two lessons I took paid off. I was able to impress your brother. I hit the damn targets!"

Nat laughed. "Good for you."

"I wasn't so great when I tried to shoot *his* gun. I mean, they're both his guns, I shot them both. The one he prefers is the .458. Geez, that's an elephant gun or something. He could take down a T-Rex with that thing."

"Yeah, he gave it a girl's name."

"Mandy."

She shook her head and chuckled. "Right."

Jason was actually a little flattered that Trey had complimented him on his shooting. Perhaps there was room to get closer to his future brother-in-law after all.

"So when is the big hunt?" Nat asked.

"I don't know. When *is* the hunt, Trey?" Jason asked, as Trey came back into the room.

"Normally in September, but I like to do it anytime in the summer. We'll go soon, in August, probably."

"Isn't that out of season?" Nat asked.

Trey shrugged. "It's on our property. We should be able to kill any animal we want on our property."

"I don't know about that."

Trey jerked his head at her. "I think I know what I'm talking about. *I'm* the veteran, *I'm* the hunter, all right?"

Nat held up her hands. "Fine, Trey. Jesus."

Trey shook his head. "Anyway, you should have seen Brain Fart Man here, he was actually good with the .338." He punched Jason in the arm. "You could've been a sniper in the army. Although you'd probably want to use my M24 for that. You don't hunt big game with that, but it's not bad for hunting humans."

"Hm, not my line, Trey, but thanks," said Jason.

"You got equipment? What gear do you have?"

"Huh?"

"For the hunt. Do you have any gear? I know you don't have a gun, so you can use my Win Mag and ammo, but do you have all the other stuff you need?"

"What do I need?"

"Shit, man, you need the right clothes, and you want layers. Even though it's summer, it can get cold at night out in the woods. Good boots. A flashlight. Insect repellent. A sleeping bag. Tent—if we sleep outdoors. Fluorescent jacket and hat? Rain poncho? Knife? Maybe a hatchet. High-energy snacks, like protein bars?"

"Wow, I had no idea."

"I'll make you a check list."

A voice was heard from another room, calling for Trey.

"I'm back here in the den!"

The Russian guy Jason knew as Mack came in. "Hey. What's going on?"

"Nothing," Trey said. "Butthead and I just got back from target practice. The guy can actually shoot a gun."

"Really?" Mack grinned at Jason. "Congratulations!"

Jason rolled his eyes. "Thanks. I'm not a total dweeb."

Trey said, "I figured if Mr. Hopeless was going to be my brother-in-law, in spite of my dire warnings to my sister, I'd invite him on a hunt."

Mack raised his eyebrows in surprise. "When? You don't mean the Bacchanal . . . ?"

"*No!*" Trey shot his friend a sharp look. "We're going on a hunt."

Mack had obviously let something slip. "What's the Bacchanal?" Jason asked.

"Nothing," Trey answered.

Nat said, "Oh, it's this stupid guys' weekend that has been sort of a tradition in our family. My dad started it with his buddies when he was younger. Now Trey and some of his friends do it."

"What is it?"

"They go up to our cabin in Michigan for a weekend or whatever, and get blistering drunk, watch sports on satellite TV, go hunting . . . . You know—a rite of passage, a regular frat party where they try and see who's got the biggest dick."

Jason laughed. "Sounds like fun. I'd like to go!"

"No. You can't," Trey said with finality. "Come on, Mack. Let's get out of here." He tugged at his friend's arm and they both retreated. Mack waved at them. "*Poka*," he said. *Bye,* in Russian.

"What's the big deal about this little Bacchanal thing?" Jason asked Nat. "Why can't I go?"

Nat shook her head. "Because he's being an asshole. Besides, I don't think you want to attend. You don't have the temperament for it. Sorry, you don't, Jason. It would be Trey and Mack and their paramilitary buddies. I think they'd eat you alive."

"You're probably right. Still, if it's a family tradition, you'd think he would invite me along to be polite, even if I *didn't* go."

"I know. Don't take it personally."

He lay down beside her on the couch. "Want to go back to Chicago?"

"Why? Let's hang out here. We can go swimming."

They heard someone enter the den. It was Nat's father.

"Hey, guys," Greg Paley said.

"Hi, Mr. Paley. How was your business trip to Russia?"

Greg bopped Jason on the head as he walked by on his way to the kitchen. "It was good, and how many damn times do I have to tell you? Call me Greg."

"I'm sorry, Greg, it's just the way I was raised. I have to call you Mr. Paley. I'm wired that way."

"Well, cut it out. How was the range?"

"Fine! I did pretty well."

They chatted about the rifles and Greg asked which one he liked best. Jason did his best to talk firearm lingo, but eventually admitted he was a novice.

"That's okay, Jason. When we go on the hunt, I'll show you the ropes."

"You'll go with them, Daddy?" Nat asked.

"Sure, why not. I haven't been hunting in a while."

"Where is your cabin, exactly?" Jason asked.

"In the middle of a forest in Michigan. North of Kalamazoo and Grand Rapids. Got a nice little chunk of Manistee National Forest land that is officially owned by the Paley family and not the government. My father purchased it when Palit Wool really started to take off. It was a summer home, although the cabin isn't much. Two bedrooms. It's fine for short trips. There's a shed on the property that is essentially one bedroom, too."

"The property butts up against a lake," Nat said. "And a little river flows through it, too."

"You've been there?" Jason asked.

"Of course I've been there. Well, when I was little. I haven't been there since I was a kid."

"Why not?"

Nat looked at her dad. "I don't know. Why not?"

Greg laughed. "I think the males of the species took it over. It became a guys-only domain."

"Actually, I hate it," Nat said. "There's no hot water, you have to heat up water on a fire. TV reception sucks; there's no cable. I'm surprised there's even electricity. There's no cell phone service, is there, Dad?"

"Nope. No Wi-Fi either. It's meant to be a getaway from civilization."

"Did you start the Bacchanal?" Jason asked.

Greg did a slight double take and frowned. "Who told you about the Bacchanal?"

"Trey did."

"No, I did," Nat replied. "After Mack and Trey mentioned it."

Greg nodded. "I see. Yeah, I started it when I was in my thirties. Early nineties. I had these two buddies who hunted with me, and it sort of grew out of that. Louis and Jim. I met them in the army, and we became good friends."

"When was that? Where were you?" Jason asked.

"1976 to 1980. Europe, mostly. I did some time in West Germany and Austria. There was no shooting war on at the time. Because I can speak Russian, the brass found me useful."

"I sort of remember your friend Jim," Nat said. "He died, didn't he?"

"Yeah, about fifteen years ago. In China of all places. Louis is still around. He still works with me."

"You don't do this Bacchanal thing anymore?" Jason asked.

Greg shook his head. "Nah. It's a young man's folly. I don't particularly want to spend my nights throwing up from too much booze. I kind of outgrew it, I guess. Trey took it over. Now it's his thing." He tilted his head and looked at Jason. "You're too much of a nice boy to get mixed up with those characters. I'd stay away from it if I were you." He turned to Nat. "Where's your mother?"

"She went to the store."

"Ah." Greg moved on toward the kitchen, leaving the couple alone again.

Jason was perturbed, and Nat could see it. She reached out and squeezed the sides of his cheeks so that his mouth puckered. "Don't pout."

"What, I can't participate in a Paley family ritual? It's really hard trying to like your brother," he said.

"I know. I think you're doing a swell job, though. I love you for it." She leaned in and kissed him. "Maybe you two will end up being good friends."

"Then maybe I can go to the—" he made air quotes with his fingers—"*Bacchanal.*"

"Well, I'm going swimming." She unwrapped herself from him and stood. "You coming?"

"Yeah, I'll go change in a second."

"See you in the pool."

As she left the den, Jason couldn't help thinking about the slight. It seemed to him that Trey was hiding something.

15

End of July

Yana Kravec had spent the last three weeks in a hell on earth.

After the shocking revelation that she had been fraudulently lured to the United States by human traffickers, the horror was nonstop. At the end of the first night in the house in New Jersey, she wanted to die. The man named Bobby and the man called Abram had both taken turns with her body, used it, abused it, and torn her insides apart until she was a bloody mess. The same thing happened to Christina and Sofia. They were each kept in separate rooms. Yana knew by their screams that they were being subjected to the same torture.

The woman called Nadine told her the next morning that she would "get used to it."

They let her heal for a few days, but then it happened again the following week, and one more time at the beginning of her third week in captivity.

Her spirit was broken. She had nothing to live for. It was hopeless. She would never escape.

What were they going to make her do? Prostitute herself? Nadine had intimated that there were "bigger plans" for her, but that she had to be "conditioned" first.

Then, one morning, Nadine told the three women to pack their bags—they were moving across the country to Chicago. They piled into a different van, again with blacked-out windows. The driver was Butch, a burly, bald Caucasian man who was heavily tattooed and pierced in many places on his face. He didn't speak. With him was Fidel, a Caucasian man who claimed to be from Serbia. He seemed pleasant, but Yana sensed that he could be cruel if he wanted. He warned the three women that if they tried to escape or caused any trouble, he would "snap their necks."

Oddly, along the way, the men allowed their captives to appear in public. The van stopped at various rest stops to fill up with gas. The women were allowed bathroom breaks, but only at facilities where the restroom was just big enough for one person. Yana, Christina, and Sofia had to use it one at a time. Mingling with other travelers was forbidden. Food was bought to go and eaten in the van.

The trip had taken two days. Yana tried to sleep for most of the journey, but she found it impossible to do so. She was in despair. It had been nearly two months since she'd left St. Petersburg. What were her parents doing? Did they think about her at all? Were they worried? Yana's eyes filled with tears as she thought about them. They probably didn't even know she had left the country. Why hadn't she *told* them? How could she have been so *stupid*? *No one* knew where she was!

Even if she could escape her captors, what would she do? She didn't have her passport. They'd told her that the Immigration officers would put her in jail. At the moment, however, that sounded like heaven. Better to rot in an American prison than be raped and abused at the whims of her abductors.

At the end of the two-day journey, they arrived in Chicago. Now she sat in a room in the back of a strip club somewhere in the huge city. She hadn't been able to see much of the streets due to the van's tinted windows. She'd been separated from the other girls and ushered into the club as soon as she was dropped off, and she sat there by herself for a few hours. Music pounded through the walls . . . *boom boom boom.* She heard the sound of women laughing outside the door. The dancers. Were they captives, too? No, they were enjoying themselves. They were *laughing*. How could they laugh if they were victims of kidnapping?

Christina and Sofia had been taken somewhere else. Her compatriots were told to remain in the van as Fidel escorted Yana away and handed her off to a Russian man at the back of the building. Would she ever see them again? They had become close. Like sisters. They were family. The three women had attempted to comfort each other against the harsh realities of their new existence. Mostly they cried together. Sofia took to praying a lot, even though she had claimed to be non-religious. Yana had been raised with no particular faith, and now she knew she'd been correct.

There was no God—not in a world where something like *this* could happen.

She heard a key unlock the door. It opened, revealing a thick-necked man in his forties. He stepped inside and closed the door behind him.

He spoke Russian. "What is your name?"

She cleared her throat. Lately her speech had become very hoarse. "Yana Kravec."

The man pulled out a passport, opened it, checked the photo against her, and nodded. "From now on, your name is Nadia. If anyone asks you, you say your name is Nadia. If they ask for your family name, you say your name is 'just Nadia.' Got that?"

Yana nodded.

"In a few hours you will be taken to your new home. Wait here. Can I bring you something to eat or drink?"

She wasn't hungry. Her appetite was completely shot. "No, thank you."

"Stand up."

She did so.

"Turn around."

She obeyed.

The man nodded. "You will do fine. You are a very beautiful woman. You are worth a lot of money."

Yana stared at her feet. "Am I going to dance here? Is that what this is about?"

"No. You are special merchandise. The Bear has other plans for you." There was a knock at the door. "What?"

"Ivan, Makar is here with the car."

"All right." He placed a hand under Yana's chin and lifted her head. "Your ride got here sooner than we thought. Grab your things and let's go."

He led her out of the room, where the music was louder in the hallway. She passed an open doorway to a dressing room. Two women were inside; one was putting on lingerie, the other was sitting at a makeup table, looking in a mirror. They didn't notice her.

The man called Ivan took Yana to the back door, the same one she had entered a few hours earlier. A younger man, probably in his late twenties, stood outside in the alley by a blue Nissan sedan. It was dark outside.

"Ivan?" A voice called from the hallway.

"What?"

Yana turned to see a dark-haired woman with tattoos on her arms. Their eyes met.

"I wanted to tell you that there's a drunk customer giving Sheila a hard time. I can't find Dmitri. You might need to handle it."

"I'll be there in a minute!" Ivan snapped. "Go back to the bar!"

The woman held up her hands. "Fine." She turned to walk away, but stole another glance at Yana.

"Get in the car!" Ivan spat.

Yana obeyed. The younger man—his name was Makar?—had popped the trunk.

"No," Ivan said. "Let her ride in front. It's late enough. She can see some of Chicago."

Makar shrugged, closed the trunk, and opened the passenger side door. Had he expected her to ride in the *trunk*? Yana thought the horrors would never cease. She got in the front seat. Makar sat behind the wheel, and they drove away. Now she could see the city, the streets, the traffic, the lights . . . As they pulled out of the alley, she glimpsed the neon sign for the club.

The Den.

"What's your name?" the driver asked.

"Yana."

He back-handed her on the face as he drove. "No, it's not! What is your name?"

"Nadia. *Nadia*!"

He nodded. "That's right."

They drove for a while until they reached a dark residential neighborhood. It reminded her of that first street in New Jersey where she'd been taken. Isolated, quiet, and out of sight.

It was the same procedure as before. Makar pulled into the garage of a house. He led Yana inside and handed her over to two men—one black, the other Caucasian. The latter grabbed her roughly by the upper arm and took her upstairs. He knocked on a door and opened it.

Two other women were lying on beds. They looked up. From the dark circles under their eyes, Yana knew that they, too, were captives.

"Your roommates," the man said as he shoved Yana inside. "We'll go over the rules later." He closed the door and was gone.

The other women were young, late teens or early twenties. One was Asian, the other white.

"What's your name?" the Asian woman asked.

"Ya—er, Nadia."

"No, what's your *real* name?"

"Yana. My name is Yana." She broke out into tears. "My name is *Yana. My name is Yana!"*

She was determined not to forget it.

16

Early August

On the Monday following Annie's visit to the Den with Harris Caruthers in July, she attempted to contact Tiffany Vombrack, the bartender, to follow up and perhaps interview her away from the club. Her attempts failed and the momentum on the case slowed. She spent the last half of July on a case involving a Pakistani couple in Chicago who had apparently "bought" a maid from their native country.

Finally, she was ready to get back to the tattooed girls. As Annie stepped into her cubicle, with coffee thermos and lunch in hand, her cell phone rang with the chime it made when a person called the number on her business card. She plopped her stuff on the desk and grabbed the phone out of her jacket pocket.

It was Tiffany Vombrack, and she wanted to meet. She specifically asked to see the "photo of the dead girl" again.

They agreed to get together at a Denny's on Harlem Avenue, coincidentally, but in Oak Park, much farther north than where Karen Washington had been held. Normally, Annie would have dressed down to meet a witness, but she didn't bother to change out of her pantsuit. She did, however, stash her weapon in her purse to avoid undue attention.

Annie arrived first. She chose a booth away from the window in case Tiffany might be worried about being seen from the outside. She sat and placed her leather carrier on top of the table. The waitress brought coffee and water, and Annie waited a full fifteen minutes before Tiffany finally appeared. She was dressed the same way as she had been at the club.

"Hi, sorry I'm late," she said. "Traffic."

"I understand; it's all right."

Tiffany sat and motioned for the waitress. "Coffee, *please*."

"You have to be at work at five, when the club opens?"

"Four-thirty. Sometimes I have to open up, and today's one of those days."

When the coffee came, she ordered a full breakfast from the menu, taking it for granted that Annie was picking up the tab. Annie stuck with her coffee, as she had already eaten.

"Thanks for reaching out," Annie said.

"Yeah. I got to thinking. Do you have that picture of the dead girl in the car with you? I want to see it again."

Annie nodded. She pulled the file folder out of the case and found the photos. She glanced around to make sure no one else could see it. "Not exactly breakfast material," she said as she handed Irina Semenov's picture to Tiffany.

She looked at it and nodded. "I *have* seen her before. I thought I might have when you first showed it to me, but Ivan was there and I didn't want to say so."

"I suspected that."

"Listen, I don't want to be in a courtroom. I don't want to have to say anything on the record. Okay?"

"Tiffany, we might need you to, if it comes to that."

"Nope. I'm going to get up and leave. I can't be a witness or testify or anything like that."

"Why not?"

"It would be ratting. People in this business, they don't like rats."

"Maybe you should get in another business."

"Right. Like it's that easy. For you, maybe."

Annie didn't want to lose her. "Fine, off the record. Tell me what you know. It won't go further than this table."

"I have your word?"

"You have my word."

Tiffany nodded. "Okay, girls come and go all the time at the club. *All the time*. Some girls stay a few weeks, maybe a few months, and then they're gone. Some girls are there just a week and decide they can't handle it."

"You're talking about dancers?"

"Yeah." Tiffany pointed at the photo. "She was a dancer who was there for one day and one day only. Her name was Anastasia. I didn't know her last name. She wasn't very good; her attitude was poor, as I recall. Her English was okay. I didn't really talk to her except to say hello and welcome her. She was new. Then, the next day, she came to work and Makar was there to take her somewhere. She never came back."

Annie took the photo and replaced it in the folder. "Anastasia?"

"Yeah."

"Actually her name was Irina Semenov. She was trafficked, we believe, from Russia."

"Trafficked? Oh, my God. Really?"

"You don't know anything about that?"

"No! Jesus, I'm just the bartender!"

"Calm down. I want to ask you if you've noticed anything. Anything that sticks out, something that's out of place somehow. You said Makar took her somewhere?"

"Yeah. You remember Makar?"

"Makar Utkin. The boss's son."

"Yeah, him. I assumed he was taking her to another club or something."

"When was this?"

"Oh, I don't know. May, sometime."

"Please, can you be more specific?"

"Uh, let me think. Around the middle or end of May, maybe?"

"Maybe?"

"I don't know!"

"This is important, Tiffany. Was it before Memorial Day weekend?"

"Yeah, I think so. I'm pretty sure. Look, and there's something else."

"What?"

"There was a girl at the club a week or so ago. Week-and-a-half. I was told she was interviewing for a job, so she was in one of the back rooms of the club. She didn't come in through the front door, though. It was pretty late, close to midnight maybe. Anyway, I asked Ivan who was there, and he said 'some girl named Nadia.' I never talked to her. Well, *she* left with Makar that night, too. Ivan escorted her to the car."

"Can you describe her?"

"She definitely looked Russian, I can just tell. Brown hair. Big eyes, but that might have been a deer-in-the-headlights look. I think she looked scared."

"Tiffany, what day was this?"

"Uh"—she hid her face in her hands, and then raised it—"Thursday, a week ago Thursday."

Annie made a note of the date and nodded. "I'm going to show you the other two girls again." She pulled out Karen's and Teresa's photos. "Still don't know them?"

The woman studied the pictures, but shook her head. "No, I can say I've never seen them before."

"All right." Annie organized her thoughts. This meant that Makar Utkin had lied to her. Probably Ivan, too. Makar had known Irina Semenov—"Anastasia" to him, most likely. She would have to revisit the young man.

"Is Makar working tonight?" Annie asked.

"I haven't seen him for a couple of days. He works a crazy schedule. You never know when he's going to be there. It's like he works when he feels like it."

The food came, and Tiffany dug in. In a way, it gave Annie pleasure to see her eat. It probably wasn't often that she was treated to such a meal.

"Tiffany, I'm investigating a human trafficking operation here in Chicago. Have you noticed anything at the Den that might indicate that something like that is going on?"

She slowly shook her head. "No, I don't think so. All the girls who dance there *want* to dance there. I mean, I don't interview them or anything, I'm not the person who hires them, or fires them, for that matter." Tiffany set her jaw. "I'm trying to remember if there's anything . . . sometimes men bring potential dancers in the back door, like that Nadia girl. They meet with Ivan, or Fyodor, if he's there. Hardly ever do those girls get hired." She held up her hands. "I don't know if there's a casting couch in the office or not. I stay out of that."

"Do the men who work at the Den—do they have relationships, or *relations*, with the dancers?"

"Sometimes. But it's consensual on both parts, I'm pretty sure. Some of the girls, they're pretty loose, if you know what I mean. Others are there for strictly business, and they don't put up with any harassment. I get hit on all the time, and I don't put up with it."

"Have you ever heard anyone mention someone called 'The Bear'?"

"I don't think so."

Annie's eyes suddenly widened and she gasped, her attention focused over Tiffany's shoulder.

"What?" Tiffany asked, turning to look.

A tall and muscular man, dressed in shorts and a tank top, had just passed by their table. He was facing away from Annie and Tiffany, just a few feet away, with an arm around a blonde woman who, even from the back, looked like she could pass as a model. The man was studying his cell phone as the woman spoke, trying to tell him something.

Annie felt her stomach lurch. *Could that be? Eric? Shit, shit, shit, no, no, no . . . !*

The man turned just enough so that Annie could see his face.

"Oh, Jesus," she whispered and put a hand to her brow, embarrassed.

"What is it?" Tiffany asked.

"I, um, thought I saw my ex with his new model girlfriend. But it's not him."

The couple walked away and sat on the other side of the restaurant.

"How long has it been since you, uh, broke up?" Tiffany asked.

"Eight months. Well, almost nine."

Tiffany gave her a look. "Do you still have a thing for him?"

Annie looked back at the couple. He was still eyeing his phone, ignoring his gorgeous date as she spoke to him. *Typical of Eric,* she thought. *Two of a kind. This guy isn't interested in what* she *has to say, either.*

"Not at all. I've moved on."

"Have you?"

Annie did *not* want to discuss her private life with Tiffany Vombrack. Plus, she was a little angry with herself for reacting the way she had. "Yeah, it was just my eyes playing tricks on me. My jerk alert was going off. Look, Tiffany, let's get back to the subject at hand. I have to get going. Do me a favor. Keep your eyes and ears open, all right? If you see or hear anything, you let me know. Okay?"

"Does this mean I'm an informant?"

"Not officially."

"I can't mention on my Facebook page that I'm working for the FBI?"

"You don't want to do that, Tiffany."

"I'm kidding. Do I get paid, though?"

"No. Not unless you think you can deliver some serious evidence. Heck, if you give us evidence that will lead to a successful prosecution, we can put you in witness protection, and you can start a whole new life." That apparently appealed to Tiffany. Annie saw her eyes glisten at the prospect. After a pause, Annie said, "I'd like to know when Fyodor Utkin returns."

"Fyodor? You think he's involved?"

"I don't know. Maybe. Be careful. Make sure your bosses don't know you've talked to me. Do you know where Fyodor is?"

Tiffany shrugged. "He's in Russia, is my guess."

"Do you know when he'll be back?"

"Nope. Ivan's always in charge when Fyodor is away. Maybe it's really Ivan you want."

"I can't imagine Ivan Polzin having it together enough to be in charge of a complex and dangerous crime like trafficking, can you?"

Tiffany smiled. "No, you're right. But he takes orders well."

"That's what I'm thinking, too. Thank you, Tiffany. I hope we'll be able to speak again. You call me if you hear anything. Just be careful."

"I will. I have some hash browns left. You want 'em?"

17

Agent Harris Caruthers returned to Chicago to join Annie in questioning Ivan Polzin. She had managed to get the green light to make official requests for Polzin, Fyodor Utkin, and Makar Utkin to appear at the US Attorney's office on Dearborn. Polzin responded, but not the Utkins. She had known Fyodor was out of town, possibly in Russia, but Makar couldn't be found.

She had chosen to deliver the request to the Den in person at five o'clock on a weekday, accompanied by Harris and two Cook County Sheriff's men who provided support. Annie didn't expect there to be trouble, but one never knew.

The bouncer at the front was unfamiliar to her. Before he could protest, Annie and Harris displayed their credentials and the legal documents. "I have official FBI communications for Ivan Polzin and Makar Utkin."

The big man looked like he'd been struck. "Uh, okay. Wait here?"

"No, we're coming in." She nodded at the three men behind her. "Let's go."

They marched into the club—which had no customers at the moment, though loud music was already pounding. Tiffany was behind the bar. At first her eyes betrayed a look of alarm, but she quickly recovered and remained cool.

"See if you can get the music turned off," Annie told one of the cops. She went past the bar—merely glancing at Tiffany—and through the EMPLOYEES ONLY archway, followed by Harris and the other man. They moved beyond the dressing rooms and into Polzin's office, where she found him sitting at his desk.

"Mr. Polzin, the FBI would like you to come down to the federal building for some questioning. It's voluntary, and you can bring your attorney."

The man's expression was one of disgust, as if he'd just bitten into a rotten apple. "Am I under arrest?"

"No, sir. But you need to come in for some questioning. This is not a subpoena. It's just a request. The meeting is suggested for tomorrow, but we're here to take you there now, if you'd like to get it over with. You may call your attorney, if you wish, and have him or her meet us there."

"Now? Can you do this?"

She offered the envelope to him, but he swatted it away. "Fine," he said. "I have nothing to hide. What's this about, anyway?"

"Where is Makar Utkin?"

"He's gone. On vacation."

Annie cursed inwardly. "For how long? Where did he go?"

"How should I know where he went? He'll be gone for a week or so."

"There's a time on the letter indicating when you should be at the US Attorney's office tomorrow. Or would you like to come with us now?"

"I'm calling my attorney, but I'm not coming until tomorrow."

"Very nice to see you again, Ivan. I look forward to our chat."

Attempts to reach Makar Utkin at his Chicago residence on the south side—State Street near Chinatown—failed. Annie had to be satisfied with Ivan Polzin for now. He appeared at the Northern District of Illinois US Attorney's building on time with his lawyer, an American named Victor Plant. Annie had dealt with Plant before and knew him to be a weasel who represented underworld figures and small-time crooks. In fact, he was both Polzin's and Fyodor Utkin's lawyer.

Annie sat across the table from the two men in an interrogation room. Harris stood behind the one-way mirror, watching and listening. Despite his attempts to look composed, Annie could see that Polzin was antsy.

"A video camera is recording our conversation," Annie announced. "I thank you both for coming."

"My client has nothing to say," Plant said. "Unless you charge Mr. Polzin with something, we are leaving."

"Mr. Plant, we just have some questions for Mr. Polzin. How about we give it a shot before you go all Fifth Amendment on us?"

"Ask away. I've advised my client not to answer."

She looked at Ivan Polzin. "Mr. Polzin, you lied to me about not knowing this girl." She showed him the photo of Irina Semenov. "You *did* know her. She was at the Den in early May."

Polzin pointed his thumb at his attorney. "He says I don't have to answer, so I won't."

"Mr. Polzin, we know that Ms. Semenov was at your club for a few hours, and Makar Utkin came and took her away."

"That's not true!" he blurted, almost involuntarily.

Plant put a hand on Polzin's arm. "Don't answer her."

"Mr. Polzin, we have reason to believe that another woman was recently at your club for a few hours and was also picked up by Mr. Utkin and taken to another location."

"That happens all the time, we give rides to some of the girls . . ."

Plant said, "Ivan, stop talking."

"No, it's all right!" Polzin snapped at his lawyer. He then laughed nervously and said, "I have nothing to hide. Agent Marino, I have no idea what you're talking about. Whoever told you this is a liar."

"Mr. Polzin, we have reason to believe that you might be involved in a human trafficking operation. Is this true?"

"No!"

"Shut up, Ivan!"

Annie kept at it for another twenty minutes, but it was soon clear that Polzin's attorney was not going to let him speak.

"Very well," she finally said. "We will continue our investigation. I suggest you not leave town, like your *comrades* did."

Polzin's eyes narrowed at the implied insult.

"Are you going to charge my client? Is he under arrest?" Plant asked. "This is harassment, you know."

"No and no, and no it's not. You're free to go." She pointed at Polzin. "But we'll be watching you."

Polzin did his best to keep a straight face, but she noticed his Adam's apple move as he swallowed—a telltale sign that he was nervous.

A meeting was held in the SSA John Gladden's office. Present were Annie, Harris, and Michelle Aronson, a US Attorney who had been assigned to the case.

"I'm sorry, Agent Marino, but there just isn't enough evidence yet," the attorney said. "You have no concrete proof that the strip club is involved in your trafficking case. I agree there's *something* there, but you don't have enough to connect the pieces. You really have nothing on Mr. Polzin. I have to say I think you brought him in too soon. Now they're going to be careful."

"I know," Annie said. She turned to Harris. "What did you find out from ICE?"

Harris glanced at his notepad. "Fyodor Utkin left the country on June 8 for St. Petersburg, Russia. As far as we know, he hasn't returned. Not through legal ports of entry, anyway. He's still over there. We have in place a stop on his passport for when he tries to come home. He'll be held for questioning."

Annie turned to Gladden. "John, I know there are a lot of parts to this puzzle. I haven't quite put it together. But I'm getting close."

"What happened with the investigation of the driver of the car that crashed in Michigan?"

"We were successful in finding Vladimir Markov's real residence. It wasn't far from the Cat's Lounge. He lived in a studio apartment, not in a good neighborhood, and he worked in a newsstand in Chicago. His finances were poor, although he made a deposit of five thousand dollars into his bank account the day before his death. It was a cash deposit."

"But nothing in his house or computer?"

"Nothing useful. We're still checking phone records. The most recent calls he made on his cell phone—which survived the crash—went to now-disconnected numbers, burners, phones that could be tossed. Everything else looks legitimate. There are some calls to the Cat's Lounge and to the Den, spread out over two or three months. There's definitely a connection there, but otherwise it appears Mr. Markov lived a very lonely life since his divorce."

"The phone calls to the clubs don't prove anything except that he was a loyal customer," Aronson said. "He could have been calling to find out if a particular dancer was on duty that night."

"And the bartender . . . ?" Gladden asked.

"Tiffany Vombrack. I think she knows more, but she's going to want something in return."

"You have to find out what she knows before we can make any deals. Do you think she can connect the dots?"

"I don't know. The problem is that none of them are talking. I'm pretty certain Markov was associated with the Utkins,

Polzin, and our friend, The Bear. But we haven't caught them at anything yet. I need to step up surveillance of all these characters. I'd like to find Makar Utkin—he's still 'away,' but we know he hasn't left the country. My gut tells me that Fyodor Utkin is in charge of The Bear's US operations. He's probably over in Russia meeting with his boss now."

"Look, I'd like to catch these bastards as much as you would," the attorney said. "I just need more. I'm not convinced this 'Bear' even exists."

Annie looked at her supervisor.

He asked, "Are you in touch with one of the Russian ALATs?"

"Yeah, Colin Clark. He hasn't gotten back to me yet."

Gladden grunted. "I'll authorize the time, but I can't give you any more bodies. As for the bartender, use your judgment. If you think you can get something out of her, then keep at her. She's got to give you an indication of what she knows before we can even think about making a deal with the woman."

"I understand."

"Annie, you're free to work this case to your heart's content, but not to the detriment of any other cases. Got me?"

"Yes, sir. I'm lucky to have Agent Caruthers here working as my partner. He's on Detroit's dime."

"I know that. Let's reconvene if and when you uncover more evidence."

"Thank you, John."

She walked out with Harris and spread her hands. "What do you think we should do now?"

"We perform a little surveillance on the Den ourselves. It's just you 'n' me, kid."

"Fine." She looked at her watch. "The club is going to open soon. Watching a strip club is just my idea of how to spend a weeknight. Let's go."

18

"Why are you so quiet this evening?"

Nat and Jason sat in Pat's Pizzeria and Ristorante on Lincoln Avenue, their favorite joint for thin-crust pizza. One of the things the couple had in common was a dislike of the famous Chicago deep-dish pizza. Jason had originally hoped they would move to New York City after they were married, a superficial wish—he liked the pizza there better. He admitted that saying such a thing was sacrilege in Chicago. Unfortunately, Nat had a therapist job ready to go with a firm in the Windy City, so they would be staying for a while.

"I'm not being quiet," Jason answered.

"Yes, you are. You're acting glum. What's wrong?"

"Nothing. I'm just tired."

They ate in silence for a while, and then Nat said, "No, you're not. I know you. You're mad at me or something."

"I'm not mad at *you*."

"Then who are you mad at?"

"I'm not mad at anyone! I'm just . . ."

"What?"

Jason shook his head. "I don't know. Your . . . brother and dad and mom . . . I don't know . . ."

"What about them?"

"I just . . . I just don't think they respect me."

"Oh, come on. Don't be silly. My parents love you."

"Really?"

"Sure they do."

"I think they *like* me all right, but I always get the feeling they're really just tolerating me, and they hope pretty soon you're going to come to your senses and realize you can't marry a guy who has no secure source of income."

Nat put a half-eaten slice of pizza back on the plate in front of her. "Are we going to have this discussion again?"

"Don't be annoyed."

"I can't help it. You're so insecure."

"I'm not insecure. I'm perfectly fine with myself. It's your family that is insecure with *me*."

"That's nonsense."

"Is it? Then how come Trey *constantly* berates me? I've tried to warm up to him, I've tried to be his friend, I've tried to show him that I can be a regular guy . . . and he still treats me like dog poo on a stick."

That made her laugh. "Look, I know how Trey can be. We've talked about this before. He's got . . . problems. He's messed up. What can I say?"

"I know, I know, he's 'not right since he came back from Iraq.' I get it."

"But my parents like you. They don't berate you."

Jason sighed. "Your mom—I can hear it in her voice, and I see it in her eyes. She looks at me like I'm a lost puppy. I think she's disappointed you've picked me."

"That's not true."

"Are you sure? Have you actually talked to her about it?"

"No, but I—"

"And your dad . . . hey, I like your dad, don't get me wrong, but I'm also getting the feeling that he thinks, 'Uh oh, she's really going through with it . . . I thought it was a phase she would get over, but no, she's actually going to marry the guy.'"

"What makes you think that?"

"It's just a feeling."

"A feeling."

"Yeah. I mean, he has a sense of humor, we've laughed at jokes together and all that, but most of the time he has a pretty serious look on his face."

She paused. "Well, I think I know what you mean. Of course he has a sense of humor; he just doesn't show it very often. I think what you're seeing is that he's just worried about Trey. But he's also a very determined man, always thinking about business. He still has a lot of the army in him."

"But he didn't see combat. He was in the army, what, in the late seventies?"

"Yeah. What difference does that make? Whether you see combat or not doesn't make the army any less disciplined. And remember, he lost a brother, too. I think he blames himself for the accident."

"Does he?"

"I don't know. He doesn't like to talk about it." After a moment, she added, "Yeah, I think he does feel guilty about what happened to my Uncle David. It was a tragic accident, and Dad was right there. He saw it."

They ate in silence for a while again. Jason offered the last bit of wine in the bottle to Nat, but she shook her head. He poured the rest into his own glass and drank it.

"Nat, what's the story with your dad and your grandfather Maxim?"

"What do you mean?"

"I don't think I've ever seen your dad speak to him. Most of the time Maxim stays upstairs in that big house."

"You've seen him downstairs plenty of times."

"I know, but I think more often he's upstairs by himself. It seems as if he doesn't like to associate with the rest of the family."

"Grandpa Maxim had a stroke; he can't associate well with the rest of the family. He was once the patriarch, you know, the leader of the family, the head of Palit Wool. It was *his* father, Gregor, and his uncle Isaak who founded the company. Their last name was Palit, not Paley. My great-grandfather Gregor changed his name to Paley when they immigrated to America. My dad is named after him."

"I know. Your family tree is fascinating."

"Was that sarcasm?"

"No."

"Hm. Anyway, Grandpa Maxim took over the company and got rich. How do you think he feels now, helpless, stuck in a wheelchair, unable to speak?"

"Doesn't he write notes? Can't he communicate that way?"

"Sure. But he does so only if there's something he really wants. He doesn't 'talk' to us very much. He's a little antisocial, I'm afraid, but not in a mean way."

"I like your grandpa. Sometimes I think he's the only one in your family—besides you, of course—that really does like me."

That made her smile, too. "He's a sweet old man. Even though he can't speak."

"Yeah, but I've seen arrows shoot out of his eyes whenever he sees Trey or your father. Do he and your dad not get along?"

Nat made a face and finished the last of her pizza. After a pause, she admitted, "No, they don't. As long as I can remember, they didn't get along much."

"How come?"

"I don't know. Grandpa Maxim had the stroke the same year as my Uncle David was killed on that hunt."

"Really?"

"Well, it was a few months later. Right around the time I was born. Maybe—"

After a pause, Jason asked, "Maybe what?"

"Well, maybe Grandpa Maxim has always resented Dad for what happened to Uncle David."

"Wasn't it an accident?"

"That's what the police investigation said."

"So why would he hold it against your father?"

"Because Grandpa Maxim had named Uncle David to be his successor as the head of Palit Wool when Grandpa retired."

"Really! Wait . . . wasn't your uncle younger than your dad?"

"By two years."

"So it sounds like your Grandpa Maxim liked your Uncle David best."

Nat narrowed her eyes at Jason. "Don't you say that."

"Sorry."

"Why would you say that?"

"I said I'm sorry. Forget it."

She let out a heavy sigh. "All this talk about family is putting me in a bad mood."

"Okay, sorry. Let's get out of here."

On the way back to his apartment, Jason collected his thoughts. No, he wasn't sorry. There were still a lot of issues he wanted to work out with Nat's family. After all, if he was going to marry *into* it, he wanted to be comfortable. His sister, Miranda, had advised him on a number of occasions that having good relations with the in-laws was not necessarily a prerequisite for a happy marriage, but it certainly helped. Was it going to be possible? Was he having second thoughts?

Jason did his best to put it out of his mind as they approached his building.

19

Annie sat at her desk preparing a report from the notes of the surveillance she and Harris had performed over the past two days, but she found her mind wandering back to the brunch with Tiffany at Denny's. She'd been thrown by the appearance of the man she had mistaken for Eric. After not seeing or talking to him for eight months, the prospect of a surprise encounter—while she was with a witness—was disturbing. There was no question that the guy at Denny's resembled him—he'd had a smug, *look who I'm dating now* attitude as he showed off his blonde girlfriend, and yet his focus was on his cell phone. Later that night she probably had drunk too much wine while listening to Joni Mitchell's *Blue*—another one of her mother's favorites—and mulling over the failed relationship.

But then she'd started thinking about her mom. Julia Presetti had been a sort of hippie folk singer type when she'd met Giacomo Marino—who always went by the name of Jack—at the Woodstock festival, of all places. Julia was nineteen, Jack was twenty. He had family in New York, which was where the couple eventually married and had their first child, Annie's oldest brother, Robert. Her father's job as a philosophy professor brought them to Chicago, where their second son, Paul, was born. Annie came along next, followed by the youngest, Mary. Her mother had lived with cancer long enough to see Annie get a master's degree, but was robbed of the opportunity to witness her daughter becoming an FBI agent. It was one of the reasons Annie had requested a transfer from New York back to Chicago—her mother didn't have much longer to live at the time. The transfer—and the promotion to Special Agent—had come a month too late. Julia Marino passed away in 2014, just before Annie made the move.

Looking back on her decisions made Annie realize that her job was more important than a romance that was going nowhere. Eric had never respected what Annie did. But it was who she was. Maybe she'd feel differently about starting up a new romance if and when she met someone who understood this. She would know it when it happened.

As for Eric, Annie thought, *he can go stick his head up his ass.*

She made a mental note to phone her father and try to make a date to visit him. She didn't do it enough. Then she thought, *Do it now, or you never will.*

Annie looked at the time and noted that her father would be in his office and not the classroom. She dialed his number.

"Annie?" he answered.

"Hi, Dad. How are you?"

"Just fine. What's up, sweetie?"

"I was just calling. We haven't talked in a while. Sorry, it's been crazy busy here."

"No need to apologize, I'm just happy to know you're alive. We missed you at the cookout on July Fourth, though."

Jack Marino, after moving through a couple of institutions, now taught at College of DuPage in Glen Ellyn, a western suburb of Chicago. Robert, a stockbroker in New York, and Mary, a schoolteacher in Bloomingdale, another western suburb, had made it out to the family home in Glen Ellyn for the holiday.

Paul, a film editor in Los Angeles, and Annie had missed the gathering.

"Yeah, I'm sorry about that. My bad."

"Don't worry about it. You still taking dance lessons?"

"Ha. Technically, I am, but I'm never in class. I keep practicing the same toe-heel shuffle combination over and over in my apartment. Aloysius thinks I'm mad."

Her father laughed. "Your mother would egg you on. You know she—"

"—she tap danced, too, I know, that's why I started taking lessons. I was just . . . I was just thinking about her. I guess that's why I called."

"Yeah, well, I think about her all the time."

"Sure. We all do."

"How's—you still seeing what's-his-name? Edward?"

"Eric. No. That ended about nine months ago. Forget him. I have."

"Oh. I'm sorry to hear that, honey."

"Don't be. He was a schmuck. Besides, FBI agents don't fall in love and get married." *Christ, had she just said that?*

"Annie . . ."

"Never mind, Dad. Really."

They small-talked for a few more minutes, and Annie said she had to get back to work.

"Okay, don't be a stranger," he father said. "Maybe we can do something on Labor Day weekend?"

"Sounds like a plan."

There was a pause. "You sure you're okay, sweetheart?"

"Absolutely. Talk to you later."

She hung up and sighed. *Of course I'm okay.*

Her gaze moved back to the computer monitor.

The report. Unfortunately, there wasn't much to write. Nothing unusual had occurred at the Den. Harris had been set up to watch the back of the building, while Annie kept an eye on the front. Customers came and went. Dancers and staff entered and left through the back door. No one brought women to the club in a surreptitious manner. The operation was proving to be of no consequence, and so on the third day Annie pulled the plug and decided to focus on other pending cases. She was about to deliver the report when SSA Gladden phoned with some news.

"Marino, you have another tattoo."

The next day, Annie and Harris drove to Milwaukee, where a forty-eight-year-old Caucasian man had been caught attempting to dispose of a body in a forest preserve. The deceased was a woman, approximately eighteen or nineteen years of age, who had been strangled. Milwaukee PD arrested the man, who confessed to killing her.

The bear claws tattoo was on the corpse's neck.

This information was processed through ViCAP, where it was flagged and sent to the Chicago FBI field office. The crime had occurred a week previously, so Annie and Harris were too late to view the body, which had already been cremated. This time, the victim had actually been identified. Helena Nikolaev was an illegal immigrant from Ukraine who had been reported missing in her home country a year earlier. How she managed to enter the US was unknown. ICE was looking into the case, but other details cropped up that necessitated the FBI Civil Rights Human Trafficking squad's involvement. Special Agent Brad Blocker, from the Milwaukee FO, was already assigned, but Annie's superiors coordinated an exchange of data.

Annie and Harris met Blocker at the Milwaukee County Jail on North 9th Street, which was operated by the US Marshals Service, Eastern District of Wisconsin. The plan was to interview the suspect and go over the evidence collected at the crime scene and the suspect's home. Agent Blocker was in his early thirties and had a rather cold, no-nonsense attitude. Annie sensed in the man an underlying prejudice against immigrants—Russian or otherwise—as he spoke of them disparagingly.

After viewing the crime scene photos and autopsy report and examining the photo of the tattoo, Annie confirmed that the victim was linked to The Bear.

"The perp says he bought her on the Internet," Blocker said. "She was to be his personal slave. Apparently, he had her confined in a shed that was in his backyard for three months. He used her for his own sick pleasure. He's divorced, lived alone, but he has kids reaching college age." The man shook his head. "That's what these damned immigrants get themselves into coming over here like that without proper documentation."

Annie ignored the remark and asked, "How did she die?"

"He was doing one of those asphyxiation kink-things on her while having sex with her."

"You mean raping her."

"Uh, yeah. Went too far, he says. Real piece of work, he is."

She and Harris watched the video of the suspect's confession, took notes, and then arranged to interview him.

Joseph Flanagan was a top salesman with a national insurance firm, but now he was dressed in a jumpsuit with a depressed look on his face as he was brought into an interrogation room.

Annie and Harris sat across from him at the table. Annie introduced herself and Harris and told the man why they were there. "We've heard and read the statements you've made, but we'd like you to please tell us again everything you know. We're especially interested in how you obtained the woman. Who you spoke to, what kind of money you paid . . . anything at all?"

"I've already told the police what I know."

"That's all right. You can tell us now."

Flanagan told a story that was not unfamiliar. He had been a patron of a strip club called Cherries Jubilee, located in the western outskirts of Milwaukee. In Annie's classification of strip clubs, it was one of those middle-level B-clubs that catered to a working-class clientele. The dive featured dancers of all ethnicities, but the Eastern European and Russian women, Flanagan claimed, were the "most attractive," which was why he went there. After being recognized as a regular customer, a man approached him in the club.

"He asked me if I might be interested in owning a girl like them," Flanagan said. "At first, I was, like, *what*? What do you mean? He explained that he knew of a website where you could buy a woman—like a mail-order bride—only she would be, in his words, 'your personal slave.' I thought he was crazy, but he was slick and charming and acted like he knew what he was talking about."

"Please describe him. Was he American? Russian?"

"Russian, I think. He spoke with a heavy accent. He said his name was Petyr, spelled P-E-T-Y-R. He actually spelled it out loud, just like that. He never told me his last name."

"Did he work at the club?" Harris asked.

"I don't think so. He was sitting in the club like a customer."

"Had you seen him there before?" Annie asked.

"A couple of times. We'd said hello to each other, acknowledged that we liked what we saw on stage. I remember he asked me if I liked Russian women. I told him yes. It was the next time I was there, after that, that he told me about the website."

Annie consulted her notes. "I see you provided the website URL to the other investigators. Did you know that this was an address in the dark web?"

"I know that now. I didn't at the time. I didn't even know what the dark web was!"

The FBI, of course, knew all about the darknet, as it was also called. The organization had special personnel in the Cybercrimes Division who monitored it. The darknet functioned primarily as a black market for illegal transactions, an online shopping mall of worldwide illicit and criminal behavior. Terrorists used the darknet to communicate with each other, and child pornographers were active in it. While some legitimate business was conducted in the dark web, chances were that anything going on there was seriously questionable.

"Tell us how it worked," Annie ordered. "What convinced you to try it?"

Flanagan shrugged. "I guess it was just the idea of having a . . . oh, God, I'm really sorry. I never should have done it."

"Too late for that," Harris spat. "Just talk to us. Maybe you can help yourself when it comes to your sentencing. I know they're talking about the death penalty for what you did. We'll see if what you tell us leads to any convictions of the people running this thing. It could help."

Annie knew Wisconsin didn't have the death penalty. She shot Harris a look, and he winked at her.

The threat worked, though. Flanagan nodded and said, "Petyr told me I need this special software called I2P. Once I had that on my computer, I could access the site. The URL he gave me just went to a screen where you filled out a form—your name, address, and what you were looking for. It said that all the information was confidential and would not be shared."

"And you believed that?" Harris asked.

"I know, I'm stupid. Really stupid."

"Go on, Mr. Flanagan."

"So, a day later, I got an email with a code, and that allowed me to get past the front door of the site. Then I was asked questions about my living conditions, like where I would keep a woman if I got one, how I would keep it a secret, what risks I might have to take. Stuff like that. I guess they wanted to be sure I wasn't going to get caught easily. I also had to affirm that if I *did* get caught, I was on my own. I had to take the fall. After that, I waited a day or two, and then I got another email with a new code and URL. This sent me to a different site for another set of questions, this time about the type of woman I was looking for. You know, blonde or brunette, that kind of thing. A day or two later, another email arrived with a new link and code. This one took me to a picture of . . . Helena. She looked . . . great. I didn't ask to see any others."

The prisoner hung his head and started to cry.

Annie and Harris shared a glance, and then she asked, "Do you need a break, Mr. Flanagan?"

He shook his head. Annie found some tissues in her suit jacket pocket and handed them over. The prisoner wiped his face and blew his nose.

"Then what happened, Mr. Flanagan?"

"The cost was fifteen thousand dollars. I had to come up with the money. That took a couple of days."

Harris interrupted. "Didn't you have any qualms about paying money to strangers with no recourse if something went wrong? What if it was just a scam?"

"It was to be an in-person exchange. Once I agreed, I got another email with instructions. I had to get the cash and put it in a suitcase. I was told to go to a motel—it was the Shady Grove Motel out on I-94—and go to a particular room at one in the morning. They said I had to back up my car right in front of the room and open the trunk. I knocked on the door. There was a man there with a clown mask on—and Helena was sitting on the bed."

"Did she appear as if she'd been mistreated?" Annie asked.

"I don't know. She looked just fine to me, better than her picture. She was scared, I guess. She didn't say anything."

"The man," Harris interjected, "can you describe him?"

"He was dressed in black and had that creepy rubber clown mask on. He had a big gun, too. Made me very nervous. When he spoke, it was not a Russian accent."

"American?"

"Yeah. Sounded like it."

"And then what?"

"I was told to open the suitcase. The guy counted the money. He then told Helena to get in the trunk of my car. I objected, but he told me I could do what I wanted after I'd driven at least ten miles away, but he advised me not to let her out until I was home."

Annie glanced at the police reports. Investigations had been made at the motel in question. The room had been rented by a "J. Smith." The manager had been interrogated for a day, but ultimately it was clear that he hadn't known what was going on in the room.

"So . . . you had Helena there in your shed for three months," she said.

Flanagan nodded. "I didn't mistreat her. I fed her, I made sure she wasn't bored when I wasn't around; I even gave her a puppy."

"You didn't *mistreat* her? You kept her captive in a shed, you raped her repeatedly, you used her for your own selfish purposes . . . and then you ultimately strangled her to death?"

Flanagan hung his head and started to cry again.

"Jesus . . ." Annie looked at Harris. "Come on, let's go. We're done here."

Annie and Harris continued to go over the case with Agent Blocker.

"We were all over that club, Cherries Jubilee. The manager's a guy named Chuck Dzenko. American, born and raised.

Actually, he's only the assistant manager but he ran the place. Get this—Flanagan was still coming to the club, even with the woman already at his house. Dzenko knew him as a customer. Dzenko has lots of arrests on his record, including a couple for pandering, but that was over a decade ago. A while back he was manager of another club that burned down called Marvel Girls. There was some insurance fraud suspected there, but nothing was proven. As for Cherries Jubilee, it appears he keeps the business clean, so far, if you can call what he does clean. He swore he didn't know a customer named Petyr or witness any encounters between Flanagan and anyone else other than the dancers."

"Of course not. Did you find out who actually owns the club?"

"Yeah, looks like it's a shell company based in Belize called—"

"Eyepatch, LLC."

"Yeah."

Annie nodded. "We already have our Financial Crimes people looking into it. The company has no TIEA so we can't find out who the principals are. But we're still trying. Has the name Fyodor Utkin come up in your investigation?"

"Yeah, he's the real manager of Cherries Jubilee, but he's missing in action."

She looked at Harris. "We really have to find that guy."

For grins, Annie and Harris stopped at Cherries Jubilee before heading back to Chicago. The club hadn't opened for business yet, but they found Chuck Dzenko behind the bar, restocking the booze. He was in his fifties, had red hair, and sported a pot belly.

"And what can I tell the FBI that I haven't already told the FBI?" he asked when they revealed their IDs.

"We'd like to show you some photographs," Annie said, pulling out her expanding collection. She showed him pictures of Vladimir Markov, Irina Semenov, Karen Washington, and Teresa Wang, and then shots of Makar Utkin, Fyodor Utkin, and Ivan Polzin. He reacted negatively to them all except Fyodor.

"I know him, he's the boss."

"How well do you know him?"

He shrugged. "Known him a few years. He doesn't live in Milwaukee, though. Lives in Chicago, doesn't he? He isn't here much. I've pretty much managed the place for him. You know, a while back I had a club of my own, the Marvel Girls . . ."

"We know that," Harris said.

"Yeah, well, Fyodor's club was competition—friendly competition, I guess. We knew each other. Sometimes dancers from his place came over to mine, and sometimes mine went over to his. It's an incestuous business. Uh, I didn't mean it that way . . ."

"We know what you mean." She pointed to Makar's photo. "This is his son. You ever seen him?"

Dzenko frowned. "I don't think so."

"Have you ever seen this before?" Annie showed him the photo of the bear claws tattoo.

"Nope."

As it was before the club officially opened, there were no dancers or other staff to interview, but Annie didn't think it would matter. She thanked Dzenko and they left. Before hitting the road, she made a call to SA Sally Bertram in Financial Crimes.

"Hey, Sally, I just wanted to know if you've made any progress on uncovering anyone behind Eyepatch, LLC, that shell company we talked about before?"

"No, but have you heard from Colin Clark?"

"The ALAT in Russia? No, I've been waiting to hear from him."

"Well, he called me to ask the same thing. The Russian government busted a bank in St. Petersburg that was allegedly moving dirty money for some drug runners located in some of the southern states—Texas and Arkansas and Louisiana, I believe. Let's see . . . it's called Karpovka River Bank. In the course of auditing it, they discovered that Eyepatch, LLC was listed as a client. In a gesture of uncommon goodwill, the Russians shared that information with our embassy."

"Holy shit, that's good news. Thanks, Sally, I'll get on to Clark right away." She hung up and told Harris what she'd learned.

"I hope that leads somewhere," he said. "But I tell you, this operation . . . how in the world have they kept it so well hidden? This guy, Flanagan, if he hadn't been careless, he might still have Helena Nikolaev in his shed. How many buyers are there? How many victims? We're lucky Flanagan screwed up. Other buyers could be more careful. Are there dozens of other trafficked victims out there being held *privately* by The Bear's customers?"

Annie frowned. "I hope it's limited to just dozens."

20

Yana wanted to scream.

Not because of the abuse she was subjected to, but rather from the sheer helplessness she felt. She had lost count of the days since she was first brought to the house. It had been at least a month. One of the other women, the Asian girl, was sold two weeks into Yana's stay. Now it was just the two of them—Yana and the Serbian girl, Mira.

She wished she could find the courage to attempt an escape.

The captors were two men who lived in the house, too. Very bad, very cruel men. The only good thing was it was now prohibited by their bosses to touch the merchandise. So, sexually at least, the torment had let up. The first month of captivity had been a constant barrage, such a terrifying ordeal that Yana was fully aware that even if she did find a way to flee, she would be forever damaged.

She wanted to die.

One night, the call came. The black man, Alexander, answered his cell. "Yeah?"

"Yeah?" Then his eyes went to Yana.

Immediately she knew this was about her.

"Right. One hour. Right." He hung up and addressed her. "Get your things ready. Pack up. You're leaving in an hour."

"I've . . ." She had to clear her throat. "I've been sold?"

"Nah. Just a rental. A few days, that's all."

"A . . . rental?"

Alexander looked at her coldly. "You've been deemed rental material on the website."

"What?"

"The Bear—he decided to open up the business and allow rentals as well as permanent sales." Alexander shrugged.

"Where am I going?"

"Nice place. You'll love it. Nice cabin in the woods. Beautiful."

The threat of isolation somewhere remote scared Yana even more.

She did as she was told. She packed and exchanged a tearful goodbye with Mira. They had become close in the past month.

The other captor, Freddie, came by her room. He was a British guy with multiple tattoos, and Yana couldn't stand him. He had made numerous comments about how he would have had her if she hadn't been off-limits.

"Well, some lucky guy hit the jackpot with this one," he said in his East London accent.

"Fuck you," she murmured.

Freddie tensed and straightened. His right hand balled into a fist.

Yana suddenly felt emboldened. "You can't hit me, especially now, asshole," she said to his face.

He struggled to restrain himself. Finally, he walked out of the room.

Yana's heart was beating furiously. How had she summoned the courage to confront him like that? He could have killed her.

But what would it matter? She was off to her eventual death in a matter of minutes anyway.

She sat on her bed and waited.

Over the past few weeks she had learned a great deal about the organization that was luring women into a trap and selling them as slaves to sadistic customers.

The Bear was the big boss, but Yana had never seen him. She had heard his name mentioned a few times and was told he was in charge. From what she understood, The Bear was based in Russia. He employed recruiters all around St. Petersburg, and even in areas deeper into Russia and across the border in Ukraine. Recruiters made up the bulk of the Russian end of the operation. From a logistical point of view, it was relatively easy to get the women aboard a cooperative container ship. Only one accomplice was needed to oversee them during the journey across the ocean. At the ports, Customs men were most likely bribed to get the women through.

The American end of the operation was much more complex. The first house in New Jersey, where the wretched woman Nadine and her thugs resided, was where the serious assaults took place. Bobby was actually in charge there, and Yana knew now that he took his orders from someone in Chicago.

There were three houses she knew about in the Chicago area. Men who ran local strip clubs were in charge of "distribution." Women were kept locked up in the houses until a sale came through. A driver then transported the "merchandise" to the buyer. Full service. Kind of like free delivery and installation. What Alexander had just told her confirmed the financial options for customers. Women who were sold to "keep" cost a lot more money—fifteen thousand dollars or more, depending on their age and looks. A "rental" was less, a low four figures.

There were more members of the organization in the US than in Russia, and they seemed to be based in Illinois. She couldn't be certain, though. Ivan, the man at the strip club, was a kind of mid-level manager, she figured, having only met him once. Yana could tell he was just a subordinate. She had never met the one called "Fyodor," but from what she had gathered, he might be the boss of the US side of the network. She had overhead Freddie and Alexander talking one night about how Fyodor had fled to Russia because the "heat" was on him and The Bear wasn't happy about it. He'd been "recalled."

Yana had to remember all of it, every detail. She would tell the world what had happened to her when she got out.

For that was what she decided, then and there. To get out. Escape. In whatever way she could.

Right on cue, the one called Makar arrived. She had met him once before when he had driven her to the house from the club. She didn't like him one bit; he was the one who had struck her when she failed to say her name was "Nadia."

"Go to the bathroom one more time," said Alexander. "It's going to be a long ride." She obeyed. Then, Makar and Alexander ordered her to get in the trunk of Makar's car, which was parked in the garage. There was nothing she could do to resist.

She climbed into the trunk, and Makar shut the lid.

21

"Is this SA O'Horgan?"

"Yes?"

"Hi, this is SA Annie Marino over in Civil Rights—Human Trafficking."

"Uh huh?"

"I just sent you an email with a file attachment. It's a case I'm working on."

Melanie O'Horgan worked in the Cyber Division of the FBI. During her twenty-one months so far as a Special Agent, Annie had not yet worked with anyone from Cyber.

"I see it, it just popped up. Hey, I know John Gladden, he's your SSA?"

"Yep. He's the one."

"We were at Quantico together. How can I help you?"

Annie gave O'Horgan a quick rundown of the case and explained the need to hack into some websites on the darknet. "I have the URLs to the various pages that the killer in Milwaukee viewed on his computer. I have his emails. I'm hoping it won't be too awfully difficult to try and find out who's behind them and where the bastards are located."

"I can't imagine what those women are going through. It's awful. Let me take a look at all this and get back to you on whether or not I think we can get into those sites. Is that all right?"

"Sure. Like I said in the email, if this trafficking operation is as big as I think it is, then we need to expedite stopping it. Like you said, those women are surely suffering. I've come across some pretty disgusting trafficking cases so far—and it hasn't even been two years since I became an SA—but the misogyny of these traffickers is inhuman, if you ask me."

"I hear you. I promise to get back to you as soon as I can."

"Thanks."

Annie phoned Harris next. He had resumed watching the Den on his own, but he had recently been recalled to Detroit. There just wasn't enough for him to do in Chicago, and he would be leaving soon.

"How's it going?" she asked.

"Snoresville. Ivan's at the club, but no one else is. It's pretty dead in the middle of the day since the place isn't even open. I'm calling it quits. Want to have lunch before I head back?"

"Sure."

They sat in the Rosebud Restaurant on Taylor Street, relishing old-school Italian food. Annie insisted on treating, and they ended up ordering dishes that were much too heavy for lunchtime. It was certainly satisfying.

"God, that was great. Too bad we couldn't have had some wine with that," she said, noting the time. "I guess you have to take off, huh?"

"Yeah, probably should. But, hey, I'll be back as soon as something else breaks. You're making progress, Annie."

"Not fast enough. I keep thinking about those women—" Her cell phone rang, and she recognized the caller ID. "Hold on, it's Tiffany, the bartender at the Den." She answered. "Anne Marino."

"Annie, I have some photos you need to see!" the bartender whispered with urgency. "I found them in Ivan's office."

"What are they, exactly?"

"Pictures of girls who have come and gone, you know, actor-dancer headshots. You have to see them. I think one of the girls you showed me is there."

"Really? Where are you?"

"At home."

"Okay, wait there. I'll be right over. What's the address?" Tiffany told her. "Okay, give me a half hour." She hung up and told Harris what was going on. "You want to accompany me?"

"Sure."

Annie paid the bill and gave Harris the address. "Follow me. We'll park on the street in front of her residence."

Tiffany Vombrack lived east of Oak Park in the area of West Chicago known as Austin. Not a particularly upscale area, it was a neighborhood of closed businesses, homes that were boarded up, and housing for lower-income families. Tiffany lived in the upstairs space of a two-story house divided into two apartments. Directly across the street was an empty three-story brick building that was surrounded by construction equipment. It looked as if the city was going to take the structure down soon.

Annie and Harris got out of the car. It was a sunny, hot day. The street was deserted.

"You sure she's home?"

"Said she was." Annie opened the common front door, which revealed a short hallway with an entrance to the bottom residence on the left, and a stairway straight ahead leading up to Tiffany's door. There was no mechanism for ringing a bell. "Come on," she said to Harris. "You getting a buzz that something's not right?"

"As a matter of fact . . ."

They climbed the stairs and drew their weapons. Annie approached the door and started to knock on it—but it was ajar. Annie pushed it open slowly. "Tiffany?" She stood a few seconds and listened. "Tiffany, you in there?" she called louder.

Annie turned to Harris and whispered, "Shit." She raised the Glock 27, assumed a Weaver stance, and pushed the door open the rest of the way with her foot. Harris, his weapon high as well, followed her into a small living room and kitchen. The ash tray on a small Formica dining table was full of butts, the place was smoky, and there was an unmistakable burnt odor to the apartment. Dirty dishes lined the small counter next to the sink. There was no stove, only a hot pad and a microwave oven.

She went to the bedroom door, which was wide open. Annie's sharp intake of breath was audible. "Search the bathroom, Harris."

He moved past her, registering the shocking scene that lay before them.

Tiffany Vombrack was lying on her back on a blood-soaked bed. Someone had shot her in the right temple, and the splatter decorated the headboard and part of the wall behind it.

"Clear. No one else is in the apartment," Harris said, emerging from the bathroom.

The room was small, but it had a large window that faced the street. It was open, and a warm breeze wafted in.

Annie looked under the bed and all around it. "No weapon. She didn't kill herself. I'm calling it in."

She stood in the middle of the room, looking out the window, as she put in the call to 9-1-1. Annie relayed her credentials and said that she and another agent would remain on the scene until the cops arrived.

"Christ, she just called you, what, a half hour ago?" Harris asked.

"Yeah. She was shot right before we got here. But I bet the killer is long gone." She stood by the window. "And it doesn't look like there's anyone around who might have heard the gunshot." Annie scanned the street below and then looked at the face of the abandoned building across the road. The windows were boarded up. The front door had a city notice pasted on it, and on the roof . . . a figure was crouched low, holding something in his hands—

"Get down!" she cried, shoving Harris away.

The loud report outside was accompanied by a *zzzzt!* that abruptly ended in Harris Caruthers's torso. He grunted loudly and fell to the floor, blood seeping over his three-piece suit. Annie crouched, making sure she was out of the sightline.

"Harris!"

The wound was below his right ribcage, right in the gut. He growled in pain, gritted his teeth, and said, "Go . . . *get* . . . him!"

"I'm not leaving you."

"No! . . . Go . . . !"

"You're going to bleed out." She placed her hands over the hole in his clothing and pressed hard.

"Annie . . . !" Harris gasped and cursed. "Go . . . get . . . the bastard!" He placed his own hands over his abdomen. "Ambulance will be here . . . soon. Go!"

She knew he was right. Annie turned, crouched by the window, and peeked. The figure was gone from the rooftop.

"All right, I'm going. Hold on, Harris."

She bolted out of the room, redialing 9-1-1 as she ran down the stairs. Reaching the ground floor, she halted at the door, opened it a crack, and peered out. The street was empty. Quiet. No sign of someone running from the building across the street. Was the sniper still inside?

The emergency operator answered and Annie delivered an update to her previous call—an agent was down and she was in pursuit of the suspect, although there was still a possible sniper situation. She hung up and stepped outside, carefully scanning the roofs and windows of all the buildings across the road. Nothing stuck out, so Annie took off, running through the tiny front yard, past their Bucars and across the road, then up to the front door of the abandoned building. She flattened her back against it and listened. The street was dead silent. She thought she heard sirens in the distance. Annie slowly moved along the exterior to the right side of the building, her weapon pointed in front of her. She reached the back and looked up and down the alley. Nothing. No moving vehicles. A back door was completely off its hinges, revealing a gaping entrance.

The sirens grew louder. *Good*, she thought, *help is on the way.*

Confident that she would have seen or heard the sniper if he'd left the building, Annie went inside, commando style. It was an empty foyer with a powerful stench—the place had been used for squatters and was littered with garbage and food remains. The structure was an old office building with a stairwell connecting the three floors and the roof, where the shooter might have left some crucial evidence.

Annie ascended the stairs, her weapon leading the way. She continually looked behind her as she went, in case the sniper showed up below her. When she reached the second floor she paused, opened the door, and peered into the hallway. Nothing but darkness, with some dim illumination coming from office windows. She continued climbing, repeating the procedure at the third floor. Finally, she reached the roof and stepped out. She moved to the edge where the sniper had hunkered down. Across the street, Tiffany's bedroom window was in the perfect position for a marksman who had some training.

She'd been wrong. The guy *had* left the building. She sensed it now. He wasn't there.

How the hell did he get away so quietly?

Furthermore, Annie wondered if the whole thing had been a trap. Was it a coincidence that Tiffany's killer would strike just minutes after the bartender phoned her? Or did Tiffany have a gun to her head? Could she have been forced to call and persuade the FBI agent to come to her house?

It couldn't have been happenstance, she thought. Otherwise the killer would have just left—instead, he had parked himself across the street and waited. He'd known she would be in Tiffany's bedroom.

Two police cars roared onto the street, lights blazing and sirens blaring. Annie needed to go down and meet them, but first she examined the area around her.

A shell casing lay next to the short brick wall that surrounded the roof. Annie took a photo of it with her cell phone but left it for the uniforms to retrieve.

By the time she emerged outside again, the ambulance had arrived. Annie held up her badge, holstered her weapon, and went to talk to the officers.

22

The shooting of an FBI agent sent shock waves throughout the organization nationwide. Now the Bureau's director was interested in Annie's case. The order came down from on high that the sniper must be caught—and if the human trafficking ring could be dismantled in the process, even better.

Harris Caruthers had been transported to Rush Oak Park Hospital, which luckily was only minutes away from the site of the shooting. The agent was in critical condition. Forensics analysis determined that the round had been a 7.62x51mm M118 Match Grade that caused a tremendous amount of damage to the agent's large intestine. It was a through-and-through, and the bullet was recovered from being embedded in the floor of Tiffany's bedroom. The shell casing Annie had found on the roof was a match. Thus, the weapon was most likely a bolt-action sniper rifle used by the military. Harris was in surgery for nearly twelve hours. Annie waited at the hospital the entire time, despite admonitions from her SSA to go home. The doctors proclaimed that the agent would live, but that he would be out of action for months. Harris had been extremely lucky. If Annie hadn't pushed him out of the way as she had done, he would have been gone.

And he could have been *her*.

The local police were handling the shooting, per protocol. Preliminary investigation revealed that there were footprints other than Annie's in the dirt alley behind the old office building. They led across the alley and into the backyard of the house directly behind the structure; there was no fence. From there, the prints were lost. It was speculated that the sniper had taken the shot and then immediately run down the stairs and into the alley. He kept going, through the yard and around that house to the street parallel with Tiffany's. Perhaps he had continued through the yards and alleys—there was very little in the way of fences around properties—to a parked car. Maybe he'd had an accomplice with a waiting automobile. Surveillance cameras in the area were being checked, but unfortunately it was not a community where many such devices were installed.

As for Tiffany Vombrack, she had been killed with a handgun. She had been standing by the bed and shot at close range. The round had tunneled through her brain and made a hole in the wall above the headboard amid the splatter. Where the bullet had gone from there was anyone's guess. Because of the massive exit wound, investigators thought it was a 9x19mm Parabellum, which prompted an initial conjecture that the weapon was possibly a Beretta 92 F, but no shell casing was found at the scene. The killer could have scooped it up after performing the dirty deed.

All this prompted Annie to wonder if they were dealing with one shooter or two. One man *could* have shot Tiffany in her bedroom with the handgun, and then gone across the street to the roof to await Annie's arrival. He'd had the time to do so. Maybe the sniper rifle had already been planted there. Annie also had to assume that the killer wasn't expecting her to show up with a partner. If all those things were true, then it meant she had indeed been set up and targeted. The traffickers were on to her, and there was no question that she had made herself visible to them by personally showing up at the strip clubs and interviewing various personnel.

A few days after the shooting, there were tense discussions between SSA Gladden and SAC Tilden, who said aloud that he thought Annie was too new at the job to continue being the point person on the case. Gladden went to bat for her, citing how she had handled the shooting incident with professionalism. "She saved Agent Caruthers's life," he reiterated. "That says something." Finally, it was decided that Annie would remain in charge of the case. It was unfortunate that her regular partner, SA Ed Barnley, was still deeply embroiled in a special task force looking into several "color of law" cases regarding police misconduct and was unavailable to resume working with Annie.

"I hate to say it, Marino, but you're going to be on your own for a while longer," Gladden told her. "That said, I don't want you going out on interviews and such on this case without a partner. You'll need to grab someone who isn't busy."

"That's going to slow me down, boss," she answered. "I'm not afraid. I don't think I'll be talking to any suspects or witnesses in an isolated location like Tiffany Vombrack's house. It will always be in public spaces."

Gladden relented. He told her to use her own judgment, but also to be damned careful.

Late weekday evenings. Overtime on weekends.

Annie worked tirelessly, putting minor cases on the back burner and concentrating on the "Bear Claws Case," as it was now informally known. ALAT Colin Clark had been in contact, saying that his "man" in St. Petersburg had some interesting leads. He didn't want to get Annie's hopes up until he had something more concrete, but Clark felt that he was closing in on some answers. He had also been in touch with Sally Bertram in Financial Crimes. The Karpovka River Bank that had been raided by Russia's FSB—the Federal Security Service of the Russian Federation, which was the successor of the KGB after the fall of the Soviet Union—had been operated by members of the Novgorod mafia, a small but formidable organization that had its tentacles wrapped around the northwestern area of the country, including St. Petersburg. Investigators uncovered evidence of money laundering for various enterprises. Many of its "clients" were shell companies on island havens or in remote countries such as Belize. Eyepatch, LLC was one of these patrons. At the moment, authorities were unsure what role Eyepatch played in the grand scheme of things, and they still hadn't produced any human names to go with the company. However, the fact that Eyepatch popped up among other questionable offshore accounts was enough to continue deeper scrutiny.

Melanie O'Horgan in Cyber had also made some progress on the darknet websites, which were now offline. Shadow pages had been recovered from Joseph Flanagan's hard drive in Milwaukee. From what Melanie and her team could assess, the URLs and emails had been routed through many servers and countries before ending up on Flanagan's computer. This was typical of dark web subterfuge, making it extremely difficult for law enforcement to trace cybercrimes to their sources. She was confident, however, that with some time they might be able to reconfigure the protocols involved and eventually come up with an ISP address or two.

In the meantime, Annie busied herself in her cubicle on the tenth floor. On this particular day, she planned to visit Harris at the hospital after she got off work, but first she had to write a report concerning Tiffany Vombrack's next of kin. Her mother was still alive and lived in Florida. She had an ex-husband and twelve-year-old son who lived in the Chicago area, and Tiffany had apparently seen the boy off and on over the years. Because she had once been a heroin addict—something Annie learned after the fact—the ex had received sole custody. Annie had spent that afternoon speaking with the former spouse, but he had little to do with Tiffany's life since the divorce, which occurred when their son was two. Nothing to see there.

Annie couldn't help feeling some guilt for what had happened. Could she have prevented the murder? Probably not, although she'd been careless in meeting Tiffany in public. Most likely, the culprits had been watching the bartender and maybe somehow found out that she was supplying information to the feds.

Staring at her computer screen, Annie got an idea. She brought up Facebook and searched for "Tiffany Vombrack." She distinctly remembered Tiffany joking about her Facebook page when they'd met at Denny's.

The profile picture was a recent one. Tiffany looked happy, smiling broadly at the camera. Under "Employment" it said she was a bartender for the Den, which had its own Facebook page. Annie spent some time going through Tiffany's photos, although there weren't many. Most were candid shots of her with various men. There were a few with her mother. One of Tiffany and her son, who appeared to be around seven in the photo.

Annie clicked on the link to the Den's page. Like most pages for businesses, it consisted of photos and information about the club. She scanned the timeline and looked at the pictures taken both inside and outside the building. There were many shots of the dancers—scantily clothed, of course, but nothing too risqué for Facebook. Annie scrolled down, eyeing each picture, until she came to one of Tiffany and a couple of the bouncers. Makar Utkin was in the frame with her, grinning at the camera.

So far, attempts to find the younger Utkin or his father had been futile.

She stared at Makar's picture and once again felt the nagging tug in her gut that she'd seen the young man prior to meeting him at the Den. This time, his likeness was *very* familiar. Those blue eyes were distinctive. His cocky self-assurance was—

"Oh, my God."

Viewing him in a photo was just the context that Annie needed to remember where she'd seen him before. She typed "Jason Ward" in the search box, and her coffee buddy's page appeared. Annie was already Facebook friends with Jason, so she had access to all of his posts. She clicked on "Photos" and scanned the album in thumbnails. Going back to May, she found what she was looking for.

They were snapshots from Jason's graduation party at his in-laws' house. She recalled their conversation at Starbucks when he'd first shown her the photos—about his future brother-in-law, whom he had described as a jerk and a bully. He had pointed to Trey Paley, whom Annie recollected and quickly found. Standing next to him, his arm draped on Paley's shoulder, was Makar Utkin.

The guy Jason called "Mack."

Makar didn't have a Facebook page, but Trey Paley did. Annie clicked on his name, but nothing happened. She wasn't "friends" with Trey. Instead, she typed his name in the search box, and the man's page popped up. There was enough visible public information to pique her interest.

His bio stated that he was a veteran of the US Army, and there were several pictures of him in fatigues—now called ACUs—and holding various assault rifles.

One caption read: "Here I am with my pride and joy, a .458 Winchester Magnum with a 19-inch Mag-na-ported barrel, detachable scope, and pop-up peep sights. Great for bear hunting." The picture portrayed Trey proudly holding the rifle across his chest. Another snap showed him with a .338 Winchester

Magnum. "Another fine Win Mag hunting rifle that serves as my backup weapon," the post proclaimed. It was obvious that Trey Paley owned an impressive collection of firearms.

In a picture that brought Annie forward in her chair, Makar held a Beretta 92 F handgun.

Well. It's a leap, but . . .

Could *that* have been the weapon that killed Tiffany Vombrack?

It was the last picture that sent a surge of electricity up Annie's spine. Trey held an M24, a bolt-action sniper rifle employed by the military, which used 7.62x51mm cartridges. The caption stated, "This is me with one of the weapons I carried in Iraq. Twelve confirmed kills!"

What had Jason told her about his future in-laws? Their ancestors were originally from Russia.

She dug her cell phone out of her purse, found Jason in her contacts, and stopped.

Wait.

It was an incredible coincidence. Or was it?

Annie reviewed what she knew about her writer friend and whether or not she could trust him. Was it even possible that *he* was involved in some way?

No. She thought she was a pretty good judge of character, and she had always sensed that she could trust Jason. He had already told her a lot about his new family, and he was not remotely close to Trey Paley. He didn't *like* him. In fact, Jason might know something that could help her.

She dialed and waited until he picked up.

"Annie?"

"Hi, Jason. Am I catching you at a bad time?"

"Not at all. I was online looking at Craigslist. I figure I've wasted enough time this summer being a lazy bum, so I thought I'd start looking for a job."

"I thought you were going to be a writer."

"I am! But unless you're James Patterson or Stephen King, you don't make a lot of money writing novels. I'm afraid I'll have to get a teaching certificate after all just so Nat's parents will respect me."

"I'm sure you'll be a big bestseller. I'm looking forward to reading your first book."

"Oh, you're the one! Thanks, I appreciate it. So what's up? Are you still at the office?"

"Yes. Jason, remember when you were showing me photos from your graduation party?"

"Yeah?"

"Remember the Russian guy who you said was your future brother-in-law's friend? Someone you called 'Mack'?"

"Yeah? Mack."

"Did you know his name is really Makar? Makar Utkin?"

"Uh, yeah, I think so. I've heard Trey call him Makar once or twice, but usually he goes by Mack. Why?"

"What does he do? Do you know?"

"Whoa, Annie, why are you asking? I mean, does this have to do with your, uh, work?"

"Jason, I'm just looking into something, and I'd appreciate it if you'd just keep this conversation between you and me. All right?"

"Sure."

"What do you know about him?"

"Nothing, really. He and Trey are best buds. He's nice enough to me, but we never really talk. I want to say he works at a bar. Or his father owns a bar, maybe more than one. I'm not really sure."

"What if I told you he works at a strip club?"

Jason laughed. "Really? Are you shittin' me?"

"No, I'm not. You've never heard him talk about that?"

"No. I'd remember that, believe me."

"And what about Trey Paley? What's his story? I know you don't really get along with him."

"Oh, he's a real nutcase, in my opinion. He was in the army, over in Iraq. Came back kind of psycho. Nat says he has post-traumatic stress disorder."

"Was he a sniper for the army?"

"Uh, yeah, I think he was. He always brags about how 'good' he was in the army. I remember him saying he was a sniper and that he killed, I don't know, a bunch of people."

"Does he have a job now?"

"I think he works for his dad at Palit Wool. Well, sort of. He says he works there, but I don't think he really does anything. I don't know what he does. I don't keep tabs on him. I like to stay as far away from him as possible."

"I thought you were going hunting with him."

"I am! That makes a lot of sense, doesn't it?" He laughed. "I don't know when that's happening, though." He chuckled again. "How do you like that? I say I want to stay as far away from him as possible, and yet I'm going hunting with him."

"Okay," Annie said. "Thanks, Jason. I appreciate it."

"What's this about, Annie?"

"I don't want to say. Just please keep this to yourself, all right? Don't tell anyone what we've talked about, not even Nat. Promise?"

"Uh, sure."

"Thanks, I'll see you at Starbucks."

"Okay, see you later! Oh, wait!"

"What?"

"Miranda—my sister—she still wants to call you. Remember I had asked you before—something to do with her work. Is that okay?"

"I told you she could."

"Right. Okay, I'll tell her. Thanks. See you!"

She hung up and stared at her phone.

What kind of coincidence is it when a case is indirectly connected to a friend who lives down the street?

Her eyes went to Trey's photo on her screen.

Could Trey Paley be . . . ?

She studied the man in his various poses with the guns. The military experience was evident in his posture and demeanor. Smug. Self-confident. A little wild-eyed in some of the pictures, perhaps.

Annie went back to Makar's page and examined his photo.

This guy is a second banana type. No way he could be management.

Was Paley connected to him in all this?

Where are you *hiding, Makar Utkin, my blue-eyed friend?*

She looked at her watch. There was just enough time to go visit Harris for a few minutes before visiting hours ended.

23

It took several days, but after jumping through hoops with the USAO and securing subpoenas, Annie was able to take a look at Trey Paley's rap sheet and military records.

He was born in 1989, Highland Park, the first child of Greg and Angela Paley. Greg was owner and manager of Palit Wool, the textile company Jason had told her about. Apparently, Trey was a difficult teenager. Annie could have requested further subpoenas to view Trey's sealed juvenile records, but she would have needed a lot more evidence and serious probable cause. However, by reading between the lines, Annie suspected there had been at least a couple of arrests when he was under the age of sixteen. There might have been a stint in a drug rehabilitation program while he was in school. Perhaps it was no surprise that he enlisted in the army in 2007, when he was eighteen. Annie made some calls and learned that Trey never graduated from Highland Park High School—he had dropped out at sixteen.

Reports from army physicians shed more light on the young man's history. It was acknowledged that Trey had a violent streak. He was disciplined three times for fighting while at basic training. Notes from commanding officers indicated that he was an unruly soldier once he was sent overseas. However,

Trey Paley displayed a talent for marksmanship. He was sent back to the US to Fort Benning, where he enrolled in a seven-week sniper training course. It wasn't clear how Trey qualified, due to his juvenile arrest record and former drug use, but he graduated, received security clearance, and joined the Airborne Rangers.

Back in Iraq in 2008, Trey saw action in a number of locations. His official record claimed there were twelve confirmed kills as a sniper. However, Trey's file contained unflattering reports from army psychiatrists. He was prone to anger, often started fights with fellow soldiers, and was especially hostile to Iraqi civilians. He had been written up a number of times for roughing up nationals, even women.

The most disturbing document was a 2009 arrest report from an MP. Trey and two other soldiers had been arrested in a Baghdad brothel in an area off limits to US personnel. Iraqi police were involved because a woman—a prostitute—had been beaten and killed. Details were unclear, and the report never claimed that Trey or any of the others were responsible. Annie smelled a cover-up.

In 2010, Trey received an OTH—Other Than Honorable—discharge from the army as a result of this incident. From what Annie could gather, there was not enough evidence to prosecute Trey or the other men in a court-martial and bestow upon them a more decisive dishonorable discharge, which would prevent the subject from receiving veteran benefits and such. An OTH discharge could go either way. According to the records, Trey was indeed receiving benefits, mostly for psychiatric therapy. He had been diagnosed with PTSD by the time he was sent home.

That explained a lot—why Jason thought his future brother-in-law was a bully. It didn't, however, prove that Trey Paley might have been the sniper who shot Harris Caruthers and possibly murdered Tiffany Vombrack. Annie knew she could be exploring an avenue that was simply in her head; perhaps someone else completely unknown was responsible.

She even spent a little time checking out her neighbor. Annie had felt guilty doing so, but in the interest of being comprehensive in her investigation, she ran his name through the data bases. As her gut had told her, Jason Ward came up squeaky clean.

The fact remained that Trey Paley knew Makar Utkin and that they were "best buds." Annie's instructor in the Behavioral Science Unit at Quantico had told her at least twice that she had good instincts. She remembered his words to her: "Marino, sometimes an agent's instincts are all there are that solve cases, and sometimes they even keep him or her alive. You should trust them. It's your brain's way of telling you to look *here* or look *there*. And it never hurts to look."

A call came in at her desk.

"Marino."

"Annie, it's Sally Bertram in Financial."

"Hey, Sally."

"The financial records for Fyodor Utkin just came in from his US bank and the IRS."

"Oh, great! That was really fast." Along with attempting to figure out who was behind Eyepatch, LLC, Financial Crimes had met with the US Attorney's Office to get subpoenas for Utkin's records.

"I know, right? That process usually takes a month or two, but we got lucky! We're going to dig into these spreadsheets, and I've got our top forensic accountant on it. With a cursory glance, Utkin's tax returns look legit. Where is he now, do you know?"

"He's in Russia, supposedly. He has dual citizenship. He left at the end of May."

"He does have regular deposits of sizable amounts on his bank statements, but not so large that they'd trigger red flags. It's possible he's getting other income elsewhere, though."

An email popped up on her computer monitor from Colin Clark.

"Hey, I just got an email from the ALAT in Russia. Let me call you back, okay? Thanks."

Annie hung up and opened the email.

Agent Marino—

Our investigator in St. Petersburg has uncovered significant information on Fyodor Utkin. In fact, he has been murdered. His body was found washed up on the shore of Neva Bay near Big Port container terminal, wrapped in plastic, and his throat was cut. Investigators believe he was in the water at least a month.

Informants have stated that Utkin was in the city in early June but he hasn't been seen since. His last known public appearance was at a restaurant on June 10, where he dined with Evgeni Palit and another man who may have been an American. Palit is a legitimate businessman who runs a company that also has a Chicago outlet—Palit Wool. It's a textile company that specializes in wool products. Do you know it? Evgeni Palit runs the manufacturing plant in St. Petersburg. The retail distribution part is in Chicago.

However, my contacts in local law enforcement say that Evgeni Palit has been an associate of Nikolai Babikov for a long time. Babikov is believed to be in the Novgorod mafia. This organized crime outfit operates out of the Novgorod area in northwest Russia, not far from St. Petersburg.

In the 1980s, Palit was suspected of using his shipping infrastructure to smuggle black market goods in and out of Russia, including drugs. A Palit Wool employee was caught smuggling jewelry and fine art in 1988. Evgeni Palit was cleared of wrongdoing, but the suspicion remains.

I suggest you look into Palit Wool in Chicago.

Yours,
Colin Clark, Assistant Legal Attaché

"Holy shit," Annie said aloud. She felt her pulse pick up. Her instincts were red hot, and she felt that familiar surge of excitement when she knew she was right. She opened the attachments, which were crime scene photos of Fyodor Utkin's bloated, decomposed body, local police reports, and newspaper clippings about the incident.

She shot back a reply, thanking Clark for the information and asking that Utkin's finances in Russia be carefully examined. She also asked for more information on Evgeni Palit and Nikolai Babikov, as well as the Novgorod mafia, although the FBI would surely have plenty of files on the organization.

Annie then sent the email attachments to all her colleagues who were actively involved in the Bear Claws Case to bring them up to date.

It felt good. Progress at last. Annie stood, looked out of her cubicle to make sure no one was watching, and performed a little of the tap routine she'd memorized. The flats she was wearing weren't the best shoes for dancing, but they'd have to do. She recited the steps in her head as she moved—

Right paradiddle, Left paradiddle
Right para para, Right paradiddle
Left paradiddle, Right paradiddle
Left para para, Left paradiddle

"Marino? What are you doing?"

Annie gave a little shriek and turned. SSA Gladden stood with his hands on his hips, but a smile played on the edges of his mouth.

"Sorry, John, just letting out some tension, heh heh." She felt her face flushing. "Uh, I heard from the ALAT in Moscow. There's some progress!" She pointed to her computer screen. "Look, I just sent you an email, but let me show you the—"

"That's okay, I'll read the email. Right now I have to rush to the SAC's office." He turned away but Annie could tell he was stifling a laugh.

"Well, shit," she muttered aloud as she sat at her desk. Then she snorted aloud at the absurdity of it all.

Oh geez, Annie, great job, you've succeeded in embarrassing yourself, now get back to work!

Again she studied the face of Fyodor Utkin's son, Makar, on her screen. The question was—where the hell was he? How much should she tell Jason, her friend and neighbor, about these revelations?

She was convinced more than ever that Trey Paley just might be a suspect.

What was it Jason had told her about the Paleys and Michigan? The family owned a cabin there, somewhere in the forest, in the "middle of the state."

Annie pulled up her contacts and dialed Chief Daniel in Lakeway. Was it possible he might know the Paleys?

"Police department."

"Chief Daniel?"

"No, this is Captain Mike Baines."

"Captain Mike, hello, this is FBI Special Agent Annie Marino. Remember me?"

"I sure do! You're not somebody I'd forget too easy."

Annie cringed. She thought the man might have had a little crush on her. He'd had a goofy puppy-dog attitude around her when she was up there investigating the Irina Semenov incident, and she had felt it again when she was in touch with Captain Mike and the chief a few times later during the month of June to follow up on their progress.

"How are things going there?"

"Oh, it's been pretty quiet this summer so far. Nothing too bad. Your usual traffic violations and domestic quarrels. Had two robberies and a stabbing. We helped county boys raid a meth lab in the woods, and that was pretty exciting. Otherwise, it's been a slow summer, crime-wise."

"I was really asking about the Irina Semenov case. I guess I would have heard if you'd made any progress on that."

"No, that hit a dead end, that's for sure. The county sheriff and his men are handling it now, with some of our help when we have the time. We've been slowly going around to all the people who live out in the forest, you know, asking questions, but there are only two of us here; four, if you count the part-timers. We only get them on weekends, or sometimes during the week if someone's lost in the woods or something."

It was what usually happened when there was a case in an extremely rural area. Unless the solution to a crime was in front of their faces, or it didn't take longer than a few days to reach a conclusion and arrest a suspect, most rural law officers tended to classify a case as cold and move on.

"Listen, I wanted to see if you know anyone by the name of Paley? In particular, a young man named Trey Paley. His family supposedly has property in the woods up there somewhere."

"Trey Paley? Sure, I know him. I know his whole family!"

"You do?"

"Yeah, they have a cabin not too far from here. They own a lot of land that was carved out of the national forest. They use it for hunting—it's real good for bear and deer hunting. Trey's granddaddy made some kind of huge deal with the government for the property quite a while back for it."

"Have you seen Trey recently?"

"No, ma'am. Well, not since June. He was up here in June. Why do you ask?"

"Are you *friends* with him?"

"Well, I guess. I mean, we don't hang out or anything. We know each other. I've actually had to talk to him a couple of times about hunting out of season. He tends to do that."

"Have you seen his father recently?"

"Greg Paley? No, ma'am, I haven't seen him up here too recently. When was it . . . maybe last April or so he was at the cabin for a little while. He doesn't come up here much. By the way, I did talk to Trey about that girl we found. He wasn't even in the state when it happened. Nobody was at their cabin when all that happened."

"I see."

"They're good people. I can vouch for that. Shoot, Trey's a war veteran."

"Okay, thank you. Uh, please tell the chief I called, will you? I'd like to talk to him, too."

"Sure thing. Bill's going on vacation in two days, though. It'll just be me minding the fort for a week."

"Better get you some of those volunteers."

"Nah, I don't need 'em. Not unless we have a terrorist attack or something, and I don't think that's too likely in our neck of the woods. I'll have Bill give you a call."

"Thanks."

She hung up, frustrated. *Damn.* Had she been hoping the captain would say that Trey Paley was a very suspicious person, possibly running a human trafficking operation out of his cabin in the woods?

Unfortunately, nothing was ever that easy.

24

Yana looked at herself in the mirror in the shed's bathroom. The tattoo on her neck stung. It felt as if she'd burned herself a little. It wasn't terrible, but it was sore. The man who had applied the tattoo told her to wash it with antibacterial soap and to not use a towel to dry it. Paper towels were best, and she should blot the area, not wipe. He said the soreness would go away after a few days since it was a small tattoo on an area of her skin that wasn't as sensitive as other places. Large tattoos like arm sleeves or elaborate ones on the stomach and back could take two weeks to heal.

She felt the urge to cough again. When she did, dark phlegm projected into the sink. She washed it away with the faucet. For a while she'd felt sick, as if she had a bad cold. She wheezed a little when she breathed. Not good.

It was her fourth day in the forest. Yana had no idea if she was still in Illinois or not—she didn't think so. Time, like her spatial movements, was blurry.

She remembered riding in the trunk of Makar's blue Nissan Altima from Chicago to their destination, wherever it was. The trip had taken around four hours, maybe more—it had been difficult to keep track of the time while curled up in the darkness of the trunk. It was night when they arrived. Makar let her out, and she saw that they were in a heavily wooded area.

Her first thought was that she was so far from civilization that no one would be able to hear her scream.

A log cabin stood in front of them, and she had never been so happy to be able to use the bathroom. For such a structure in the woods, it was very nice. It had two bedrooms, a living area with a fireplace, kitchen, bathroom, and storage space. A family could live there comfortably.

But no family lived there, and neither would she.

After she'd relieved herself, she saw Makar take a small ring of keys out of a drawer in the kitchen, and then he led her away from the cabin along a dark path through some trees, maybe thirty yards or so, to a small wooden shed. Makar used a key on the ring to unlock a padlock on the door. He removed it and opened the door. He then reached in, switched on an overhead light—a naked bulb—and pushed her inside.

"This is your home for a few days," he said.

It was basically one room, maybe twelve by sixteen feet, with an adjoining tiny bathroom. A queen bed occupied most of the floor space, along with one chair and a nightstand with a reading lamp. The bathroom had a toilet, a sink, and a mirror. On the sink was a single tube of lipstick. There was nothing else, not even a bathroom door. No fireplace, heater, or air conditioner. The only window was a small skylight in the ceiling, which was just high enough that she couldn't reach it even if she stood on the bed.

A long, thick chain was attached to the wall at the head of the bed. At the end of the chain was a cuff. Makar ordered Yana to remove her blue jeans. She did so, knowing that if she didn't obey he would strike her. He then told her to sit on the bed. Makar attached the chain cuff to her right ankle and locked it with another key on the ring. The chain was long enough for her to get up and go into the bathroom, but too short for her to reach the door of the shed. She supposed that was to keep her from attacking someone who entered. She was also unable to reach the light switch on the wall next to the door. The only light she could control was the lamp on the nightstand.

Once she was "settled," Makar turned off the overhead light and left her alone with some blankets and a stack of magazines. She heard him lock the padlock on the outside of the door. There was nothing to do but lie down, and she slept poorly. In the morning, he brought her breakfast. She was starving, having not eaten since the previous afternoon. A little later he brought her some lunch, and that evening came dinner. It wasn't terrible food, but it wasn't cooked by a gourmet chef, either.

On the third full day of her captivity in the woods, the tattoo artist arrived. Makar had come, unlocked the cuff, and let her out of the shed. They walked along the path to the main cabin, which was a different experience in the daylight. Tall trees were *everywhere*. She could barely see bits of the blue sky overhead. In another life, she might have asked what kind of trees they were, but at the moment she didn't care.

A black pickup truck was parked in front of the cabin next to Makar's Nissan. It obviously belonged to the tattoo artist, who was inside, setting up his equipment. He didn't speak to Yana. He was an older man, around sixty, and was tall, fit, and bald. He didn't tell her his name. He'd brought a portable machine and containers of ink, laid out on a table beside a chair.

Makar ordered her to sit and be still. He said he would tie her to the chair if she didn't cooperate. The tattoo application hurt, as she had always heard they did. The process took about an hour.

At one point, Makar asked the other man in English, "Have you heard anything about when I can go home?"

The artist merely replied, "No." Even from the one-word answer, Yana could tell the man was American.

"Have you heard from my father?"

Again, "No."

Makar muttered something under his breath and moved away from the chair. For a moment Yana considered jumping up, wrestling away the artist's little machine, and trying to use it as a weapon. But of course, that would be futile. She'd never be able to overpower two strong men. She was weak from fatigue and hunger. She didn't have the willpower. It wouldn't work.

When he was done with the application, the artist spoke to her for the first time, giving her the aftercare instructions. Makar would make sure the antibacterial soap was in her bathroom. Then he packed up his things and left.

It was back to the monotony of the shed and the chain. Long, boring days of nothing to do. Makar bringing three mediocre meals a day. He told her that "pretty soon" there would be a special guest coming that she was expected to "entertain." At least Makar wasn't bothering her. Not yet, anyway.

Now, it was her fifth day in the woods. Yana stood in the tiny bathroom and examined the tattoo, which was healing nicely. The claws of a bear, with a few droplets of blood. To her, though, the droplets did not represent blood—they were tears.

The tube of red lipstick they had supplied her was for *their* pleasure. She knew she would be required to apply it.

Lipstick and bear claws.

It was the ultimate humiliation, to be branded as someone's property. She attempted to cover the tattoo with her hair, but the edge was still visible in the mirror. She was permanently trademarked. Made in Russia.

25

Annie arrived at the Palit Wool headquarters in Northbrook on time for a one o'clock appointment with CEO Greg Paley. He had been cordial on the phone and said he would be happy to speak to her. When he asked why the FBI wanted to talk to him, she said it concerned matters on the Russian end of his business. He offered no resistance; in fact, he seemed genuinely concerned that something might be wrong.

The office took up the entire third floor of a six-story building that housed other businesses. When Annie stepped off the elevator into a foyer, she faced a large frosted glass wall and door with the legend PALIT WOOL tastefully embossed on it. She went in to find an attractive female receptionist sitting at a fancy marble desk. The waiting room had modern, European furnishings. In some ways, it reminded her of a clean and bright bank lobby. After giving her name to the receptionist, Annie was told to have a seat.

Paley didn't keep her waiting long. Within a minute after her arrival, he appeared through the door that led to the rest of the office.

"Agent Marino? Greg Paley."

Annie stood and held out a hand, which he shook. "Good afternoon, Mr. Paley, thank you for seeing me."

"You're quite welcome. Come on back to my office."

She was struck by his height and good looks. The full head of white hair really did give him that "distinguished" appearance. The Slavic, rugged features of high cheekbones and a strong jaw were pronounced, and he had deep-set almond-colored eyes.

They went through the door into an open-designed space not unlike her own tenth floor of the field office. People sat in cubicles working at computer terminals. Paley led her down a carpeted path and into a hallway past the staff.

"This is, of course, our administrative headquarters, where all the pencil pushing happens. We have a warehouse in New Jersey where all the goods from Russia are stored and from where they are shipped to retailers. We also have a small manufacturing arm in Glenview, although 90 percent of our manufacturing is done in St. Petersburg. Can I get you anything? Something to drink? Coffee?"

Coffee sounded good, she said. Paley said something to a secretary who sat at another marble desk outside the CEO's office, and then he gestured for Annie to enter.

His private inner sanctum was much different from the rest of the layout. Annie felt as if she'd just walked into the Explorers' Club, a gentlemen's abode decorated with mounted stuffed animal trophies, dark leather furniture, and a bar. She almost expected its occupants to wear Victorian-age British Empire hunters' clothing, complete with pith helmets. A black bear and two large deer heads adorned one wall. A grizzly bear head and a deer with massive antlers were on the opposite side. Most impressive was the expansive black bear rug, complete with head, that lay on the floor.

"Oh, my," Annie said. "Someone likes to hunt."

Paley laughed. "Yeah, I suppose you could say that. Do you hunt, Agent Marino?"

"Only criminals."

"Touché. Please, have a seat." He gestured to the comfy chair in front of his desk. Instead of sitting behind it, he sat on the sofa near her, beneath the grizzly.

Annie briefly thought of her neighbor Jason and the fact that he might be going hunting with Trey Paley. She had to be careful not to let on that she knew this man's future son-in-law.

"I must say, you have me very curious as to why you wanted to have a talk," Paley said. "It's not often that I get a visit from the FBI."

The secretary knocked on the door that was ajar, bringing in a tray with coffee cups, cream, and sugar. She set it on the table between them. "Thank you, Dorrie. Close the door on your way out, please."

"Yes, sir."

Annie took a moment to doctor her coffee with cream, while he did the same. Finally, she launched into it.

"Mr. Paley, I understand you know a man in St. Petersburg, Russia, by the name of Evgeni Palit? You're related, is that right?"

"Yes! He's my father's cousin, so that makes us, what, second cousins? He's my partner in the business. He runs the Russian side of Palit Wool. It was his father who founded the company with my grandfather."

"And you took over the US operations from your father?"

"That's right."

"When was that?"

"1994." Paley frowned. "What's this about, Agent Marino? Is that what I'm supposed to call you? Agent Marino? Mrs. Marino?"

"Agent Marino or Ms. Marino is fine. Mr. Paley, do you know a man named Fyodor Utkin?"

Paley made a little face. "Um, yeah. I do. I think I know where this is going. Is it about his strip clubs?"

"In a way. How do you know him?"

"Through Evgeni. Fyodor is Evgeni's nephew on his wife's side of the family. So I suppose you could say Fyodor and I are related, too, but not by blood. Fyodor immigrated to the United States not long after the Soviet Union fell, when he was, I don't know, thirty-something. Because I'm sort of a relative, he looked me up. At first he did a little 'consulting' for Palit Wool in terms of distribution and business contacts. That didn't last too long. We're really just acquaintances. I can't say we're necessarily friends. I don't really approve of what he does for a living now."

Annie's instincts weren't throwing red flags. He seemed to be telling the truth. "I see. Mr. Paley, I'm sorry to have to tell you this, but Mr. Utkin is dead. He was murdered in St. Petersburg."

"What?"

"His body washed up from the bay and was found recently. Investigators think he was killed as far back as June or early July."

"No. Really?"

"Yes, sir. You didn't know?"

"No, of course not. Evgeni hasn't said anything about it. Does he know?"

"I don't know if he does or not. It's in the news over there, so if he's paying attention, then he knows by now."

Paley sat back after placing the coffee cup on the table. The frown never left his face. "Jesus. Why hasn't he said anything? I need to call him."

"Mr. Paley, we have reason to believe that Evgeni Palit may be involved with some unsavory elements over there in Russia."

"What do you mean?"

"Criminal elements. Organized crime."

"What? No way."

His eyes stayed on her. A good sign. He was genuinely concerned. "Have you ever heard of the Novgorod mafia?" Annie asked.

"Uh, yeah, I believe so. They're in St. Petersburg, aren't they?"

"Yes. We suspect that your second cousin is associating with a man named Nikolai Babikov. Have you heard of him?"

Paley hesitated, looked away, and slowly shook his head. "Not that I know of."

Was that a lie? "Are you positive?"

"Yes."

"Nikolai Babikov is a major figure in the Novgorod mafia. We know that he and Fyodor Utkin were friends."

Paley looked as if he was at a loss. "I had no idea. How was Fyodor killed?"

"Throat cut. Wrapped in plastic and thrown into the bay."

"Jesus."

"I understand you may also know his son."

"Mack? Yes, I do. He's one of *my* son Trey's best friends. Jesus, does Mack know about this?"

Annie was glad he mentioned his son's name. That would help her. "I don't know. As a matter of fact, we're trying to find Makar Utkin. Do you know him as Mack or Makar?"

"Both. We call him Mack, usually."

"Do you know where he is?"

"No, why? Is he gone?"

"He's missing. Supposedly he went on vacation, but that was a couple of weeks ago. No one seems to know where he is. Do you think your son—Trey, isn't it?—might know where he is?"

"Yes, Trey is my son. I don't know if he knows. You want me to call him?"

"Maybe in a minute. Let's talk about Trey for a moment."

Now Paley squinted his eyes. His body language told her he didn't like the direction the conversation was going. "What about Trey?"

"Did you know Makar Utkin works at one of his father's strip clubs?"

"Yes."

"Well, if your son is good friends with him, then he probably visits the establishments that Fyodor managed, doesn't he?"

Paley nodded. "Yeah, I'm sure he does. But Trey's an adult. He's a war veteran. He can go to a strip club if he wants. Nothing illegal about that."

Annie figured it was time to come to the point. "Mr. Paley, we believe that Fyodor Utkin was involved in serious criminal activity—namely human trafficking."

Paley's jaw dropped. "Human—what? No, no way. Wait—what do you mean?"

"Illegally bringing women to this country from Russia and enslaving them to be prostitutes or . . . whatever. Against their will."

"No, I don't believe it." He vigorously shook his head.

"And if Fyodor was involved and somehow using his strip clubs in the racket, then Makar may be involved, too."

Paley was quiet for a moment. She let him stew on that until he said, "This is very disturbing. You have proof of this?"

She didn't address the question, but Annie felt the man was shaken. Did he really not know? "I'm probably going to want to talk to your son, but I thought I'd speak to you first."

"I appreciate that. Agent Marino—"

"Yes?"

Paley made another face and shook his head. "Trey . . . he's, well, Trey's got some problems. He's not well. He came back from Iraq with severe post-traumatic stress disorder. He's being treated for it, and I think it's under control, but he often makes . . . bad decisions. I try to look out for him. He lives at home right now, with Angela—that's my wife—and me."

Annie didn't want him to know how much she knew. "Trey was in Iraq?"

"Yeah. Airborne Rangers."

"You must be proud."

"Oh, I am. I was in the army, too, back in the seventies, but I didn't have a war to fight then. Trey served his country well." He stood and walked over to a bookshelf where several framed photos sat. He grabbed a couple and came back, showing her one of Trey in uniform. "This is Trey."

Annie simply nodded. Paley wasn't telling the whole truth—he was covering up for his son's checkered record. She sensed it was the first time during the conversation that he had intentionally lied. Was it because he was ashamed of Trey's OTH discharge? Or was he simply in denial? Perhaps he was just being protective of his boy.

Paley then showed her the other photo—five hunters in the woods with the carcass of a black bear. Greg Paley was in the center, and he looked twenty years younger. Annie also recognized Fyodor in the picture. "I thought you might want to see this picture. It was taken not long after Fyodor came to this country in the early nineties. We went on a hunt up in my property in Michigan. That's Fyodor."

"I recognize him. And you."

He pointed to one of the others, a rather coarse-looking fellow with long hair. "That's Evgeni. He came over for a visit when we were setting up this office in Northbrook. My dad was still running things then, but he had a stroke, and I took over not long after we bagged this bear." The other two men in the picture were a tall, balding man and a stocky wrestler-type.

"Who are the other two?" she asked.

"That's Louis Freund and Jim Dixon. I've known them since our days in the army. Louis has worked for me a long time, and still does. Jim did for a while, but he died in a tragic accident in China in 2002." He pointed to the bear rug on the floor. "That's this bear in the picture."

Annie had no admiration for hunters who killed animals for sport. All she said was, "Huh." Why was he showing her this photo? "How did Jim die?"

"Fell off a bridge. He was drunk."

"That's too bad."

"Yeah." He placed the photos on the table and remained standing over her. "What is it you're looking for, Agent Marino? Why did you want to talk to me? Just to find out if I knew this Babikov guy?"

Annie remained sitting but looked up at him, focusing on his eyes. "Mr. Paley, have you ever heard of someone called The Bear?"

"The Bear?"

"He's a human trafficker. Russian. He's running a very large criminal enterprise that stretches from St. Petersburg to Chicago. And I think your cousin Mr. Palit might know him. I also think your pal Mr. Utkin *did* know him."

Paley smiled. "I really don't know what you're talking about. He calls himself The Bear?"

She glanced down at the animal hide on the floor. "The Bear. Like your rug."

Paley spread out his hands. "Sorry. I don't know anything about it. But if Fyodor had anything to do with human trafficking, then frankly he deserved to die, I'm sorry to say. That's a horrible business. It makes me sick. And if Evgeni . . ." He shook his head, snatched the photos off the table, and replaced them on the bookshelf. He stood with his back to her for a moment, silent, until it prompted her to say something.

"Mr. Paley?"

"Aw, hell." He turned to face her. "I suppose I better 'fess up. I wasn't telling the whole truth when you asked me about that man Babikov."

"Oh?" She'd thought so earlier.

"I better confess it now, Agent Marino, since you'll probably find out anyway."

"What's that?"

"Evgeni . . . yeah, I know he's had some dealings with the criminal underworld in Russia. Damn it." He walked slowly back to where she was sitting. "I was afraid this might come back to haunt my family. It was all in the past. Actually, it was his father, my great-uncle Isaak, that initiated it. He got involved with Sergei Babikov, the founder of the Novgorod mafia."

Annie felt that buzz of satisfaction when she realized she was on the right track. "So you *do* know Nikolai Babikov."

"Me? No. I've never met him. But, yeah, I know who he is. I'm sorry I was being deceitful before. I don't know why I was. I guess . . . I guess I didn't want Palit Wool to be mixed up in anything . . . sordid."

"So far it isn't," Annie said. "Is it?"

Paley went to his desk and sat in the big chair behind it. He leaned forward and said earnestly, "No, it's not. Look, this is not a very nice story, I'm afraid. But I'll tell you anyway. The year was 1910. My grandfather, Gregor Palit, and his brother Isaak founded Palit Wool in Russia. My grandfather changed his name to Paley when he immigrated to America in 1923. In order to get around the Communist government's strict rules regarding imports and exports—especially to a country like the United States—Isaak had to make some deals. He got to know

Sergei Babikov. I don't know what my great-uncle Isaak did to gain Babikov's favor, but that's what happened. Babikov greased palms, he bribed officials, he did whatever it took to help my grandfather and great-uncle. Without the Novgorod mafia, there wouldn't be a Palit Wool operating in the United States since the 1930s. Great-uncle Isaak died in 1963, and his son Evgeni took over the Russian end of the operation. I'm afraid he got tight with Sergei's son, Nikolai, who I suppose you already know is now the leader of those crooks. My father—" Paley stopped and took a breath, as if it pained him to talk about it.

"Maxim Paley."

"Yes. My father refused to work with mobsters, and I'm proud he stood up to them. But for a while the company faltered. There were financial problems. After my military service, he sent me to Russia to try and straighten things out. I think I was successful. I turned the company around. I cut off ties with Babikov. *I* did that. Unfortunately, what my cousin Evgeni does in *Russia* is out of my control."

"I understand you take frequent trips to St. Petersburg. Three or four times a year?"

"Yes. Strictly for business. I check on the plant and make sure everything's running smoothly. I go down to southern Russia, near Kazakhstan, where the wool comes from, and verify that the goats are well cared for and no one's skimming off the top. We have a small facility there that shears the wool. Anyway, I make sure there's no corruption going on, because that happens a lot in Russia. Especially after the Soviet Union collapsed."

"I realize that."

"So obviously, from what you're telling me—with Fyodor being murdered—something's still not right over there."

"Yes."

Paley stood. "Well, you can count on me to help you find out what's going on."

His honesty impressed her, and she felt that perhaps she had gained an unforeseen ally in the case. She was glad he'd come clean. She now understood why Jason had said he liked his future father-in-law. Annie got to her feet as he came around the desk and held out his hand. She shook it and said, "I do want to talk to your son."

He nodded, and then his eyes welled up. "I understand. I'll make sure he cooperates with you. He can be . . . troublesome. He is a troubled young man. You want me to call him?"

He's really upset about Trey. "No, please don't say anything to him. I mean, he's your son, you can say whatever you want to him, of course, but I'd *prefer* that you didn't. If you could just give me his cell phone number or another way to get in touch with him, I'll make the contact."

Paley nodded. He returned to the desk, took a pen, and scribbled a phone number on a note pad. He tore off the sheet and handed it to her. "I do want to help with this," he said. "I don't want the Paley name or Palit Wool mixed up in anything illegal. And if Trey . . . no, I'm sure he's done nothing wrong. At least I hope to God he hasn't. His mother will be heartbroken. Will you keep me informed?"

"I will." Annie folded the note, put it in her jacket pocket, shook Paley's hand, and said goodbye.

26

The Paleys' butler let Jason in the front door and directed him to the back. "Miss Natalia is by the pool, sir."

"Thank you, Dudley." He moved through the expansive foyer and into the living room, where Angela Paley reclined on the sofa with a washcloth covering her eyes and forehead. She was dressed in skimpy shorts and a halter top, her bare feet resting on the arm of the furniture.

"Who's there?" she asked.

"It's Jason, ma'am."

"Oh, Jason, hi. Pardon me for not getting up. I have one of those headaches that make you rather want to fall on a sword."

"I'm sorry. Have you taken anything for it?"

"Yes, yes, I've taken more painkillers than I should. Nothing works."

"Well, if it's any consolation, Mrs. Paley, despite the headache, I must say you are looking very well this afternoon."

She lifted an edge of the washcloth so she could peer at him. "Ha. Thank you, you sweet man. At my age, every compliment is welcome, I don't care what the feminists say. I think Nat's out by the pool." She replaced the wet cloth over her eyes. "I tell you, it was one knock-down, drag-out this morning with Trey. It's why I've got this monster of a headsplit."

"Trey? What did he do? I'll show *him*! He can't mess with my favorite future mother-in-law and get away with it."

That made her laugh a little. "Oh, he went off to Michigan this morning. He was supposed to go with me to my mother's house this weekend. It's my mother's eighty-second birthday and he couldn't bother to be respectful to his grandma."

"Eighty-second? Wow, that's great. How's she doing?"

"She acts like she's forty and she's meaner than *he* is."

"Well, tell her 'happy birthday' for me. I enjoyed meeting her at the graduation party."

He left Angela and found Nat in a bikini and sunglasses outside on the recliner by the pool, a half-empty cocktail of some kind in her hand.

"Hey, hon."

"Hi," Nat said with a downbeat timbre.

"What's wrong?"

"Oh, nothing. Just my job starts on Monday, remember? I don't want the do-nothing-summer-after-graduation to end."

He sat on the edge on the recliner and slid his hand up and down her smooth, sunscreen-oiled leg. "I'm still looking for something, but I haven't had any luck. I might have to ask your *dad* for a job."

"He'd probably give you one, but you'd have to give up your dream of being a writer."

"Yeah, well, that's not going to happen. I'm up to thirty thousand words of the new masterpiece. I ain't stopping now!"

"You bring your swimsuit?"

"Of course. I'll go change. So Trey went to Michigan?"

"Yeah, he left this morning. Why?"

"He went hunting without me?"

"This isn't a hunt. It's one of his stupid Bacchanals."

"Really? Who else is going to be there?"

"Hell, I don't know. Mack, I guess, I don't know who else. I don't keep up with Trey's friends."

"Is your dad going?"

"He told you he stopped doing those a long time ago."

Jason sat with his chin on his fist, like Rodin's *Thinker*.

Nat sipped the dregs of her drink through a straw and handed him the glass. "Another, please, when you come back out?" He took the glass but didn't move. "Aren't you going to change?"

"I think I should go up there and surprise him," Jason said.

"Who, Trey?"

"Yeah. Damn it, *I* want to go to the Bacchanal!"

"No, you don't. You'd hate it."

She was right. He probably would. Still—it was an opportunity for him to prove his mettle not only to Trey, but to Nat as well. "Maybe so, but I want to be more of a brother-in-law to him. I mean, he's a war hero and all. I really want him to like me, Nat."

She lowered her sunglasses with one finger and looked at him. "Are you serious?"

"Yeah, I think so. What would he do if I showed up at the cabin?"

Nat replaced the sunglasses and shrugged. "Not much he *could* do once you're there. He'd have to let you join them. He couldn't very well kick you out and send you home after driving all that way."

"That's what I think. Maybe I should. I could go home right now, pack a bag, and drive up. Can you give me the directions?"

"No, wait, Sunday is my grandmother's birthday, and I want you to come with Mom and me to go see her."

"Aw, why should I spend the weekend seeing relatives, when instead I could be up in the woods getting drunk as a skunk?"

Nat sat up and put her feet on the concrete. "You really *are* serious, aren't you?"

"Yeah!"

She was silent a moment.

"What?" he asked.

"I'm just thinking . . . maybe it would be good if you and Trey bonded. It would make our lives easier."

"I can always see your grandmother another time. I'm sure she's going to live to be a hundred."

"Hm."

"And what the hell, if it turns out to be a disaster, I'll just write about it. It can be my next book—a comedy about how a knucklehead tries to be as cool as the big boys."

That made her smile. She stood, took the empty glass from him, and said, "Let's go inside. We have the directions stuck to the fridge or somewhere. I'll find them for you. It's not like you can plug an address into your GPS. There are a few unmarked back roads. Come on."

Before he left the Paley mansion, Jason stopped by the living room to say goodbye to Nat's mother, but she was no longer lying on the sofa. Instead, Maxim Paley sat in his wheelchair, watching a golf game on the large widescreen television.

"Hey, Mr. Paley, how are you?"

The old man's eyes went to him and twinkled.

Jason took a moment to sit next to him. "What are you watching?"

The man's eyes shifted, as if to say, *isn't it obvious?*

"Oh, yeah, I guess you're watching golf, huh. Hey, guess what. I'm going up to see your cabin in Michigan."

Again, there was a subtle change in the man's eyes. *What?*

"Trey's up there having one of his weekend soirees, so I'm going to surprise him and show him I can be one of the manly men, too."

Maxim Paley moved his hand on top of Jason's and squeezed it. Hard.

"Whoa, that's quite a grip you have there, sir. You're as strong as an ox!"

It seemed the man's eyes were on fire.

"What? What's wrong?"

Again, the squeeze.

Was the old man trying to tell him something?

Jason's phone rang. He gently removed his hand from the older man's grasp and said, "Excuse me a sec, Mr. Paley." It was his sister, Miranda. "Let me take this."

He walked away from the wheelchair. From where he stood, he could see the old man taking the marker off the Velcro on the little notepad in his lap. He started to write something down.

"Miranda?" There was static on the line, so Jason turned away and moved toward the door. "Are you there?" The line disconnected. He looked at the phone. "Huh."

It was either a butt call or the service isn't good where she is, he thought. He turned back to Maxim Paley and waved. "I'll see you when I get back, Mr. Paley. Take care of yourself! Enjoy the golf game!"

With that, he left the house, not noticing the one word the old man had scribbled on the top slip of the pad—

Don't.

Jason arrived at his apartment in Chicago and quickly unlocked the door.

What to take, what to take . . .

He didn't want to be an idiot. What was it Trey had said he needed? Jason didn't own a gun, but he had a knife. A Swiss Army knife. Trey and his buddies would surely laugh at him if he brought that.

Am I crazy for doing this?

He was setting himself up for ridicule. He'd never live it down. When the weekend was over, Trey Paley was going to tell the world what a pussy Jason was.

No, he's not. I'll show 'em. I can drink as much beer as they can.

Jason went into the bedroom and opened the closet. He started to get his carry-on suitcase but put it back. It would look more rugged if he took his old backpack he used in undergraduate school. He dug it out and put it on the bed.

What do I take to wear?

He grabbed a few pairs of socks and underwear, a couple of T-shirts and long-sleeved button-downs, a pair of sandals, and a sweater. He found a flashlight in a dresser drawer and checked the batteries—they seemed to be good. Next, he went into the bathroom to grab a toiletries kit and stuffed it with a toothbrush, toothpaste, and some sunscreen.

What else?

He opened the medicine cabinet and examined what was available. Some antibiotic ointment wouldn't be bad, so he threw that in. A bottle of ibuprofen. A few band-aids.

Stop it! They're really going to think you're a major wimp or something!

Jason took the kit back to the bedroom and threw it in the backpack. He found his cell phone charger and dropped it inside.

Is there electricity up there?

Jason pulled out his phone and dialed his parents' store. His mother answered.

"Hi, Mom, just letting you know I'm going up to Michigan for the weekend with Nat's brother, Trey."

"Trey? What for?"

"Just a guys' weekend out in the woods. You know, some good ol' male bonding with six-packs, poker chips, and wild animals. It'll be fun."

"Oh, my. Be sure to take some insect repellent. There could be ticks up there, you know. You don't want to get Lyme disease."

"I'm not sure if insect repellent keeps ticks off of you, but that's a good idea anyway." He went back into the bathroom and searched the medicine cabinet. There was no insect repellent.

"When will you be back?"

It was Thursday. Would Friday and Saturday be enough time? "I don't know. Sunday night, I guess. Maybe Monday. I'll call you from there."

"All right. Oh, your sister said she was going to talk to you. Why don't you give her a call? It's something to do with her work."

"She tried to call a while ago but we got disconnected. I'll call her back. Bye! Tell Dad 'hey.'"

"I will. Be careful. Love you!"

"Love you, too."

He hung up and dialed Miranda.

"Safe Haven, Miranda Ward speaking."

"Hey, Sis, it's me. Did you try to call me earlier?"

"Yeah, but I hung up before you answered. Sorry. I got another call I was waiting on. Didn't mean to leave you high and dry."

"It's okay. Mom said you wanted to talk to me?"

"It was nothing important. I was going to give you a call later when I got off work."

"What is it?"

"You know your friend, the FBI agent?"

"Annie? Yeah?"

"Did you ask her if I could call her? I know she works with crimes against women and stuff like that."

"What I understand is she works on civil rights crimes. Hate crimes and the like."

"Human trafficking?"

"Yeah, she's told me a little about all that. I told her you're starting up a division for human trafficking, and I did tell her you wanted to talk to her. She said it was fine if you call."

"Oh, great. I want to pick her brain."

"Here, let me give you her phone number. I put her card somewhere . . ." He found it on his dresser and quickly read off the number to his sister. "That's her FBI office number. I think she'd prefer you not share it."

"Well, duh. Thanks, I owe you."

"No problem. Hey, guess what."

"What?"

"I'm on my way up to the Paleys' cabin in Michigan. I'm going to hang out with Nat's brother and some other guys for the weekend."

"Really? Are you nuts?"

"No, it'll be fun."

"You're lying. Jason, do you know what you're doing?"

"Sure."

"Are you going hunting?"

"I don't know exactly what we'll be doing. Probably just drinking a lot of beer and telling sexist jokes. Hey, I'm just trying to be better friends with my future brother-in-law."

"God, be careful. I have to admit I got a very bad feeling about that guy when I was at their house."

"I know, he puts off a lot of people. It's okay. I can handle him. We broke some ice when we went shooting before."

"I hope so. Well, uh, have a good time?"

"I will. Thanks. Talk to you later!"

He hung up and decided he was ready. Jason looked around the room one more time and then down at his feet. He didn't own hiking boots—just the kind of heavy boots for winter in Chicago. Those surely wouldn't be appropriate. He decided to keep his tennis shoes on.

Anything else?

He saw Annie's business card on the dresser and decided to enter her phone number into the contacts on his cell phone. As he picked up the backpack, ready to leave the bedroom, he stopped. He turned, opened a dresser drawer, rummaged around, and found the Swiss Army knife.

Screw 'em.

He stuck it in his pocket and left the apartment.

27

The email from Colin Clark in Russia arrived that afternoon as Annie was assembling all the pieces of the puzzle that she had thus far. Opening it, she read—

Agent Marino—

Autopsy report on Fyodor Utkin is attached. Further investigation by St. Petersburg has shown that Utkin was in the country from May 27. He owned an apartment in the city which was found to be ransacked. Files and other personal documents had been taken from a desk, whereas clothing and other items were left alone.

Our financial investigators have discovered that Utkin kept money in Karpovka River Bank—surprise, surprise—and that a sizable deposit had been made last April 5 of a little over US$100,000. We are gathering evidence and will send you complete reports ASAP.

As for Greg Paley, we have his Russian entry/exit information. He has visited Russia twice since January 1, three times last year. Paley owns an apartment in St. Petersburg in a nice section of the city (see attached documents for address and photos). He was in town when Utkin was murdered, but there is nothing that ties him to the crime. I have forwarded the photo of him to our investigator in St. Petersburg, who is still attempting to identify the American who was at the restaurant with Evgeni Palit and Fyodor Utkin. So far, though, Paley checks out clean as a whistle and is likely not involved.

In the meantime, I am attaching in a separate email documentation on several missing Russian women. Your information on Irina Semenov checks out. We are attempting to locate another woman, Yana Kravec, whose parents say she left their home some time ago and was living in St. Petersburg when she vanished. ICE has confirmed her entry in the US on June 28, but there are questions about her admittance. Proper procedure was not followed. ICE is interrogating the Customs official who stamped her passport and visa.

Palit Wool continues to be a dead end in the investigation. Evgeni Palit is scheduled to be interviewed by St. Petersburg police in the next few days. My investigator will report on what they learn.

Yours,
Colin

Annie studied the attachments and read the reports. The photo of Yana Kravec struck her as important. Could she be the "Nadia" that Tiffany Vombrack had claimed to see at the Den? The woman who had been shuttled away by Makar Utkin? Of course, Yana Kravec could be anywhere in the United States. After coming into the country through the Port of Newark, the funnel could have led to a million different places. Annie's instincts, however, told her differently. The woman was Russian, she had seemingly been admitted into the country under questionable scrutiny, and she was now off the radar. It sounded too much like Irina Semenov's situation.

As for Fyodor Utkin's deposit of $100,000, why would he deposit it in Russia and not in his US bank unless it was dirty money, income that he didn't want to declare to the IRS? It was entirely possible. According to Sally in Financial, his American records were clean. It made sense to do the money laundering in Russia as it was probably easier and less likely to be noticed.

Clark's assessment of Greg Paley was comforting, but his son was a different story. It was beginning to look like Trey Paley might be a senior manager of the operation, especially since Utkin was dead. Greg Paley's face had revealed genuine concern when she had emphasized the connection between him and Makar Utkin. Did the father suspect his son of being up to something unlawful—or immoral?

She dialed Trey Paley's number again. Annie had been trying to reach him since her conversation with his father. She got the same voice message—"This is Trey. Leave a message." *BEEP*. Annie hung up without leaving one. She then dialed Greg Paley's office. If the man truly wanted to help, he'd get his son to talk to her. She reached his secretary, the woman he called Dorrie.

"Is Mr. Paley in?"

"No, he's in New Jersey at our warehouse. Is there something I can help you with?"

"Tell him that Special Agent Marino called and that I'd like him to phone me, please." She gave out both her cell and office numbers. "When do you expect him back?"

"It'll be a few days. He's supposed to be back on Monday, but you never know."

Ugh, great. "Okay, thank you."

Annie looked at the time. As it was close to five o'clock, she thought she might visit Harris at the hospital. There wasn't much else she could do at the office that day. Her other cases had stalled or were resolved. The Bear Claws Case was now dependent on what other FBI divisions and other agencies around the globe could uncover. It might be her case, but there wasn't a lot she could do to move it forward. The wheels of justice often rolled so slowly that it was a wonder any criminals were arrested, tried, and convicted.

The desk phone rang just as she was starting to shut down her computer and call it a day.

"Marino."

"Annie? Melanie O'Horgan."

Ah. Cyber Division. "Hi, Melanie, what's up?"

"We have an ISP address for the darknet websites you found on that guy Flanagan's computer."

"No way! Really?"

"Yep. It's located in a building in St. Petersburg, Russia."

"That's not surprising. I was hoping it would be in the US, but I was dreaming. What's the building?"

"A storage facility. We've alerted the ALAT, so I imagine the St. Petersburg police will descend on the place within twenty-four hours and seize the servers. Hopefully, we'll find out who owns or rents the space pretty quickly."

"That's fantastic news, Melanie. Thank you. Please call me as soon as you hear anything." Annie gave her the personal cell number and hung up.

She gave herself a fist pump before leaving the cubicle.

"How are you feeling?" Annie gently asked.

Harris peered at her through squinty eyes. His skin was pale, but he looked better than he had the last time she'd seen him.

"Like I have a big, gaping hole in my stomach," he whispered.

"When are they going to let you go back to Detroit?"

"The doctor said I can be moved next week. I'm looking forward to it. I want to go home."

"I can imagine." Annie sat in the chair beside the bed. "I think we've had some progress in the case."

"Yeah?"

She outlined everything she'd learned. "I'm still trying to find Makar Utkin and Trey Paley. They seem to have vanished."

"I think they're the ones, Annie," Harris said. "They're the ones doing this, at least over here. It just fits. When you look at all the pieces . . . don't you agree?"

"Yeah, I do. I think Fyodor Utkin was actually running it here in the US, but Trey and Makar were his henchmen. This fellow Babikov in Russia . . . he must be The Bear."

"Or maybe he *works* for The Bear."

"I think we'd know if Nikolai Babikov was just an underling. The ALAT says he's the big kahuna in the Novgorod mafia. How much do you want to bet that the storage facility where the website servers are located are owned by him or someone connected to him?"

Harris reached over and took her hand. "You're going to crack this case, Annie. I know it."

She nodded. "I think I am, too." He winced a little. "Are you in pain?"

He nodded slightly. "They pump me full of drugs but they don't completely cover it up. I don't know, Annie, I don't think I'm going to come back to work after this."

"You mean the Bureau?"

"Yeah."

She understood. It was unfortunate, but these things happened in the FBI. "What will you do?"

"I have no clue. Maybe I'll change my mind, but I don't think so. When your job almost kills you, you tend to re-think your employment a little."

"Harris, no one's going to blame you if you resign. If this was the military, you'd get a Purple Heart."

He grinned. "That'd be nice." After a pause, he said, "Thank you for coming."

"I'll be back, Harris. Hang in there. This, too, shall pass. And don't go back to Detroit without saying goodbye first."

"Don't worry about me. You just get the bad guys. And when you find the asshole who did this to me, I want you to kick his butt, okay?"

Annie laughed and stood.

"With pleasure."

28

Jason drove his silver 2012 Hyundai Elantra through the small town of Lakeway, Michigan, just as dusk was morphing into darkness. He had used the GPS to get that far, but now he had to go by Nat's written directions and a crude map she had drawn of the Paley property that indicated the cabin in relation to the adjacent lake and the road leading to it. He was to take Highway 82 going east until he saw an old faded billboard that advertised a defunct gas station from the sixties. Six miles past that, there would be a turnoff to Garden Road to the left. That was the warning that he was getting close. Three miles beyond that and to the left, he would see a cattle guard at the head of an unmarked dirt road heading north into the forest. That was it.

In the dark, it was more difficult to find than Jason had expected. After a while, perhaps ten miles past the billboard, he came to another north-south thoroughfare, so he figured he'd passed the turnoff. He cursed to himself, slowed down, and turned the car around in the middle of the two-lane road. There wasn't much traffic at that time of the evening. He'd encountered perhaps only three vehicles, all going in the opposite direction.

Man, this really is *in the middle of nowhere . . .*

Heading back west, Jason managed to find the cattle guard and turned right onto a muddy, one-lane road. There must have been a recent rain. He wished now that he had brought his winter boots, heavy or not.

The tall trees formed an eerie tunnel illuminated by the Elantra's headlights. The forest was populated by jack pine, oak, soft maple, and paper birch trees that, during August, were fully leafed and dense. The concentration of trees was so thick that Jason imagined they surely formed a solid fortress around the Paley property, even in the winter when the leaves were gone. He was already beginning to get a sense of isolation, and he hadn't yet driven a quarter mile into the woods.

Jason didn't know what he would do if a car came down the road toward him from the opposite direction. There was no room for two vehicles side by side. He figured there wasn't enough traffic on the path to warrant such a worry. Still, it was creepy. Nat had said the road would twist and turn for a good five miles. He followed it slowly, praying that the car wouldn't get stuck in the mud. That would be all he needed—and as soon as the thought occurred to him, sure enough, he hit a pothole in the road that was full of wet, tar-like sludge. The car stopped and the back wheels spun.

"Damn it!" he yelled and hit the steering wheel with his fist. He stepped on the gas, but the tires continued to sound like buzz saws. After nearly a minute, he let up, fearing that he'd hurt the engine. "*Now* what . . ." he muttered. He sat there for a moment, contemplating the situation. How far had he gone on the road? Was the cabin close? He looked at his watch. A little after nine. "Aw, hell . . ."

He turned off the car, grabbed his backpack, opened the door, and stepped out into about six inches of mud that covered his sneaker. "Oh, *man*! Yuck!" Nothing to do but get out and shut the door. Would it be hazardous to just leave the car in the road like that? Would anyone else be coming? There was no way another vehicle could get around it. He didn't want to leave his blinkers on all night—would the battery be dead by morning? Would Trey be willing to come and help him move the car before they went to bed?

It was a chance he'd have to take. Jason reached back in and turned on the hazard lights. The steady blinking cast strange, yellow-colored staccato illumination over the trees towering around him. He looked back at the rear tires and, of course, the driver's side was a foot submerged in muck.

He locked the car and dug into his backpack for the flashlight. Flicking it on, Jason realized he probably should have loaded it with new batteries. The beam was good enough for him to see where he was going, but it was dimmer than it could have been.

He strode forward, slipping the pack on his back. Ironically, the mud leveled out ten feet ahead of the car and the road was solid again.

The forest was eerily quiet. No insect sounds, no crickets, no cicadas. Jason thought that was odd. In Chicago the cicadas were out in full force, even in the city, and they made a terrible racket at night. Here, where trees took up 99 percent of the space around him, there was not a single bug-sawing to be heard. It was creepy.

He began to wonder if he might run into a bear or a wolf or something else that might eat him alive. Now he wished he had one of Trey's guns with him. He began to wonder if it had been an incredibly foolish notion for him to come uninvited.

Nothing jumped out of the woods to get him. He trudged onward, following the wet road around curves and in straight lines for nearly thirty minutes—and then he heard the heavy bass beat of rock music. The closer he got, the more definition the music had—the guitars, drums, and singing became clearer.

Heavy metal, head-banging stuff. It wasn't Jason's cup of tea. He'd go crazy if he had to listen to that all weekend, but in light of abandoning his car and other possible misfortunes that might occur, he knew it was absurd of him to think that.

Then—he arrived.

The cabin stood in a clearing, set apart from the trees by approximately thirty yards all the way around. Lights in the windows were on. The music inside was blasted loud, but the cabin itself served as a bit of a muffler. Still—Jason was sure it was scaring away any wild animals that might be near.

He recognized Trey's red Ford pickup truck and Mack's Nissan Altima parked in front. They were both caked with mud splashes on their sides.

Steeling himself, Jason approached the door and knocked. Nothing happened, so he knocked again, louder. A few seconds later, the music volume went down and he heard footsteps clomping to the door on the other side. It opened.

"What, did you forget your k—?"

It was Makar Utkin. His eyes registered surprise.

"Hey, Mack," Jason said. "Hope it's okay that I crash your party?"

"What the fuck, Jason! What are you doing here?"

He shrugged. "I wanted to join you guys for your Bacchanal. Is that okay? Where's Trey?"

"Man, you can't be here!"

"Uh, why not?"

"You just can't!"

"Well, I *am* here. I drove all the way from Chicago." He pointed back toward the road. "My car got stuck in the mud a couple of miles back. I need help getting it out. I'm sorry, man, I wanted to surprise you guys."

Makar continued to stare at the visitor, his mouth gaping.

"Well, can I come in?"

Makar stepped aside. Jason wiped his shoes on the mat in front of the door, but it didn't do much good. "Aw, hell, I'll just take 'em off." He slipped off the shoes and left them outside. The cabin was warm and cozy, although it reeked of tobacco smoke. A stuffed black bear head was mounted above a fireplace, which was roaring with flames. The furniture was old, but in decent shape. It was rustic and homey, everything Jason had imagined a "cabin in the woods" to be.

Makar appeared to be the only person there.

"Where's Trey?"

"Uh, he's . . . he's outside."

"Outside? In the woods?"

"Yeah."

"Isn't it, like, *dark*?"

"He'll be back."

Jason thought that was odd. "Mind if I use your bathroom?" He didn't know why he hadn't just gone while he was walking along the road, out in nature and all.

"I guess."

He dropped his backpack on the floor and looked around the room. Makar pointed to a door that was between what were obviously the entrances to the two bedrooms. Jason went in and did his business. When he emerged, Makar was standing in the same spot where he'd left him.

"Look, if you guys don't want me here, come back with me and help me get my car out of the mud, and I'll leave."

"No, no . . . just wait until Trey comes back." Makar finally moved toward the kitchen area. "You want a beer?"

"Sure."

Makar opened the fridge—it was *full* of beer bottles. Jason wasn't sure if there was anything else in there. Surely there was food tucked away somewhere. Makar tossed a bottle to Jason, who surprised himself by catching it without fumbling. "Thanks." He attempted to twist off the cap, with no luck.

Makar smiled and threw him a churchkey. "Try this."

This time, Jason missed it, and the thing flew across the room, landing on the floor. "Sorry," he said. He picked it up, opened his beer, sat, and placed the churchkey on the wooden coffee table in front of a sofa. There were already over two dozen empty bottles on the table next to the ashtray.

"Trey's not going to like you being here," Makar said, coming around and sitting on a chair next to the table. He picked up his own beer.

"Why not? What's his problem, Mack? Why doesn't he like me? I've never done anything to *him*."

Makar just shrugged. No one spoke for a moment.

"The road sure was muddy. Did you have rain?"

"Yeah."

More silence. Jason was beginning to feel uncomfortable. It really *was* a bad idea to come.

Finally, Makar set his bottle down and stood. "I'll be right back. Stay here. Don't go anywhere."

"What, in the woods at night? You think I'm nuts?"

Makar didn't laugh. He opened the door and went out. The discomfort in the air was palpable.

Jesus . . . ! What the hell *is going on here?*

The music was starting to get on his nerves. Jason got up and went to the stereo system, which was on a shelf near the fireplace. It was an iPod with a tuner and speakers the size of carry-on suitcases. He turned the volume down to a near ambient level and returned to the sofa, chugging at his beer. A few more minutes went by. Jason pulled his cell phone out of his pocket, thinking he'd call Nat and tell her he'd arrived.

No service.

He tried dialing anyway, but there was no luck.

At that moment, the door opened and Trey and Makar came in.

"What the *fuck* are you doing here?" Trey growled.

"Hey, Trey. Nice to see you, too."

He slammed the door shut. "I mean it, writer-boy, what are you doing here?"

"Christ, Trey. I wanted to be, like, *friendly*, and come hang out with you. I'm sorry. Like I told Mack, if you help me get my car out of the mud, I'll turn around and drive back tonight."

Trey stood there, his face turning all shades of red. Jason could practically see the wheels turning in his head.

"No," the guy finally said. "No, you can stay. Tonight. You might have to go back tomorrow, though. We'll help you get your car out in the morning, okay?"

"Sure, whatever. Sorry. I just thought . . ." Jason held out his hands and then let them drop. "I'm sorry."

Trey remained as still as a statue, except for his heavy breathing. Makar stood slightly behind him, his eyes darting back and forth between his friend and Jason, ready to follow Trey's lead.

After what seemed like an eternity of seconds, Trey's shoulders relaxed. He removed two beers from the fridge, handed one to Makar, and scanned the kitchen counter for something.

"Here's the churchkey," Jason said, holding it up.

Trey nodded and strode toward the sitting area. He plopped down and opened his beer.

Makar asked, "Uh, you have the, uh, keys?"

Trey nodded. He dug into his pocket and pulled out a ring with several keys on it. He pitched them to Makar, who put them in a drawer in the kitchen. He then returned and sat in the other chair. Both of them lit cigarettes. Jason noted that the ash tray on the coffee table was overflowing with butts. Jason's eyes went to Makar, who seemed as if he was a little afraid of Trey, too.

Jason dared to speak first. "So . . . it's just the two of you?"

"Yeah," Trey answered.

"So, why can't I join you? What's the big deal?"

"The Bacchanal is *private*," Trey answered.

"Oh."

"*But* . . . maybe you can stay."

Makar opened his mouth. "But, Trey, what about—?"

"Shut up!" He glared at his friend and looked back at Jason. "This is my future brother-in-law. God knows why my sister loves him, but she does. I guess I better start being nicer to him, huh."

Jason didn't say anything. He just fiddled with his useless phone.

Drunkenly, Trey leaned forward. "Okay, listen. You can stay. But you have to follow the rules."

"Uh, what rules?"

"Whatever I say. There are dos and don'ts. First of all, don't go exploring on your own. It's dangerous. And stay away from the shed."

"The shed?"

Trey nodded. "In the morning, you'll see a trail that goes through the trees behind the cabin. That's off-limits, okay?"

Jason swallowed. "Okay. Can I ask why?"

Trey took a long swig of beer and let the question hang. Finally, he answered, "Actually, it's full of hornets. There are hornets' nests in there and we have to get them cleaned out. Big fucking hornets that'll attack you if you even go near the place."

"Really?"

"Yes, really! Stay away. If you get stung, we're too far away from civilization to get you medical attention. I saw you playing with your phone. You notice we don't have cell phone service here."

"What do you do in case of an emergency?"

"We avoid emergencies!"

Trey sat back in the chair and took a long drink. "If you play by the rules, we'll have a good time. There's a TV, we do have a satellite dish. We have a bunch of DVDs—mostly porn. Maybe we'll go hunting tomorrow. There's a bear den not far from here. A mama bear and cubs that are about six or seven months old. She'll fiercely protect them, so you don't want to go running into her. Papa bear?—who knows where he is. He's an *intelligent* male, he leaves the mother and her babies and goes searching for other females to mate with." He laughed. "That's the way it *should* be, right?"

Makar laughed with him, but Jason didn't.

The rest of the night had been nothing but a beer-and-cigarettes fest. Trey and Makar smoked a lot, consumed several bottles, and became drunk and boisterous, but Jason took it easy. He didn't smoke, but he pretended to be a party participant as far as the beer was concerned. He had the sinking feeling that perhaps he really *would* go back to Chicago the next day after they got his car out of the mud. No question about it. At least he had tried.

Sometime after midnight, Trey and Makar retired to their rooms. Jason was relegated to the sofa. The fireplace had died out, but embers illuminated the living room in that night-light glow that was actually comforting. But Jason couldn't fall asleep. He could hear both of them snoring loudly through the doors of their bedrooms. Jason tossed and turned, replaying in his head some of the outrageous things Trey and Makar had said during their revelry. Distasteful jokes, complaining about this or that, but especially saying terrible sexist and racist things about women and minorities. Jason felt as if he was in the lion's den. If he'd had more gumption, he'd have argued with them. He knew, though, that it would only get his ass kicked. Plus, he was alone with them in a cabin in the woods.

Sometime in the middle of the night, Jason awoke to a noise. Someone was coming out of the bedroom. It was Trey. The former soldier went into the bathroom and threw up. After a while, the toilet flushed and he emerged. He stood there in the dark for a while. Jason felt Trey watching, so he feigned sleep. Finally, Trey moved quietly across the room to the kitchen and opened a drawer, where he retrieved the key ring Jason had seen earlier. Trey crept over to the door of the cabin, slipped on shoes, and went outside.

What the hell? Where is he going?

It certainly wouldn't be for a smoke; Trey had no qualms about puffing his stinky cigarettes inside the cabin.

Jason sat up and listened. All was quiet. He got up and went to one of the windows and looked out.

Nothing there.

It was perplexing.

He went back to the sofa and waited. Fifteen minutes went by, and Trey didn't return. Very strange.

Wait . . . what was that?

Jason heard it in the distance. A sound in the night.

Was that a woman screaming*?*

No, it couldn't be.

It was the wind. An animal howling in the night.

Jason cocked his head to listen.

Nothing.

He got up and went to the door. Quietly and carefully opening it, he stuck his head outside. The air was cold and damp.

There were no sounds except the breeze and the rustling of leaves in the trees.

Chalking the scream up to his imagination, he closed the door and went back to the sofa. Jason lay down, turned over, and closed his eyes. It wasn't long before he really did fall asleep, and he never heard Trey return.

29

It always seemed to occur in the hush of the night.

When the darkness was silent and still everywhere else, when other people were complacently sleeping in the comfort of their own beds, Yana was subjected to unimaginable horror.

Now the skylight above her bed revealed a starry, black sky. On some nights the moon passed over the small window. She loved that moon. Its brightness provided her with a focus, an energy that she needed to get through the pain. She hoped she would see it again; for the past couple of nights there had been no moon. The sky had been cloudy and dark, even during the day. It had rained a lot, but it was clear now.

It was pathetic how she measured time by the weather.

The horrible American had just been in to "visit" her again. Why was he so intentionally cruel? If he had to take what he wanted, why couldn't he just do it? There wasn't much she could do to resist. Did he have to hurt her?

She knew it gave him some kind of sick pleasure.

He was a monster.

She thought her spirit was completely broken, never to be repaired. She wanted to die. Every day, under that skylight, Yana actually prayed for God to kill her. It never happened. She lived another day . . . and another . . .

Was this to be her fate forever? To be the plaything of this . . . *beast?* To her, this man was the devil incarnate.

"I am so happy that The Bear sent you to me," he had told her. "You are my *therapy* for the month." She didn't know what that meant, but it proved to her that the man was insane. He had said he was a soldier. That he had killed many people. Apparently, she was supposed to be impressed by this. All it did was reveal his sickness and depravity.

It was even more disturbing when he said that his "friends" would have their turns later over the weekend.

She'd been told back at the house in Chicago that her assignment was a "rental." Surely that meant her ordeal here was temporary? She would eventually be sent back, *right*?

Or would she never leave the woods alive?

If God wasn't able to kill her, Yana vowed to find a way out of this hell. For weeks, she had yearned for merely an opportunity to escape. Now she was so frantic and desperate to act that she knew she would kill them if she had the chance.

30

On Friday morning, Annie walked in to her cubicle and noticed the red light blinking on her phone. She set down her thermos and lunch and punched the buttons to listen to the message.

"Um, hello, Special Agent Marino, this is Miranda Ward. I'm Jason Ward's sister. You might remember that we met when I was with my brother at Starbucks a while back? I believe I told you then that I work in Indianapolis at Safe Haven, a not-for-profit that provides support and assistance for women and children who are victims of domestic abuse and other crimes. I've recently been put in charge of a new initiative that deals with human trafficking. Jason told me about your job with the FBI and I was wondering if we could talk. I'm going to be reaching out to the FBI field office here in Indiana, but I thought since there was a personal connection between you and my brother that perhaps I could start by talking to you. If you could find some time to get back to me, I'd love to have a chat." She ended the message by giving out her phone number and email address.

Annie was pleasantly flattered. After putting her lunch in the community refrigerator and checking her email, she dialed Miranda's office.

"Miranda Ward."

"Hi, Miranda, it's Special Agent Annie Marino, FBI Chicago."

"Oh, hi! Gosh, thank you for calling!"

"My pleasure. So your brother revealed classified information and gave you my phone number, did he?"

"Oh dear, was he not supposed to?"

Annie laughed. "I'm kidding. No problem at all if he did. Jason's great, by the way. I couldn't ask for a better coffee buddy."

"Yeah, well, for a younger brother, he's not bad. Well, let's get to it, shall we?"

Annie spent the next fifteen minutes talking about the Civil Rights Division and specifically some of the Human Trafficking Squad's efforts to combat the crimes. Miranda outlined what she had planned for her organization, and Annie gave her feedback. Once that business was completed, Annie said, "I look forward to seeing you again in person at Jason's wedding, assuming I'll be invited."

"Oh, I'm sure you'll be invited. Jason says he really likes you. I look forward to seeing you again, too."

"I don't think I've run into him much lately. He must be spending more time at his fiancée's house."

"Well, this weekend he's up in Michigan with Nat's brother at their cabin in the woods. They're doing some kind of macho male bonding thing."

"Oh, *really*? I didn't think he got along too well with Trey Paley."

"You know Trey?"

"I don't. I've met his father, and I've met Nat." She almost said that she'd been looking for Trey, but caught herself.

"Well, he's a piece of work. Between you and me, that guy has some problems. In fact, I'm a little worried about Jason being up there with Trey Paley and a bunch of alcohol and guns."

Annie thought about that. "I'm sure he'll be all right. Jason's got a good head on his shoulders."

"Yeah, I guess so. Well, it was nice talking to you, Annie—may I call you Annie?"

"Sure. Don't hesitate to call again if you have any more questions."

When she hung up, Annie got a bad feeling. Jason was alone with Trey Paley. She dug out her cell phone and dialed Jason's number. It went to voice mail, so she left a message for him to call her.

Surely it wasn't possible that Jason was involved. No way.

Was it right to recognize the shadow of doubt that was instinctual? She had been trained to read people. It was absolutely appropriate for her to suspect him, she was just being *thorough*. Jason was an innocent soul, she knew it in her heart.

It was that thought process that led her to—

"Oh my God . . ."

Jason was very possibly in danger.

Could Makar Utkin be up there with them in Michigan as well? She didn't believe he was "on vacation," like she'd been told. He was probably in hiding, and what better place than a remote cabin in the woods? He was, after all, a close friend of Trey's. She needed to talk to them both. Could she kill two birds with one stone? That prospect appealed to her, but there wasn't much she could do sitting in Chicago. She pulled up Chief Daniel's contact info and made the call.

"Police department."

"Is Chief Daniel there?"

"No, ma'am, he's on vacation for a week. Can I help you?"

She winced, having forgotten about that. "Captain Mike?"

"Yes, ma'am."

"It's FBI Special Agent Anne Marino."

Aside from part-time officers on call, Captain Mike Baines was all alone at the station.

Annie drummed her fingers on the desk. "Listen, there's a person of interest at the Paley cabin that I'd like to talk to. I *think* he's there. I know Trey Paley is there, and another man by the name of Jason Ward." She didn't want to give it away that she knew Jason. "Is there any way you can find out if Makar Utkin is there? Do you know him?"

"I know Mack. He's a good friend of Trey's. He's been up at their cabin a few times."

"Do you know if he's up there now?"

"Well, Agent Marino, I don't know. I didn't even know Trey was there. It's his property, he can come and go as he likes."

"I realize that. Just wondering if maybe you saw him in town, picking up supplies or something."

"No, ma'am, I ain't seen him."

"Can you find out without, you know, tipping your hand that I'm interested in talking to him? If he's there, I'll drive up, and we can go visit the place. Maybe take another officer with us?"

Mike Baines was silent for a moment, then he answered. "Yeah, I think I can sneak up there, like, and see what I can see. You going to be around later?"

"You can reach me on my cell phone. Let me know, okay?"

"I'll try to get up there this afternoon and call you back."

"Thanks, Captain Mike."

"Sure thing."

Annie hung up. Captain Mike was a country bumpkin, but at least he was a law officer who knew the area. She got up from her desk and walked to SSA Gladden's office. She knocked on the frame of the open door.

"John?"

"Good morning, Annie." He was going over reports, not looking up at her.

"I might have a chance to interview Makar Utkin and Trey Paley. I think they're both up in Michigan at the Paley property. I'm waiting on a call-back from the police captain up in Lakeway. He's going to let me know if they're there. If they are, I think I'm going to drive up and talk to them. I'd have at least one or two officers for backup."

Gladden's eyes went up to her. "I'll let you be the judge on that. There's no one out of Detroit that can do it?"

"Agent Caruthers is still in the hospital. I don't know who's handling his workload. Look, it's my case, sir, I'd like to be on top of it."

Gladden shrugged, said "Fine," and went back to his work.

Annie returned to her cubicle and found an email from the Russian ALAT in her inbox.

> Agent Marino—
>
> St. Petersburg police raided the location of the buy-a-slave website servers. The storage unit was rented by a man named Eduard Volkov, who, on further investigation, was revealed to be a non-existent entity. However, security cameras on the street were examined, and guess who visited the storage facility in June?
>
> Our friend Fyodor Utkin!
>
> Computers were seized and are now being torn apart for evidence.
>
> Will be in touch.
>
> Colin

Things were falling into place. She hadn't heard back from Greg Paley, but that was probably a moot point now. Annie knew it was likely that his son was at the cabin in Michigan. Considering what she just learned about Fyodor Utkin—if *his* son Makar was involved with *him*—then Trey Paley could be implicated as well. Was Trey working for The Bear? Was *he* The Bear? If any of that were true, then there was nothing Greg Paley could do to stop the wheels of justice. His son was going down. Sometimes bad things happened to good families.

She checked with Cyber and Financial to see if there was any news on their ends, but there was nothing she didn't already know.

Now she just had to wait to hear from Captain Mike.

31

Trey and Makar slept late on Friday due to the previous night's consumption of alcohol. The cabin was quiet when Jason awoke around eight. The sofa had been surprisingly comfortable once he settled in to sleep. He must have been conked out when Trey returned to the cabin. Jason was usually a light sleeper, so he found it odd that someone coming through the front door didn't wake him.

He got up and dressed. Then he sat on the sofa in the common area and thought, *Now what?* He didn't want to wake the other two, and there was no telling what kind of a mood Trey would be in. Jason figured since Trey wasn't very nice when he was sober, he probably wouldn't be very personable with a hangover.

Although he would have liked to have prepared breakfast, Jason didn't want to make any noise in the small kitchen area, and he questioned whether or not he had permission to scrounge around for food anyway. His curiosity got the better of him, and he moved quietly to the cabinets and opened the drawer. The ring of keys that Trey had taken the night before was back in place. He contemplated it for a moment, and shut the drawer.

He decided to go outside. The cabin door was unlocked, and he stepped out into a crisp, bright morning.

The smell of the air was the first thing that struck him. It was so fresh and clean, as if he'd just placed an oxygen mask over his mouth, especially after the foul tobacco-heavy stench of the cabin. The leaves in the trees rustled pleasantly with a light breeze. Birds chirped and insects cricked. Jason had never felt such an overwhelming sensation of *nature* than at that moment. No wonder people bought cabins in the woods. Even though getaways such as this held stereotypical reputations of a place where the boogeyman usually got you, there was something to be said about this location's serenity and beauty.

The ground around the cabin was damp but solid. The road back to the highway, however, was still muddy. Jason walked along the edge of the road in an attempt to limit the amount of mud he would pick up on his already caked shoes. It was a pleasant hike, the temperature being moderately cool. It took him twenty minutes to get to his car, and he found the blinkers still going. Jason turned off the hazard lights and tried starting the car. The engine kicked on, which was a good sign, but when he attempted to free the car from the sludge puddle, it was still no good. The rear tires continued to spin. He'd definitely need help pushing it out.

This time he left the blinkers off. Jason walked back to the cabin along the opposite side of the road this time. He quietly opened the door and stuck his head inside. All was quiet; it appeared that the sleeping beauties weren't up yet. It was about nine o'clock. Softly, Jason shut the door and continued to explore.

First he went around the perimeter of the clearing where the cabin stood. Beyond that demarcation was the thick, foreboding forest in every direction. The illumination amid the trees was fine, although it was significantly dimmer here than in the clearing. Jason knew it would get very dark in there once the sun went down.

Now he had all day—to do what? He was considering leaving as soon as he got his car freed. Trey really didn't want him there. His thoughts lingered on the events of the night before. He couldn't be *hiding* something, could he?

The thought bounced into Jason's head, and he felt a jolt. What if he *was*? When Trey saw him yesterday, the guy looked like he would explode. Jason detected a note of guilt in Trey's admonitions, as if there was something that was scheduled to happen that he didn't want Jason to know about.

He entered the path behind the cabin that led into the woods, where the alleged hornet-infested shed was supposed to be, off-limits. Jason walked slowly, imagining that at any moment Trey would jump out from behind a tree and yell at him for disobeying his rules. The path was damp, but not muddy. Boot tracks were plainly visible, going back and forth.

It wasn't as far as he'd expected. Just straight ahead, thirty yards or so, and then around a bend. The shed. It stood still and lonely, surrounded by the encroaching forest. No windows. Just a door.

With a padlock on it.

Jason moved closer and thought he heard something. It was a high-pitched sound that had a lyrical quality to it.

Birds? No . . .

It was a human voice. A girl. A girl singing. A girl singing to herself. In another language . . .

Oh my God—she's inside the shed!

Jason approached the door and knocked. "Hello? Is someone in there?"

The singing stopped. Silence.

"Hello?" He knocked again. "Is someone in there? Can I help you?"

The woman's voice called out. "Hello?"

"Hello? Who's in there?"

"Are you . . . one of them?"

"What? One of who?"

"Oh God, oh God, are you here to rescue me?" she cried out.

"What?" She had a foreign accent of some kind. Russian?

"Help me, help me, please! I am a captive! They are keeping me prisoner and . . . abusing me! Help me!"

Jason's heart froze. He couldn't speak. He could barely breathe.

"Hello, are you still there?" the woman cried. She sounded desperate.

"Yes, I am. Are you . . . are you serious? You're a prisoner? Can you get closer to the door?"

"I am chained to the wall near the bed. I can't reach the door! Please get me out! These men will kill me!"

Chained to the wall?

"Hold on. Stay calm." Jason, however, was about to burst. His adrenaline was pumping furiously and his heart pounded in his chest. "What's your name?"

"Nad—my name is Yana! Yana Kravec!"

"Yana Kravec."

"Yes!"

"All right, Yana. My name is Jason."

"Jason."

"I'm going to try and get help. I think I know where the keys are. But the guys who did this are still here. If they're up, I don't know if I can get to them. I'll try. Or I have to get away and get help. Hang tight, all right?"

"Please. Please hurry. I do not think I can take another night of that man. The soldier. He is a monster!"

She means Trey. Jesus.

"Okay, try to keep calm. I'll be back." He turned and hurried back up the path to the cabin. Along the way, he pulled his cell phone out of his jeans pocket and tried to call 9-1-1. Still no service. He didn't know why he thought there might be any during daylight. They were as isolated as an island in the middle of the sea.

Before he reached the clearing, he stopped moving, observed the cabin, and noted that there was no sign of movement. He went around to the front and carefully opened the door—

—and found Trey and Makar sitting in the common area with coffee cups in their hands.

"There you are," Trey said. "We were wondering what happened to you."

"I, uh, went to check on my car. It's still stuck. I hope maybe when you're ready, you'll help me get it out of the mud. I think I should just go on back to Chicago. The sooner we get my car out, the sooner I'll be out of your hair."

Trey wrinkled his brow. "Why are you leaving? Come on, stay. We're going hunting."

"Nah, I think I'll get on back."

"Jason, we're going hunting, and that's that. Now shut the door and come inside. We'll get your car out later. You want coffee?"

After a mediocre plate of scrambled eggs and bacon that Makar had prepared, Trey said, "Technically, the best time for hunting is early in the morning. Get out before dawn and be in place when the sun comes up. But this time of year, the black bear sows are in prime instructional mode to their six- or seven-month-old cubs. They could be out looking for food. I've encountered bears in the middle of the day before."

Jason did not want to go hunting. He'd been suffering through breakfast, wondering how he was going to get away and get help for Yana. At the same time, as he looked at the faces of Trey and Makar, he couldn't fathom the cruelty and inhumanity in front of him. To think that the man she had called a "monster" was going to be his brother-in-law! Jason had to tell Nat. He had to let Mr. Paley know what his son was doing. There was no way around it. He thought he should contact Nat first, and persuade her to get her father involved. Mr. Paley would know what to do.

The thought did cross his mind—*how much did Nat know about her brother?* She was smart, perceptive, had received a degree in *psychology,* for Christ's sake. Surely she could see that Trey was way beyond "psychological problems." Was she in denial? Was her entire family in denial?

Had her old grandfather Maxim been trying to tell him something with the distinctive squeeze of the hand? Trying to *warn* him?

When he was finished with his meal, Trey took the plate into the kitchen. He scraped the remains into the trash and turned on the faucet to rinse the dish, but there was no dish soap on the counter. Instinctively, he opened the drawer—but the key ring was no longer there.

Damn!

"What are you looking for?" Trey snapped.

"Dish soap. You got any?"

"Look under the sink, doofus."

Jason shut the drawer and did as he was told. As he cleaned his plate, Trey walked over and handed over his and Makar's dishes. "Here, you can do these, too, kitchen boy."

As Trey walked away, Jason noticed the bulge in his front pants pocket—the key ring. Surely the key to the padlock was on that ring. If he couldn't phone for help and wasn't able to leave in his car, the only other option was to somehow get the key and help Yana escape. Through the woods. Back to the highway. It wasn't that far. Surely someone would see her on the road.

But how was he going to get that key?

"You have your hunting license?" Trey asked him.

Jason looked at him as if he were nuts. "Uh, no."

"You can't go hunting without one. How are you going to go hunting if you don't have a hunting license?"

They were standing in front of the cabin, decked out in hunter garb and carrying their weapons. Jason had the .388 Winchester Magnum that he had shot before. Trey carried his .458 Win Mag, and Makar had a .388 like Trey's. Jason was dressed in what he'd had on since morning, except he'd added a light jacket and the orange hunter's vest. Both Trey and Makar wore plaid shirts and heavy boots, along with the orange vests and caps that no one could mistake for anything other than something a hunter would wear. Jason thought the two men looked like lumberjacks, but he didn't say that.

"I guess I can't go hunting, then. Look, if you'll just help me with my car—"

"What's your hurry?" Trey playfully punched Jason on the upper arm, but hard enough to make Jason wince. "I'm just messing with you about the license. Hell, we're hunting out of season; it won't make no difference whether or not you have a license. This is private property. So—we're going to spread out. Mack, you go that way. I'll go this way. Jason, you stay between us. That way we'll cover a wider area."

"What do you mean?" Jason asked. "Just walk straight into the forest? What if I get lost?"

"Just walk straight. Time yourself. After ten minutes of walking, stop and find a tree to climb."

"*A tree to climb?*"

"Yeah, it's the best perch for shooting a bear."

"A bear can climb a tree."

"Not if you shoot him first."

Trey winked at Makar and smiled. Jason felt they were having him on; they wanted to make a fool out of him somehow.

Fine. I'll go alone. Maybe I can get away, get to a road, flag down a car . . .

As Jason's thoughts swam in his head, he actually entertained the possibility of shooting Trey and Makar. Would it be justified in order to save the captive woman in the shed? The problem was he didn't think he could ever kill anyone. It wasn't in his blood.

They proceeded to march into the woods. Jason looked right and left and watched Trey and Makar head in their respective directions. They soon disappeared into the trees. Jason kept going, glancing at his watch every now and then. How far should he really go? He wanted to circle back and move in the direction of his car. At least he knew that the muddy road to the cabin went to Highway 82. That was his best bet to reach civilization.

He stopped and peered around him. No sign of the guys. Jason turned around and headed the way he had come. If he could get back to the cabin before them, he would run down the road to his car and beyond.

Jason soon found, though, that he must have misjudged the course. The cabin was still nowhere in sight—just trees. Had he somehow veered off the route?

No need to panic yet. Just angle more this *way . . .*

He walked for five more minutes, over brush and around trees, and then knew he was truly lost. Did he have a compass? No. Should he shout out and hope that Trey or Makar would hear him? Did he want to depend on them? That would be crazy—Jason wanted to get out of there, away from those crazy bastards.

At that moment, a gunshot cracked in the distance. Jason felt the heat of the bullet zip in front of his face and strike the tree to his left, splintering a piece off the bark. Startled, he yelped, "*Fuck!*" and jumped to the ground.

Jesus! Were they shooting at him*?*

"Hey!" he called. "What are you doing?"

He lay face down for a moment until he heard someone coming from his right.

"You okay?"

It was Trey. Jason raised his head. "You almost shot me!"

"Sorry, man! Jesus, I thought you were a bear!"

"Thought I was a *bear*? I'm wearing *orange*!" Jason got to his feet as Trey approached. Makar soon appeared from the opposite direction.

"I said I'm sorry! Don't get your panties in a wad. It was an honest mistake. Happens all the time."

"Happens all the time? Really, Trey?"

Trey's eyes flared. "Yeah, *really*. You want to make an issue out of this?"

Jason instinctively knew to back down. If he'd been the type of guy who *could* fight, he might have taken him on, but he knew it was hopeless. Trey would make mincemeat out of him, and then Jason wouldn't be able to escape and get help for Yana.

"I think I'm done hunting," he said. "Show me the way back to the cabin. I'm serious, Trey. I don't want to do this. You guys can go hunting all you like. Not me."

"Fine." He pointed in the direction Jason had been going. "It's this way."

But Jason was still stuck there. When he asked about moving his car, Trey put him off again. "We'll move it tomorrow. No worries. You don't want to miss the big party tonight."

Party tonight? What the hell did he mean by that?

Jason spent the rest of the afternoon in the cabin as Trey and Makar drank beer after beer and watched first a baseball game on television and then a particularly graphic and violent bondage and S&M porn movie on DVD. Jason was disgusted by the images on the TV, and the comments the two made during the "action" were vile and sexist. Jason simply sat there, nursed one or two beers, and hoped no one wouldn't notice how few he was consuming. He didn't want them to think he was staying sober on purpose.

As the dinner hour approached, Makar opened two big cans of beans and heated them in a pot on top of the small stove. It wasn't long before Trey brought a bowl and spoon over to Jason.

"Here's chow. You know, you could have been killed today."

"You think?" He took the serving. "I still don't see how you thought I was a bear."

"The woods play tricks on your eyes, man. Said I was sorry. It was an accident. Drop it, okay?"

Jason ate silently. There was no way it had been an accident—he was sure of it. Trey *had* tried to shoot him—or at least scare him with an intentional miss.

Although the sun didn't set any earlier in the woods than it did back in the city, it seemed to get darker sooner. Of course, it was an hour later, Michigan being in the eastern time zone. The days were getting shorter, even though it was still daylight saving time. Jason came to accept that he wouldn't get out of there before nightfall.

If Trey got drunk enough and passed out, maybe Jason would be able to get the key ring off his belt.

32

It was late Friday when Annie finally received the call from Mike Baines.

"Okay," he said, "I confirmed that Trey Paley and Makar are at the cabin. I saw them with my own eyes. I drove up there, but there was another car stuck in the mud on the road that led to the cabin."

"What kind of car was it?"

"Uh, an Elantra. Hyundai Elantra."

That's Jason's car, Annie thought. *Stuck in the mud?*

"Anyway, I got out of my patrol car, and I walked up the road to get a look-see."

"What time of day was this?"

"Oh, three o'clock or so. I couldn't call sooner because I had to deal with a traffic accident on Main Street."

"Go on."

"I didn't want them to see me, so I crouched in the bushes around some trees, just so I could see the cabin, you know? Well, I saw both of them. They had rifles, and they were just coming out of the woods. Looked like they'd been out hunting, although I don't know why. Middle of the day isn't a good time for hunting."

"Did you see anyone else?"

"No, ma'am."

"I'm pretty sure at least one other person is there. The owner of that Elantra."

"I didn't see him."

Annie didn't know whether that was a good or bad sign. "All right. I'd like to come up there and talk to those boys. Can you back me up?"

"Sure thing. I was going to suggest it. I can round up at least one other part-time officer. We'll put together a task force!"

This is probably more excitement than the captain's had since he found Irina Semenov in the trunk of that car, she thought. She looked at the time; it was already after six. Would it be better to wait until the morning? If she left now, she wouldn't arrive until late at night.

"Captain, I might not get there until ten o'clock or so. Maybe later. That's probably too late. Perhaps I should leave bright and early in the morning."

"Oh, uh, hold on a second, will you? I have to answer this . . ." He put her on hold. Annie waited nearly a full minute before he got back on. "Sorry about that, Agent Marino. Where was I? Oh, yeah, I don't think I can get the manpower tomorrow to provide backup. There's this ballgame in town that me and the other officers have to work. If you want my opinion, I think those boys will be up late in that cabin. A surprise visit from the FBI after ten at night just might be what it takes to put them off their guard, if you know what I mean. I can make sure you have a room at the Lakeway Hotel."

It wasn't ideal, but she could live with it. "All right. I'm going to grab some food real quick and hit the road. Should I just come to the police station where we met before?"

"That's fine. We'll be here waiting for you. I got to say, though, I sure hope Trey isn't in trouble. Him being a veteran and all. He's a hero to our country."

Annie didn't comment on that. "We'll see what he has to say when I question him. I'll see you soon, Captain Baines."

"Didn't I tell you everyone calls me Captain Mike?"

"All right, Captain Mike."

She dialed SSA Gladden's office to inform him of her plans but got his voice mail. He'd probably left for the day, it being the start of a weekend and all. Such was the privilege of supervisors. She left a message saying she was driving to Michigan.

Annie changed out of her pantsuit into the field wardrobe—jeans, a polo shirt, and sneakers. She strapped the Glock 22 on a drop holster attached to her outer thigh and picked up the bulletproof vest as an afterthought. Annie didn't think she'd need it, but it was prudent to throw it in the Bucar. She didn't expect the confrontation with Trey and Makar to turn into a shooting match, but one never knew. The vest wouldn't provide much protection against a rifle round, anyway.

Annie drove the Ford Fusion out of the lot and stopped at the first Subway sandwich shop she saw. She picked up a six-inch tuna on whole wheat and a bottle of water and hit the road. She ate her meal after she got out of the Chicagoland metropolitan area and continued driving onward as the sun began to set.

By the time she reached Lakeway, it was pitch dark.

33

By ten in the evening, Trey and Makar had consumed more than a six-pack of beer each and smoked a dozen cigarettes as they watched more porno DVDs. Jason didn't think he could take it anymore. He sat away from the TV set, nearer the kitchen. The smoke was suffocating him and the videos made him ill. He had to get those keys from Trey or try to get help for the woman in the shed. At the very least, he had to leave that cabin.

"What are you sitting way over there for?" Trey slurred. "Don't you want to watch? What, you gay or something?"

"That stuff doesn't do anything for me, Trey. And you know I'm marrying your sister, right?"

Trey nudged Makar and laughed. "You'd have to be gay to marry my sister."

"Jesus," Jason said, standing. "I'm going out to get some fresh air." Trey shot him a look. "What?"

"Don't go too far. There're bears in the woods."

"Yeah, yeah."

He stepped outside. Again, he was struck by how dark it was. The starry night sky was visible in the clearing where the cabin stood, but beyond that, the forest was a black, ominous backdrop.

Should he try to go to the shed? Provide some words of comfort to Yana?

No, not while those bastards are awake.

Jason sat on the wooden stoop in front of the door, dug out his phone, and noted the charge—45 percent. There was no point plugging in the charger cord since there was no service anyway. He shut off his phone and shoved it back in his pocket.

He heard Trey and Makar talking through the door, even over the moans and groans of the DVD. Were they arguing? Carefully, Jason approached the window. He could see them in front of the TV. Makar didn't look happy. Jason moved to the side of the window, out of sight, and put his ear to the log wall of the cabin. The voices were clearer, albeit muffled. Some words were unintelligible.

". . . supposed to be a Bacchanal! How are we . . . with him here?"

"Shut up, I'm working on that."

"Won't . . . be here later tonight?"

"I didn't tell him Jason is . . ."

"Because she's supposed . . . for you and me and . . . *my turn*!"

"Then go! Here're the keys!"

". . . when he's asleep."

The TV was turned off. Jason moved away from the wall and found his seat on the stoop, just as the door opened.

It was Makar. "What have you been doing out here?"

"Just looking at the stars. Breathing in the fresh air."

"You don't like our cigarette smoke?"

"Not really. To be honest."

"Sorry, man. Well, *we're* going to bed. You coming?"

Jason knew what he actually meant. *We want you to go to sleep so we can go have our fun with the prisoner in the shed.*

"You guys go ahead. I'll be in soon."

"No, come in now."

"Huh?"

"We want you to come inside *now*."

Jason sighed and stood. "Fine. Look, tomorrow morning, you guys have to help me get my car unstuck. All right?"

"Sure."

Trey was already in his bedroom when they entered the common area. Jason spread out a blanket on the sofa as Makar stumbled toward his room. It was obvious the guy was plastered.

Jason lay in the darkness, the room dimly lit by the fireplace embers. There was no way he was getting to sleep. He felt so helpless, unable to do a damned thing about the woman in the shed. What would a movie hero do in his place? Sure, if he had the physique and the fighting chops, he'd waltz into Trey's room and beat the snot out of the guy. Same with Makar. Unfortunately, he was no hero. He was a lowly bookworm, just like Trey always said.

The minutes passed quietly—and then the snoring began.

Jason sat up.

There was no question about it. The snores came from both bedrooms. The two had drunk so much beer that they had unintentionally passed out.

He knew that Trey had given Makar the keys. Should he take a chance?

He stood and quietly stepped toward Makar's door. He listened and heard steady, rumbling breaths. He had sleep apnea.

Jason placed a hand on the doorknob and turned it at a snail-like pace. Luckily, it didn't squeak. He pushed the door open and peered inside. Makar was on his back, his mouth open, his eyes closed. Jason's eyes darted around the room. His clothes were piled on a chair near the door.

The blue jeans.

Jason squatted and reached in. His fingers barely touched the garment. He moved farther inside and clutched the pants. He didn't notice, though, that the key ring was sitting right on top of the jeans. As he pulled the trousers off the chair, the keys fell to the floor with a *clank* that sounded to him as loud as an atomic blast. Jason froze, winced, and prepared himself for a beating.

Makar snorted and rolled over.

Jason waited a full thirty seconds before he dared to move again. He let go of the pants, got on his hands and knees, and crawled just far enough into the room to grab the key ring. He then backed out, stood, and closed the door as quietly as possible.

He found that he was trembling.

Shit, shit, shit . . . can I do this?

He moved back to the sofa, found his own pants and shirt, dressed, and put on his shoes. Was there anything else he needed? He left his bag on the floor but he dug out the Swiss Army knife and the flashlight. He grabbed the only jacket he'd brought. His cell phone was already in his pants pocket, even though it was useless. He had his car keys. There was nothing else he could possibly need . . .

Wait!

The guns. Where were they?

He didn't see them around the room. The two men must have put them in the bedrooms. He couldn't risk going in there again and trying to grab one.

I should just get the hell out now, while I can!

Jason slipped outside. He looked at his watch—it was only 11:30, although it felt much later.

He turned on the flashlight, which cast a dim beam in front of him as he moved from the front of the cabin to the back. He found the path through the trees and hurried along through its gauntlet-like tunnel. Straight ahead, and then the curve, and there was the shed.

Jason knocked on the door. "Yana?" he whispered loudly. "Yana? It's me, Jason!"

Silence.

He fumbled with the key ring, trying to hold the light on it and attempt to pick out the correct key for the padlock. He tried one, but it didn't fit. "Yana? You awake?" He tried another key. No luck.

"Jason?"

"Yes! It's me! I'm going to get you out!"

He tried a third key. Still no good. There were only three left. What if he had been wrong about the key ring? What if the padlock key was somewhere else entirely?

"Hurry, please!"

"I'm trying!"

The fourth key slipped in perfectly. Jason's adrenaline spiked as the padlock snapped open and fell to the ground. He opened the door and entered a small, dark room occupied by a bed and not much else.

"The light is there by the door," Yana whispered.

Jason found it and switched it on. The naked bulb was bright and nearly blinded them both. Nevertheless, he gasped at what he saw.

The near-naked woman on the bed looked as if she'd been through the wringer. She was bruised about the face, her hair was wild and knotted, and her skin was pale. Blood stains spotted the sheets she sat on. The chain was cuffed to her right ankle.

"My God," Jason muttered.

"Hurry! Oh, thank you, Jason, thank you."

"We're not out of the woods yet," he said as he went to her. "Out of the woods . . . sheesh, I didn't mean that literally. . . oh, never mind. I'm sorry."

He sat on the bed and fumbled with the key ring. His hands shook uncontrollably—he couldn't seem to grasp any of the keys between his fingers. Yana leaned over and took the ring from him. She knew exactly which key unlocked the cuff. She inserted it and the metal piece fell away, exposing a raw, red ankle.

Their eyes met, and Jason was hit with the reality of what was happening. Could he do this? Yana threw her arms around him, squeezing him in a strong embrace. She almost sobbed. He patted her on the back and gently pushed her away. "Come on, let's get you out of here. Do you . . . do you have more clothes?"

She pointed to the floor near the bathroom. He handed her blue jeans, a torn shirt, and sneakers. That was it. Yana put them on and stood unsteadily.

"Here." Jason handed her his jacket. "Can you walk?"

She nodded. "I feel very weak. But, yes. Thank you." She put on the jacket.

He took her by the hand and led her into the night. They moved down the path and back to the clearing, his flashlight beam pointing the way. "Be very quiet," he whispered. "Don't make a sound."

Jason slowed his pace, stepping softly as they moved around the side of the cabin to the front. He pointed to the road that disappeared into the woods. "That way," he whispered. They reached the opening in the trees and then there was a sudden illumination. Everything became a little brighter.

Jason swiveled and saw that the lights had been turned on inside the cabin.

"Run!"

34

Annie reached Lakeway at 11:00 p.m. She would have arrived sooner had it not been for a massive three-car pile-up on Highway 37 that backed up traffic for nearly an hour. She had tried to call Captain Mike but only got his voice mail. It was frustrating, but she finally made it to the small, sleepy town that was a gateway to the Manistee National Forest—where the Bear Claws Case had first become a part of her daily life over the summer. It had been only three months, but already it seemed as if Memorial Day weekend, when she and Harris had first visited Lakeway, was in the distant past.

The town was indeed quiet. With a population of two thousand, there wasn't much to do on a Friday night. There was no traffic on the roads. Street lights revealed a deserted "downtown" that might have been the setting for a Hollywood movie set in the 1950s—complete with barbershop, movie theater with the vertical neon sign attached to the facade, a gas station, a couple of clothing shops, and a drugstore—there was also a Starbucks and a McDonald's. Annie knew that Lakeway, like many communities in Michigan, was "dry"—no open bars.

She pulled into the police station lot. Two patrol cars, a black pickup truck, and a Lincoln Continental were also parked outside the station. She noted that the Continental was a rental. She locked the Fusion, checked her weapon, and walked toward the front door.

No one was in the front entry area of the building. The desk was unmanned, but the lights were on and Annie sensed the presence of people back in the Employees Only offices and the jail.

"Hello?" she called. "Captain Mike?"

"Coming!" She heard him in the back. The sound of boots running on the linoleum floor grew in volume, and the door opened. Baines held it open for her. "Glad you made it! Everything okay?"

She walked forward. "Yeah. Did you get my message? About why I am late?"

"I did. It's quite all right. No worries. We're in the back here talking strategy, if you'd care to join us. You need anything there from the vending machine?" He pointed to the contraption that held chips and cookies. "Sorry, I didn't make any coffee. Probably should have."

"No, I'm fine, I'd rather dive right in with you." She started to move through the open door, but Baines stopped her.

"Whoa, whoa . . . remember the rule? You have to leave your weapon in a cubby. Sorry."

Annie thought it was unnecessary, considering the time of day and urgency of the matter. "Really? I need to do that?"

"I'm sorry, Agent Marino, but it's my job and I was specifically told to enforce this rule, no matter what, by Chief Daniel."

"Is Chief Daniel here?"

"No, ma'am, he's on vacation. Didn't you know that?"

"I did."

"You can pick it back up as soon as the meeting is over. Chief's orders: All visitors must surrender any firearms on their person. It's just for back there, ma'am. You know it's standard operating procedure. Please."

She knew he was technically correct, although it seemed a little ridiculous at this juncture. Annie rolled her eyes, unsnapped the holster, removed the Glock, and placed it in one of the safes behind the desk. She locked the door and pocketed the key.

"There we go. Safe and sound. Anything else? That's your only weapon?" he asked.

"That's it."

"Didn't you have an ankle holster last time you were here?"

"That's right, but I don't have it today. Do you see it, captain?" She held her leg out a foot above the floor, revealed the lack of a gun, and lowered her limb.

"Okay, I'll trust you." He winked at her.

Jesus, Annie thought.

"Oh, let me get the front." He crossed the foyer, removed keys from his pocket, and locked the door. "No one can bother us now." He then gestured for her to go ahead of him. Captain Mike followed her into the hallway toward the open office door. "We're just there in the conference room," he said. She walked on and entered.

Greg Paley sat at the head of the table.

Before she was able to react, Mike Baines grabbed her left arm, and another man, who had been standing just inside the door, grasped her right. She struggled to free herself, but the men were strong. The FBI training of defensive tactics moves kicked in and she stomped hard on Baines's right foot, followed by a backward kick with her right heel into the other man's left shin. Both of them yelped and nearly loosened their grips on her arms. She slam-wiggled her way out of Baines's clutches and thrust the mound of her left hand into the captain's chin. She had aimed for the Adam's apple, but he had lowered his head and blocked the blow. Annie continued to tug with the man to her right, and she delivered a punch to his abdomen with her left fist. But by then, Baines had recovered, and he attacked her from the left.

She felt what could have been the wallop of a sledgehammer on the side of her head as the captain hit her hard. Stunned, she fell forward. The men took the opportunity to bend her at the waist and ram her on top of the table, face down. The new man held her with her arms behind her back while the captain zip-tied her wrists together. Baines then expertly frisked her, removing her cell phone and car keys from her pocket. Then they released her. Baines threw the keys to the other guy.

It was a nearly flawless takedown.

"She's feisty," Baines said, breathing hard and rubbing his chin.

She rolled on to her side, shimmied off the table, and landed on her feet. It was then that she had a chance to look at the new man. He was older, in his late fifties or early sixties. Tall, bald, and quite fit—probably a former military man.

Annie caught her breath and stared at Paley, who was obviously the man in charge. His demeanor had definitely changed since she had met him in his office. This was a very different Greg Paley.

"What the fuck's the meaning of this?" she spat.

"Why don't you have a seat, Agent Marino?"

"Why should I fucking have a seat?"

Paley shook his head. "My, my, *language*, Anne Marino. How unbecoming of the Federal Bureau of Investigation."

"You're committing multiple felonies."

"Sit down, Anne. Or can I call you Annie? That's what your friends call you, right?"

Baines hovered to her left, still nursing his chin and stepping lightly with his right foot. She had at least hurt the guy. The bald man was a lot tougher.

"Oh, I'm sorry, you don't know Louis," Paley said. "This is my colleague, Louis Freund. Louis, meet Special Agent Marino."

"Pleasure," Freund said with no warmth.

"Mr. Freund works for Palit Wool. And he's my closest friend and confidant. He's also a terrific amateur tattoo artist, aren't you, Louis?"

Annie looked at the man. *Tattoo artist?*

"He does some interesting work. There's one piece you'd especially like—it's one of those beautifully drawn and painted bear claws, with just a tasteful amount of blood on them. I think that would look real good on *your* neck, Annie. Maybe before the night's over, you'll have one. What do you think?"

"Fuck you."

"We may get around to that, but I thought I'd explain to you what this is all about, since it's what you asked for. Do you want to hear?"

She looked at the other two men. Freund pulled out a chair so that she could sit without using her hands. He waited, and Annie resigned herself to the situation. She sat, and the men took their seats.

"Now then, that's better," Paley said.

Annie remembered that she had felt something seemed off when she'd left Lakeway the first time. Now she knew. "Captain Mike" worked for the bad guys. She doubted Chief Daniel was aware of any of it. The old man was nearing retirement, not eager to embroil himself in anything serious. He was on *vacation*.

Annie was in a grave situation, but she had the presence of mind to take advantage of it. She'd learn everything she could about Paley's organization. The best way to do that was to get him talking.

"Aren't you supposed to be in New Jersey until Monday?" she asked.

"Agent Marino, after I got Captain Mike's message that said you were thinking of coming up here tonight, I decided to catch the first flight to Detroit. I told him to convince you to make the trip, but to wait until the end of the day so I'd have time to get here. And *here* we are. Now, I understand you're looking for someone called The Bear."

She didn't answer.

"Well, he doesn't exist," Paley continued. "The Bear is a myth, a legend, a persona that serves a purpose to instill fear, perhaps, in some people. For example, take a corporation—any business gets more respect and has more mystique when the CEO is a mysterious, powerful figure, don't you agree?"

"But, in reality, *you're* The Bear," Annie said.

Paley shrugged and smiled. "I just tell The Bear what to do."

"The servers in St. Petersburg . . ."

Paley creased his brow. "Servers?"

"For the website. There are probably more, right? The websites you use to sell human beings."

"What about them?"

"They're *yours*!"

"Yes, that's right."

She shook her head. "Why? You have a successful business with wool, don't you? Why would you do this? Human trafficking is one of the sickest, cruelest crimes you can commit! Do you have no soul, Mr. Paley? For God's sake, you're an American! You should be viciously ashamed of yourself."

"Are you through?" He stared her down. She could see a fire in his eyes that indicated instability. She had been fooled by his sincerity before. The man was a sociopath; there was no question about it. "Fine. I'll answer you. Palit Wool does very well, I grant you that. But that's my father's company, or really *his* father's company. I just run it now. I make a good living." He shrugged. "But the *trafficking*, as you call it, brings in a half million dollars every three months. That's something I can't ignore. Now, you might ask how I launder my money. I will tell you. I invest in several of the nightclubs you know about—the Den, the Cat's Lounge—there are more, not only in Chicago, but in other cities, too. Well, I *personally* don't invest in them, at least it's not in my name. I have an offshore shell company that invests for me. The profits from the so-called trafficking are filtered through a complex system of banks and offshore accounts until they end up in my shell company. I'm then able to play with some of that money as I slowly drip it into my personal, 'regular' account. I even pay taxes on that part of the income."

"Eyepatch, LLC? That's your shell company?"

Paley raised his eyebrows. "Very good. You people know more than I thought you did. To make a long story short, I just had to bring a select group of people into my confidence to run things for me. You remember Fyodor Utkin? He ran the US part of the operation, the 'distribution,' if you will. Until he messed up, that is, and then I decided to close shop."

Annie cocked her head at him.

"That's right, I'm shutting it all down. I figure the feds are going to bust us." He held up his hands. "Yep, I'm admitting defeat. When the FBI got involved in that ridiculous car crash last May, I knew it was over. It was a good run while it lasted. But now my team and I have enough money to move on. I'm leaving the country in twenty-four hours, and I won't be back."

"Where do you think you can hide? Russia? They're on to you there."

"I know. I'm not going to Russia. I'll keep my destination to myself, thank you very much."

"Where you're going is *down*, Mr. Paley. The Bureau knows all about you. They know I'm here. You can't get away with holding me like this."

"It's the weekend; your people aren't going to miss you until Monday morning. You are supposedly in 'good hands'—you went up to Michigan to talk to a couple of suspects in the company of local law enforcement. No big deal. You see? We have time. Since you've wrecked my operation, I'm staying in town long enough to deal with you, Annie."

Annie's heart pounded in her chest. She had been in frightening situations before, on operations out in the field, but nothing like this.

"What happened to Fyodor Utkin?" she asked, attempting to keep the man talking.

"He was a loose end that had to be silenced. Fyodor hired that drunk to drive the car. He also did some things in St. Petersburg that caught the attention of the Russian authorities. They were starting to close in on that side of the network. Fyodor ratted on me, plain and simple, and he stole a little money. If you hadn't gotten so close to me, then the Russians would have, thanks to him." He held up his hands again. "What could I do? It's too bad, he was a friend for many years."

So it was Paley that the ALAT had been trying to identify—the unknown man in the St. Petersburg restaurant with Fyodor and Evgeni Palit. It all made sense now.

"You killed him. When you were in Russia in June," Annie said.

He shook his head. "I didn't *personally* kill him."

"You gave the order. Who did? Someone from the Novgorod mafia? How did you *ever* get involved in something like this, Mr. Paley? What about your family? Your daughter? Your wife?"

He shrugged again. "Survival is more important than family. My wife and daughter will remain here, living off a trust I've set up. As for how I got involved? You really want to know?"

"Yes."

"All right. We have some time. It really started before I was born. My great-uncle Isaak, cofounder of Palit Wool with my grandfather, was tight with the Russian mafia back then. Yes, it already existed. Ever heard of Sergei Babikov? He was head of one of the most powerful Russian syndicates that flourished all through the Soviet years, and it's still around today. His son, Nikolai, runs it now. I told you some of this in my office when we first met. Anyway, my great-uncle Isaak did some deals with Babikov, and Babikov smoothed things out with the Soviet government so that the wool could be exported to America. The government was certainly corrupt back during the time of the Soviet Union. Well, besides wool, there was a little bit of art and jewelry smuggling going on in those days. Isaak's son Evgeni took over Palit Wool later and continued the relationship with the Babikov family. My father, however, tried to clean up the operation and refused to work with Babikov. The business suffered for years, but it didn't die.

"Then, in the early eighties, after I was discharged from the army, I spent some time in St. Petersburg, learning that end of my father's business. I made the acquaintance of Nikolai Babikov, and we started working together. With Palit Wool as a cover, we continued the smuggling through that decade—drugs, jewelry, arms. Whatever would sell. By the time we got to the nineties, after the Soviet Union collapsed, we realized that the sex trade made much more money. There were plenty of girls who wanted to go to America. It was easy to get into that. We started bringing girls over from Russia in 1991. It was to populate strip clubs, mostly. Then the Internet happened, and we realized how much more we could get away with—and for even more money. So we started the brothels. That led to the buy-a-slave opportunity we offered to some very select clients. The very special girls—we found we could make a tremendous amount of money off of them."

Annie burned with anger. She struggled against the zip ties but only managed to painfully grind the skin of her wrists. "So you . . . rank your *product* by what level of exploitation you think it's good for? What *she* is good for? A human being? Grade A, B, or C? You are one pathetic son of a bitch."

"Well, it's over," Paley said, snapping back at her. "The law won. *You*, however, have lost. We're going to take a little trip to my cabin, now. Trey is already there. I figure these fellows here, and I, deserve to have a final, farewell Bacchanal. You and another girl are the guests of honor. She's the last one we brought over from Russia. The pipeline is now closed."

What the hell is a Bacchanal? Another girl? Could this be . . . ?

"Do you mean Yana Kravec?"

"Who?"

"The other girl. A woman named Yana Kravec is missing in St. Petersburg. Trafficked here."

"As far as I know, her name is Nadia."

Annie narrowed her eyelids. "You bastard."

Paley placed his hands together. "I need to warn you about Trey, though. He's got . . . well, I told you already that he has some psychological problems." The man shook his head. "In the old days of the Bacchanals, when Louis, Fyodor, me, and another former friend who isn't here anymore took part, we just brought girls to the cabin to have a good time over the weekend. When it was over, they were sent back to the brothels. But Trey . . . Trey has a sickness. He has an addiction to, well, violence. When he was in the army, he got in trouble for losing his temper and killing some civilians. Unfortunately, he still gets these urges to inflict pain. He has to exercise this *need* on someone every month or so. He would probably just go out and kill a woman in the city somewhere, and he'd get arrested and go to prison, or he'd be killed by the cops. That actually happened in 2014. Maybe you know about that case? A young woman was found in a dumpster in south Chicago?"

Annie nodded.

"Well, I'm afraid Trey would simply continue to do that kind of thing if he isn't supplied with an outlet for his urges. So I arrange for one of our girls to visit him at the cabin, and he does what he wants. That's what the Bacchanals became over the last three or four years. They're for *him*. Of course, he invites his friends to participate sometimes. Most of the time the girl goes back to the house at the end of the weekend, but I'm afraid sometimes Trey goes too far." He shook his head sadly. "Personally, I don't like it. I don't attend. But I will tonight. For old time's sake."

Annie mulled over the implication of this. "That's what happened to Irina Semenov. Trey killed her."

"Who?"

"The woman in the car accident near here, last May."

"Oh, *her*. That was unfortunate. The driver was drunk and careless. Actually, she wasn't dead. She would have recovered from her injuries, had the idiot not crashed into the truck. That's what set all of this in motion, isn't it?"

"Yes. And I beg to differ with you about Irina's condition. She may have been alive in the trunk of that car, but she was at death's door. Your son went too far."

Paley nodded. "Like I said, it's happened before. Fortunately, the forest is a great place to hide bodies." He then looked at Freund and Baines and nodded. "It's time." The three men stood. To Annie, he said, "You can cooperate, and it will be a lot less unpleasant."

Now she was afraid for her life. How was she going to get out of this? She was *not* going to let them touch her.

Louis moved forward to pull Annie out of her chair, but she stood on her own. "I'm coming." She looked at Paley and asked, "Did you know your future son-in-law is at the cabin?"

Paley furrowed his brow. "What?"

"Jason Ward. He's there. With your son."

"Jason? How the hell do you know Jason?"

"Never mind that. He's there at the cabin. Is *he* taking part in this Bacchanal?"

Paley looked at Baines. "Did you know about this?"

Captain Mike averted his eyes. "Uh, yeah. I should have told you. I thought if he was there and Trey was cool with it, then it was okay . . ."

Paley pursed his lips. "Well, this will be awkward." He slammed a fist on the table. "What, am I going to have to do something with *him*, too? My daughter's *fiancé*? Like I did my fucking *brother*? God damn it!" He stared at Baines for a moment, and then he shook his head at Freund, as if to say, *I'm surrounded by idiots . . .*

"Come on," he commanded. "Get her in the trunk of your patrol car, Mike. Louis, you drive Agent Marino's car. Let's see what's going on at the cabin. I wish to Christ cell phones worked there. I tell you, my moron of a son can really do some crazy shit."

They marched her out of the station's back door. Baines pulled up his patrol vehicle and opened the trunk. They were about to force Annie inside, but she decided to save her strength for later. She climbed in voluntarily.

They shut the lid, and Annie was plunged into darkness. It was terribly uncomfortable, lying on her side with her hands tied behind her back, vulnerable and exposed with no weapon to defend herself with. After a moment, the car started moving.

Now think, *Annie*! her mind screamed. *How are you going to save yourself?*

35

Jason and Yana were both out of breath when they reached his car, which was still stuck in the road. It had taken perhaps twenty minutes as they hurried along the cold, damp pathway. To hell with any remaining mud; it was faster to use the middle of the path than it was to move along its edges as he had done before. Besides, the closer one got to the trees, the scarier it all became.

"Let's see if I can get out now," he said, unlocking the door and slipping inside. "I might need you to push. Can you do that?"

"Push? Push where?" Her voice was hoarse and tired, her breathing rapid.

"The back end. You'll see where it's stuck." He started the engine, and then thought, *What am I doing? The poor woman is beaten and exhausted . . .*

He left the car running and got out.

"Can you drive?" he asked.

She nodded.

"I'll push."

Yana exchanged places with him and he went to the back of the car. "Give it the gas!" he yelled. The tire still spun noisily. He pushed the car with all the strength he had. The vehicle moved up and forward a few inches, but the tire continued to spray mud backward, right onto Jason's shirt and pants.

"Okay, okay, stop! Stop!"

Jason kicked the buried wheel and cursed at it. It was no use.

"Listen!" Yana said as she got out and closed the car door.

Jason stopped. The sounds of the forest were now much more pronounced than he had noticed before. All sorts of cricks, buzzes, chirps, and scratches filled the air. At first he heard nothing but the ambient noise of nature in the woods at night, but then it filtered through—an angry voice in the distance, not too far away. He only heard snatches of it.

. . . damn idiot! We better find . . . gonna be your ass! . . . not coming back 'til we do! . . .

"They're after us," he said to her.

"What do we do?"

"We keep going down the road to the highway. I forget how many miles it is. I think maybe two or three."

"Look!" She pointed back up the road toward the cabin. Beams of light were moving toward them.

"Christ, run!" he commanded. He took her hand, and they started moving. The mistake he made was turning on the flashlight again.

After a moment of hurrying along the road, they heard a voice—*Hey! Stop!*—which was followed by a gunshot. Yana gasped. As they ran, she and Jason eyed each other to confirm that neither of them had been hit. They had no idea where the bullet had gone. Jason switched off the flashlight.

He noticed she was limping, slowing them down.

"What's wrong?"

"I am so out of breath . . . I feel weak . . . I haven't eaten much. I'm sorry."

Jason halted and let her lean against him. He gazed back up the road. The two beams of light were still approaching.

"We have to go into the woods," he said. "If we keep following the road, they'll catch us. Come on."

She didn't protest. He helped her cross the drive to the edge of the forest—and they ventured in. The progress was immediately hampered, especially without the flashlight's beacon leading the way. As there was no flattened path, both of them had to step through, on, and over dark rocks, branches, and bushes. It was nearly impossible to see where they were placing their feet. Only ambiguous black shapes warned them of an obstacle, and the trees were huge, intimidating sentinels they had to dodge as they went forward.

The forest grew thicker as Jason and Yana thrust onward into the dark wild. Branches and brush tugged at their clothing or swept into their arms and faces. But they kept moving, no matter what, although Jason was aware that they weren't headed toward the highway. It was possible that they were running west, parallel to Highway 82, but he wasn't certain. If this was true, they needed to veer to the south.

"Wait . . . wait . . ." he panted, holding his arm out to stop Yana from going further. She was breathing heavily, wheezing as if she had a cold. "Catch your breath. Listen." He turned to look back toward the direction from which they'd come. There were no lights. Aside from the sound of oxygen pumping through their mouths, he heard nothing but the forest's natural overlay of insect song.

"Are they gone?" she asked.

"I don't think so." He pointed to what he thought to be southwest. "We need to go this way."

"You are not sure."

"No. I'm sorry. I really didn't have a good plan to get you out. I had to improvise."

"I understand. I am grateful."

"But we need to keep moving."

He risked turning on the flashlight. The beam seemed much brighter in the more claustrophobic surroundings of the woods.

"Will they see it?"

"I don't know." He turned it off. It was too risky. "Come on." Jason angled their forward trek to the left, but inside he was panicking. He had no idea where they were. He was frightened, lost, and very cold. As they pushed through the landscape, he was now aware of the biting chill. It must have been in the low forties or upper thirties.

"Are you warm enough?" he asked her.

"No. But I will survive."

He'd given her his only jacket, a lightweight one, more like a windbreaker. She needed it more than he did. Still, his long-sleeved button-down shirt was thin. Jason was freezing.

A gunshot echoed somewhere behind them.

They both jerked their heads at each other, wide-eyed, and attempted to move faster. Jason knew the sound had come from behind them, but he wasn't sure how far back. They couldn't stop for a moment.

A light beam abruptly appeared out of the blackness and passed over them.

"There they are!" someone—perhaps Makar—yelled.

Jason grabbed Yana's arm and they ran out of the perimeter of the illumination. It was difficult for the pursuer to keep the light on the moving targets, and soon he lost them.

They continued to move as quickly as possible, and Jason hoped they'd left their hunter far behind in the darkness. As they pressed forward, the setting began to change in front of them—the woods became thinner. A different type of topography lay ahead.

They suddenly found themselves in a narrow clearing though which a stream flowed. The open space and lack of trees allowed natural illumination from the night sky to fall over the area. A half moon registered above. They could see things more clearly, and their surroundings had more definition. The stream wasn't big enough to be called a river, and it didn't appear to be a difficult cross. Jason figured it was about twenty feet to the other side. The water rolled strongly from the left to the right, indicating the direction downhill. Jason racked his brain, trying to think about their position in relation to the map he had left in his car. He knew there were rivers in the forest, and he also knew that a lake abutted the Paley's property. He had no idea what side that would be, or if finding the lake would help them. He felt useless.

"We have to cross," he said. "It doesn't look deep."

She followed him without questioning. They awkwardly stepped over some rocks and into the rushing water.

"Yow," Jason spat at the knife-like assault of the chill that enveloped his feet and ankles.

"Oh, it's cold!" Yana yelped.

They splashed onward. The water rose up to their knees, but luckily it wasn't deeper than that. They trudged on and eventually emerged on the opposite bank. He pulled her into that side of the forest. Not daring to stop, they moved blindly onward, their calves and feet cold, wet, and sore. Several minutes went by, and they saw or heard no signs of the searchers. No high-powered beams. No shouts. They stopped to catch their breaths again. Jason figured they were now maybe a quarter mile from the stream.

"I . . . I can't do this . . . all night . . ." she managed to say between wheezes.

"Neither can I. Yana, I'm sorry, but we're lost. I don't know where we are."

"I think we have to find someplace and wait until daylight."

Jason knew she was right. He dug out his phone, turned it on, and looked at the time. It was just after midnight, and yet it felt as if they'd been running all night.

It would be a long time until morning.

"We have to keep moving. We can go slower. Let's follow the same direction the stream was moving in. It goes down to something. There's a lake nearby. Maybe more people will be around there, and we can get help."

She nodded, but Jason could see she wasn't doing well. The poor woman had been locked up in a shed for days, fed sporadically, beaten, and sexually abused. It was a miracle she could walk at all, much less slog through the forest with him as she'd been doing. Jason admired her stamina and conviction. He was aware, though, that she was right—they would need to *really* rest at some point.

They continued at a slower pace. Jason began to think about what kinds of bugs were out there, and what might bite them if they decided to sit or lie on the ground. Ants, surely. Ticks? Jason was deathly afraid of ticks, which could cause some serious damage, Lyme disease notwithstanding. Spiders and beetles and flies and cockroaches and wasps and bees and moths and mosquitoes—anything was possible. They were going to be eaten alive.

A dark, mound-shaped protuberance on the ground lay ahead. As they approached, it revealed itself to be a large tree that had grown lopsided along the earth rather than into the sky. A curvy nook in its trunk was big enough for two people.

"Let's stop here for a bit," he said. He turned on the flashlight and examined the tree. "Just making sure we're not about to lean against a wasp nest or something."

It wouldn't have been his choice to sit on dirt and nestle into a nook of a tree, but it appeared to be the best room in town. He took her hand and they both got down on the cold earth. He turned off the flashlight. Even there, he still felt they were exposed.

"Hold on a sec." He got up.

"Where are you going?"

"Wait here. Be right back." He moved to a low branch of the tree that sprouted smaller, leafy branches, dug the Swiss Army knife out of his pocket, and started sawing the base of the branch, which wasn't very thick. It took a couple of minutes, but the knife did its job. Picking up the branch and all of its tendrils, he carried it back to their cubbyhole. He backed himself in and laid the branch over the nook, providing camouflage for their resting place.

"That is smart," she said.

He was happy that the knife had come in handy, after all. "Not sure how protective it will be, but it's something. Now let's just rest, listen, and watch. If you want to try and sleep, I'll stay awake."

"I can't sleep here."

"Well, neither can I. But we can rest. You're right, we can't run all night. And neither can *they*. They'll get careless. You heard Trey. He yelled to Makar that they wouldn't go back to the cabin until they find us. They're going to search all night. The good news is this is a big forest. Maybe we fooled them when we crossed the stream. I bet they thought we'd stay on that side of it."

Her eyes were closed and her head rested against the gnarly bark of the tree. Jason stopped talking. His body was itchy. His sleeves were torn and the scrapes on his arms had bled a little. He wondered when he'd last received a tetanus shot. Then he felt something crawling on his left arm and slapped at it, startling Yana.

"Sorry."

"I was not asleep."

"Looked like you were. Close your eyes for a bit. It's okay."

"Why do you do this for me?"

Jason thought about that. He had never ever imagined that, one day, he would literally be risking his life for a stranger. But it was happening now. "It was the right thing to do," he answered. He didn't have anything better to say.

"Who are you to them?"

Jason let out a sarcastic guffaw. "The soldier one, Trey—I'm engaged to his *sister*."

"What?"

"Yeah, I know. It sounds crazy. I'm not supposed to be up here. I came to the cabin to surprise them. I thought they were just up here drinking beer and shooting squirrels. The discovery of your existence was quite a shock, let me tell you. I didn't plan on this, Yana. Jesus."

She placed a hand on his arm. "Thank you."

"You're welcome. But we're not out of the woo—uh, we're not safe yet. Better get some rest. Don't be scared."

"After what I've been through the past three months, this is a holiday."

He didn't know what to say to that.

They were quiet for a while.

36

The rough ride in the trunk of the patrol car lasted an uncomfortable half hour, but the car finally slowed and stopped. She heard the driver's door open and slam shut, but the engine was still idling. Then came the voices—she recognized Greg Paley complaining about something. After a moment, the door opened again and the engine shut off. A few seconds later, the trunk lid popped up. Baines stood over the trunk, pointing a Glock 22 at her. At first Annie thought it was hers, but apparently the captain carried one just like it.

"Get out," he commanded.

She was happy to, but with her hands tied it was difficult to wiggle and sit up, much less climb out of the trunk. When he realized the trouble she was having, he holstered the gun and hoisted her up from her armpits.

"You don't weigh very much, do you."

On her feet now, Annie spat in his face, even though he was a head taller.

"You goddamn—!" He raised a hand to slap her.

"Mike!" Paley stood nearby. "Don't."

"Bitch spit at me!"

"Wipe it off. We have to hurry."

Baines grabbed her arm forcefully and pulled her from behind the patrol car. She now saw where they were—on a wet one-lane dirt road, surrounded by dark, foreboding woods. As they moved around the car, she understood the problem. Jason's Hyundai Elantra was stuck in the middle of the road, blocking traffic from moving beyond it.

Her immediate thought was that Jason was in serious danger.

God, is he even still alive?

Paley's rented Lincoln Continental was parked directly behind the patrol car, and her own Ford Fusion was behind it. Paley, Freund, and Baines escorted her around the stalled vehicle and they began walking up the path. Baines gave Freund his flashlight, which cast a strong beam in front of them. Freund carried on his back a Winchester Model 70 bolt-action hunting rifle, which looked like a .270. Paley appeared to be unarmed, unless he was carrying a concealed handgun.

"I swear I'm going to kick that boy in the ass," Paley muttered.

With her hands secured behind her back, Annie found the trek challenging. She hadn't realized how much one's arms provided balance when walking. She stumbled several times on the uneven surface.

"How far are we going?" she asked.

"Shut up," Baines snapped.

"Not far," Paley answered. "What a pain in the ass this is."

Annie was thirsty. It had been several hours since her supper, and the last sip of water she'd had was from the bottle in her car. She trudged onward with her captors, her mind going over dozens of scenarios on how she might be able to escape. Should she just take off running into the forest? With her hands tied? No, that would be suicide, most likely. Annie continued to work her wrists back and forth in an attempt to loosen the plastic binds, but the zip ties were tight and sharp. No good. She knew it would be impossible to affect a getaway unless she first freed her hands.

Eventually they came to the clearing where the cabin stood. Lights gleamed through the windows. Paley strode to the front door and opened it without knocking. "Trey? You in here?" The four of them piled into the living area. The fireplace was burning, the place reeked of tobacco smoke and beer, and both bedroom doors were open. Paley stuck his head in each and in the bathroom. "They're not here." He looked at Baines and said, "Go check the shed. We'll watch her. You still have your key to the padlock?"

"Yes, sir." He eyed Annie as if to say, *Don't you go nowhere!* and left the cabin.

Paley closed the door and told Annie to sit on the sofa. An open suitcase sat on the floor with a few items of clothing inside. Jason's?

It wasn't long before Baines returned. "No one's there, boss."

"She's *gone?*"

"Yes, sir."

"What the *fuck* happened here tonight? Damn it!"

Freund spoke up. "I think your future son-in-law must have sprung her. Your boy and his pal are out looking for them."

Paley squinted at his friend. "That's not good. *Jesus*. We have to go after them."

"We could also cut our losses and get the hell out of here," Freund said. "Let them fend for themselves."

"And leave Trey to go to prison?" Paley shook his head and sat in one of the chairs.

Annie spoke. "What did you think would happen to him when you left the country? Were you planning to take him with you?"

"Yes," the man answered. Then he made a face. "Why am I even talking to you? I should put a bullet in your head." He looked at Baines. "Go lock her in the shed. We'll keep her on ice until we figure this out. Louis and I may have to go looking for them. You stay put here in the cabin while we're gone."

Baines nodded and gestured for Annie to stand. He led her out of the cabin and back into the night. They walked to the rear of the building, crossed the bit of clearing, and entered the path through the trees. It wasn't far—they soon came to the shed, the door of which was wide open. A padlock lay on the ground. A naked light bulb, hanging from the ceiling, glowed brightly against the blackness around them.

"Get inside." Baines shoved her. Annie tumbled over the doorstep and fell on the cold wood floor, at the foot of the bed. "Come on, get up. Get on the bed. I have to lock you in." He had a ring of keys in his hand, presumably to the shed and to the chain.

Annie gritted her teeth and said, "Baines, you're going to wish you hadn't done this."

"Shut up. Can you stand or not?" He tried to help her, but Annie shrugged him off. She managed to get to her feet.

"Are you going to leave my hands tied?"

"Of course I am. Get on the bed so I can put the cuff on you."

She reluctantly scooted onto the edge of the mattress, wincing at the blood stains that were there. They kept Yana Kravec here? "What did you do to her, Baines? Is she dead?"

"*I* didn't do nothing to her. I was going to get my turn tonight, but it's all fucked up now. Straighten your legs."

"You just need one, don't you?" She moved to face him and stuck out her right leg, but kept her left bent at the knee as she leaned back on the bed.

He was still holding his gun and the keys. Since he needed both hands to manipulate the restraint, he holstered the weapon, dropped the keys on the bed, and reached for the cuff and chain. When he did, he took a side step, spreading his legs. Annie saw her chance. She kicked out with the bent left leg as hard as she could—hitting him square in the groin.

The intake of breath he made practically choked him as his eyes bugged and his jaw dropped. The scream came a second later, but by then Annie had kicked him a second time. He went down, instinctively curling into a fetal position, as he cried, "Oh God, oh God!" Annie jumped off the bed and kicked him repeatedly in the face with her right foot. Then she booted him with her left again, this time in the chest as his arms went between his legs to protect himself. The right foot lashed out again at his head—one, two, *three, FOUR* times—until his crying ceased. He was out cold, his face lacerated and bloody.

Annie stood there panting. Her adrenaline was pumping through the roof.

Had she killed him? She thought not. She squatted closer to him and heard him breathing with a faint gurgling in his throat. He could very well come to in a few seconds.

She turned to the open door to make sure no one had seen or heard what she'd done, and then closed it. Next, she squatted backward beside him so she could remove the Glock from his holster. It was tricky. She had to use her fingers like grappling hooks in order to accomplish the task. The gun slowly loosened, and she was able to stand, holding it precariously in her hands. She carried it to the other side of the bed, squatted, and let it drop on the floor.

Now for something that could cut the plastic ties around her wrists . . . Annie looked around the room and saw nothing sharp. Of course there wouldn't be. They wouldn't have wanted their captive to slit her wrists, which was unfortunately a possibility.

She took a look in the bathroom. Nothing but a disgusting toilet, a sink, and an incongruous tube of red lipstick. Back in the room, she examined Baines. He was snoring softly, his face messed up and pulpy. She seemed to remember from Quantico training that local law enforcement sometimes carried knives, but she didn't see one attached to his belt. However, his trouser pockets bulged with some objects. Annie sat on the floor next to him and tried to position herself so that her fingers could snake into his left side pocket. She felt something metal and, after three tries, managed to fish it out.

Car keys.

There was something else inside that was solid and oblong or rectangular. It had to be a pocket knife. Once again, she inched her fingers into the pocket. Her arms hurt like hell, and her hands lost all circulation.

She couldn't reach it. Cursing silently to herself, Annie removed her fingers and tried pushing on the object through the outside of the man's trousers. It was terribly awkward and difficult to do.

Baines snorted and inhaled loudly. He moved a little.

Christ! If he wakes up, I'm dead.

Annie continued to maneuver the object higher toward the pocket opening. It took another minute or so, and then she finally wormed her fingers inside to grasp it. The index and middle fingers of the right hand wrapped around it—*yes! It was a pocket knife!*—and pulled it out. It fell on the floor.

Baines turned his head. His eyes fluttered.

Annie got to her feet and kicked him in the head three more times. That did the trick.

She squatted again and picked up the knife by its edge. Seating herself on the bed, she attempted to pull out the blade. It was tight and stiff. There was no way she could do it with her hands in the contorted posture they were in.

But the tiny *corkscrew* was easy to lever out! Cutting the plastic zip cords with the tip of it, though, was another story.

Nevertheless, Annie grasped the corkscrew with the thumb and index finger of her right hand and pointed the sharp point upward toward her wrists. By flexing the joints in her thumb and finger, she was able to produce short stabs at the binds. Over and over. Three out of five times she poked her skin, and she felt wetness dripping over her hands. Blood. She sucked in her breath and continued to poke, chipping away at the plastic binds. The process seemed to last an eternity. Her thumb and finger began to tire.

Baines snorted again. His head lolled to the side and he groaned.

Damn it!

Stab, poke, stab, poke. Her skin was increasingly pricked, but the contacts with the plastic ties multiplied as well.

In the next second, she was free.

"Oh," she gasped at the pain of pulling her arms forward. It was as if the muscles had atrophied in position, and she had just woken them up. She rubbed her bloody hands together to increase the circulation. Her wrists appeared as if she had stuck them in a grinder.

First she had to make sure Baines was no longer a threat. She released the handcuffs from his belt and snapped his wrists behind his back. Next, she grabbed the chain cuff and fastened it around his right ankle. She stuffed the key ring and his patrol car keys, which contained the key for the handcuffs, in her pockets. She then removed his belt, which contained the other gadgets and gear that officers in uniform carried, and threw it to the other side of the room.

Next, she washed her bloody hands and wrists in the bathroom. The cold water felt *fantastic*. A towel and wash cloth, both used and soiled, hung over the edge of the sink. They would have to do. She wrapped the cloth over her left wrist and pressed down hard, holding it there for at least a minute. When she removed the cloth, the bleeding had stopped. The wounds weren't terribly deep, more like pin pricks. She repeated the procedure on her right wrist.

Finally, Annie returned to the side of the bed to retrieve Baines's Glock. She checked the magazine and put the weapon in the empty drop holster on her thigh. She stuck the knife in her own jeans front pocket. Then she went over to Baines's belt and removed two extra magazines for the Glock, as well as the high-powered flashlight that the captain had replaced.

As an afterthought, she stooped and rolled Baines over. She found her cell phone in his other trouser pocket. She checked it—the battery was low and there was no service. The time indicated that it was nearly one in the morning.

She was good to go.

Annie turned out the light bulb as she left the shed, closed the door, and placed the padlock on it. Unless Paley had extra keys, that would hold Baines for a while. She made her way to the cabin without using the flashlight and found the place empty. Paley and Freund must have gone into the woods to look for the missing people. Unfortunately, Freund had *her* car keys. She wouldn't be able to take the patrol car—it was hemmed in between Jason's Elantra and Paley's Lincoln.

She did a quick reconnaissance of the cabin. There were several firearms in one bedroom, including the M24 sniper rifle she had seen Trey holding on Facebook and a Beretta handgun. There was no time to bag and store them both for evidence in case they were the weapons used to shoot Harris Caruthers and Tiffany Vombrack. Instead, she shoved them under the bed, temporarily hiding them.

Annie went outside and peered around the cabin into the woods. She heard and saw nothing. She considered running back to Baines's patrol car and using the radio to call for help. But taking that twenty-minute trek back to the car would take too much precious time—if Trey or Makar, or Paley and Freund caught up to Jason and the woman, they would die.

The only thing that made sense was to head into the forest in pursuit.

37

The hours passed. Jason stayed awake. He noticed that Yana's eyes remained open for a long time before they finally closed with exhaustion. Gunshots in the distance woke her.

"What's that?" she asked.

Jason held a finger to his lips. Were they indeed gunshots? It was difficult to tell how far away they were from the noise, and he was also unsure how many there were. But it was quiet now, and he heard no voices or rustling through the forest.

After a quarter hour of silence, they relaxed back into the monotony. Now Jason wasn't sure if it was gunfire or not. He sighed, weary of the situation. Yana had slept for at least an hour. Jason would have liked to grab forty winks, but he was simply too scared. The fatigue was also palpable. His muscles were sore and his skin was terribly itchy.

Mostly, he was cold. He thanked the stars that it was still August. He couldn't imagine what it might have been like had the season been fall or winter.

As Jason listened to the night air and the accompanying insect calls, Yana's wheezy breathing concerned him. It seemed to be worse when she was asleep.

"Do you feel sick?" he asked her, speaking softly.

"I have felt sick for weeks."

He had no response. It might have been appropriate to say something like, "We'll be safe soon," or "We'll get you medical attention as quickly as possible," but Jason was unsure how much of it would be true. He was terrified that he had no plan to save them. If they managed to stay safe in the little tree-cave they were huddling in until dawn, what then? Trey and Makar would still be out there looking for them. Moving downstream, possibly to the lake, was as good an idea as any. He wasn't certain, but he didn't think the lake itself was on the Paleys' property. If that was the case, then surely other people could be nearby.

"What time is it?" Yana asked.

Jason removed his cell phone and checked the home screen. He was surprised. "Gosh, it's nearly five. The sun's going to come up soon. Maybe we should head out. How do you feel?"

"Better. I'm just cold."

"Me, too. And I think I've been the main course for some kind of critter." He knocked the makeshift door of branches away from their cubbyhole and stood. It felt good to give himself a good scratch all over his limbs. His legs were stiff and his butt felt frozen and numb, but at least they hadn't been devoured by a wild animal. He helped her stand, and she groaned a little. "You all right?"

"I think so."

"Do you need to use the bathroom or anything?"

"Yes."

"So do I. Look, you go over there, and I'll go over here. Okay?" He pointed to opposite clumps of bushes near groupings of trees. She nodded and disappeared into the shadows. Jason moved toward his chosen latrine and relieved himself. He then returned to the tree hook and waited.

After five minutes, Jason called out. "Yana? You all right?"

No sound.

"Yana?"

He walked toward the trees where he'd sent her. Yana abruptly rushed around the foliage and nearly screamed when she collided with him.

"Yana! Are you all right?"

"He's coming."

"Who?"

"The Russian one."

Jason perked his ears. Yes—there it was, the light, steady one-two rhythm of legs pushing through the brush.

He put a finger to his lips, and Yana acknowledged with a nod.

They became statues like the trees surrounding them. The rustling grew louder and nearer. Jason felt an intense wave of fear, knowing beyond doubt that they were about to be caught. However, if they ran, Makar would surely hear them and give chase. Best to remain silent and still, and perhaps he would move on past them.

But luck was against them. Soon, Makar's noisy trekking could be heard just a few feet away, and Jason *felt* the movement amid the nearby trees. Makar was walking directly toward them.

"Run!" he whispered, grabbing her hand. They took off away from their pursuer, but it was too late.

"Hey! Come back! Trey! I found them! Over here!"

Jason and Yana ran blindly through the woodland. It was impossible to keep clutching Yana's hand, and they were forced to separate to navigate around trees and other brush.

A gunshot resounded behind them. Jason figured Makar was shooting wildly at targets he couldn't see. It was still very dark, but he supposed it was possible that, by running, they were visible against the black backdrop of the forest.

"Trey! Over here!"

The voice was moving with them—Makar was also running. Jason turned his head to look for Yana. He couldn't see her, but he heard her, scrambling ahead, tearing through the branches beside him.

Then Jason's foot hit a depression in the ground and, for a moment, he was flying. He landed hard in a shallow pit and felt something sharp rip into his trousers and cut the hell out of his right calf. He couldn't help but cry out in pain and double up, grabbing his leg. He eyed the shadowy ground behind him. A tree root stuck out of the earth, the culprit that had scraped his leg when he fell.

Jason struggled to get up.

"Hold it right there!"

Makar stood a few feet away, his Win Mag held high.

Jason raised his hands. "Don't shoot, Makar. Please, man."

"I have to."

Jason's heart nearly stopped. This was it.

I'm going to die.

Makar adjusted the rifle in his arms and aimed. Jason closed his eyes. The hunter squeezed the trigger—and the shot went wild. Jason looked up to see that Yana had bolted into Makar, knocking him off balance. She wielded a hefty broken tree branch in her hand and struck him with it as if it were a club. After the first blow landed, she raised the weapon and walloped him again. Makar went down, dropping the rifle as he attempted to protect himself with his arms. The branch swung down again . . . and again . . . mercilessly, viciously. It was as if Yana had been possessed by a demon. She cried and grunted each time she assaulted Makar, who, by the fifth bash, was no longer making any sounds.

"Yana!" Jason called, but she continued to beat the fallen predator, sobbing as she did it. She was a wild animal, her hatred boiling over and manifesting in primal violence. Jason managed to sit up and use the tree root for leverage to stand. His leg exploded in agony, but he moved forward and climbed out of the small pit. He managed to grab her arms and stop her.

Yana dropped the branch and collapsed into his arms, crying and sobbing. He held her as she buried her face in his chest. Jason gazed at the misshapen form on the ground. She had hit Makar at least fifteen times, battering the man's head and chest, assuredly beating him to death. It was a good thing the sun had not yet come up; Jason knew that Makar's skull was likely exposed and split, revealing the bloody organic matter within.

"You saved my life," Jason said, still holding her.

She tried to catch her breath, as she separated from him and wiped her nose with the sleeve of Jason's jacket.

"Thank you," he added.

"I saw him just as I finished peeing," she said.

"It's okay, he's gone now."

"His friend is not far behind."

"Maybe. Trey could be on a completely different side of the forest." He knew better, though. The sound of the gunshot had carried farther than he would have thought. There was no question that Trey had heard it.

"We can't stay here, Yana."

"Did I kill him?" She was panting. She turned to look, but Jason took her chin in his hand and lifted her head toward him.

"I think so."

She nodded. "Good. He deserved to die."

Jason reached down and picked up Makar's .338. His lessons at the range were going to come in handy, after all. He inserted an arm through the sling and wore the weapon on his back.

"Come on, let's keep moving toward the lake." He took her hand, and she let him lead her onward, just as a preview of dawn crept over the forest.

38

Some time prior to Jason and Yana's encounter with Makar, Annie thought she might be lost. After a long period of trekking through the forest, it seemed she was getting nowhere. Everything looked the same in the dark. Captain Baines's high-beam flashlight helped, but it only illuminated a circle of space in front of her. In a way, it created a kaleidoscopic effect as she moved forward, due to the similarity of the trees and foliage around her. Annie attempted to pinpoint landmarks as she went, but it was near impossible to do so. At one point, she heard shouts in the distance, but she didn't know if the voices belonged to Greg and his friend Louis, or if they might have belonged to Trey or Makar. She had turned in that direction, but a half hour went by without her hearing another sound other than the bugs and the breeze in the trees.

Finally, the effort caught up with her and she had to rest. She found a large rock and sat on it to catch her breath and rub her wrists. The wounds smarted and itched, and her legs were sore. Her sneakers weren't built for the rugged terrain, and they were taking a toll on her feet. Mostly, she was cold. Annie was astonished that it could be so frigid at night in the middle of August.

Looking at her cell phone, she saw that the time was nearly four in the morning. She'd been trudging through the forest for hours.

Christ, I'm lost.

She spent a few minutes with her eyes closed, breathing deeply, attempting to spread a blanket of calmness over her—otherwise she thought she might panic. Annie had always been a levelheaded person, someone who didn't let stress get to her. Now, however, the unfamiliarity of the alien surroundings was doing a number on her psyche. She wished she had gone for Baines's patrol car instead of diving into the woods. At least she could have used his radio to call for help.

Was there a way to make it back to the cabin? Could she possibly retrace her steps?

Not wanting to waste any more time, Annie stood and headed back in the direction she'd come. However, she was well aware that she could be completely turned around. Without a compass, she had no idea if she was walking in circles or moving *away* from the cabin. The whole thing was madness, every bit of it—the case, the revelation that Greg Paley was essentially The Bear, the fact that her neighbor Jason was mixed up in the mess, and the realization that she was lost in the goddamned woods. She could just imagine what her SSA was going to say—if she ever saw him again.

Stop it! You're going to get out of here! You're going to—

There it was again. A human shout.

This time, Annie knew exactly where it was coming from. She angled to the right and kept moving. The light beam led the way, but still the landscape continued to appear the same. It was an endless loop of moving through a dark tunnel of trees.

After twenty minutes of walking, however, the trees thinned and she came to a clearing with a stream flowing from her left to right. Annie took the precaution of using a tree for cover as she peered out into the relatively treeless corridor that ran through the woods. She aimed the flashlight along both banks of the stream and into the wall of forest on the opposite side.

Should she cross the stream? She was certain the voice had come from the other side.

Annie inched out from behind the tree and approached the edge of the clearing, some twenty feet to the water's rocky edge. The stream didn't look deep. She could probably wade across, but it was going to be damned freezing.

She started off into the open and reached the bank of the stream. Annie thought it best not to attempt the crossing while holding a flashlight, so she turned it off and stuck the end in her jeans front pocket—

—and a gunshot cracked on the opposite bank.

Annie felt the heat of the bullet, but it was a miss. She bolted back to the trees.

Another shot, another miss.

Whoever was shooting was near, on the other side of the stream.

Panting, she pulled around the nearest tree large enough to provide cover. She froze behind it and waited. Unless the shooter was wearing night-vision goggles, it was surely going to be difficult for him to see her. She stuck out her head and looked. A good section of the clearing and the other bank was visible. Annie stared across the water at the trees, hunting for any sign of movement.

And there he was. She *could* see him, for she caught a quick glint of light, perhaps a reflection off of the lens on the rifle scope. A man huddled behind a clump of bushes and a large rock. His head, shoulder, and rifle were exposed. Annie couldn't discern who it was, but she knew it wasn't Jason.

He fired the gun again, this time hitting uncomfortably close to her tree.

Shit, maybe he can see me, just like I can see him!

She knew she had to do what he least expected—and that was to attack *him*. Could she hit him from there? It would be a terribly lucky shot, but she had to try. Annie unsnapped the holster and drew Captain Baines's Glock. Throwing caution to the wind, she rolled out around the tree and assumed a Weaver stance, aiming at where the muzzle flashes had come from on the other side.

He fired again . . . and struck the tree.

Annie squeezed the trigger. The gun kicked with a loud discharge, and the man fell as he emitted a loud grunt. He dropped the rifle, too—it now lay unattended on the rock.

No way. Did I hit him? I really hit him?

There was silence.

Now what?

If he was faking, he'd pick her off as soon as she started toward him.

The problem was that Jason and the woman who had been trafficked and held prisoner were probably on that side of the stream, too. Since she had come to the river, it must mean she hadn't been retracing her steps; and if someone was shooting at her from the other bank, it made sense that Jason had already crossed himself. She had to risk it.

Holding the Glock high, she ventured out, slowly walking into the clearing. The rifle remained on the rock. No movement.

Then she heard a light moan.

"Who's there?" she called out.

"Help . . . me . . . uhh . . ."

"Identify yourself!"

"Louis . . . Freund . . ."

"You're hit?"

"Uhh . . ." His voice died out. Either he was a brilliant actor or he was truly in bad shape.

Annie continued toward the stream. She reached the bank, tested the water, and then plunged forward. It felt like ice. She drew a loud intake of breath through her teeth and suppressed a yelp as she moved forward, one leg after the other, until the water level rose to her lower thighs.

It took a couple of minutes, but she made it without losing her balance on the rocky bottom. It was the one case in which her sneakers and their rubber traction had come in handy. Annie climbed up the other bank, drew her weapon, and moved slowly toward the clump of rock and brush. She pulled the flashlight out of her pocket with the other hand and flicked it on. From twenty yards away, she recognized Freund's Winchester Model 70.

"Show me your hands!"

She heard another groan.

Annie took a few steps forward. "Mr. Freund? Show me your hands!"

"Can't . . ."

She believed him. Annie approached, skirted around the brush, and saw that Louis Freund lay on his back, one hand covering a serious wound at the base of his neck on the right side.

That was *a lucky shot!* she told herself, adding that to the list of extraordinary events that had occurred so far that night.

Annie squatted beside him, first running the beam over his body to make sure he wasn't hiding another weapon. "Where's Paley?" she asked.

Freund's eyes were clenched shut in pain. He tried to shake his head. "Don't . . . know . . ." His voice was a crackly whisper.

"Is anyone else nearby?"

"Maybe . . . Ma . . . kar . . . I think . . ."

"And the girl? Jason?"

Freund barely shook his head.

Annie gently moved his hand, telling him to let her see. He was bleeding profusely. Although she hadn't severed his spine, she had possibly hit an artery.

He was going to die if he didn't get medical attention quickly.

She hated to be cruel, but she thought . . . *tough shit.*

Annie reached for his trouser pocket, frisked him through the fabric, and felt the jiggle of metal objects. Her car keys. She pocketed them, went over and picked up the rifle, and stood over his head. "I'll get you help when I can. As you know, it's a little hard to call the *authorities* out here. I'm sorry. Is there anything you want to tell me?"

He just stared at her and bared his teeth, like a wild animal.

"Keep pressing on your neck. It's all you can do for n—"

"Hey! Come back! Trey! I found them! Over here!"

The shout wasn't far away. Near the stream.

It was followed by a gunshot.

Annie turned and moved in that direction. She slipped the Winchester sling around her shoulder to wear it on her back and drew the Glock. With the flashlight in her left hand, she allowed the beam to lead the way, although dawn was beginning to creep over the forest.

Although she tried to be focused on the task at hand, Annie couldn't help thinking, *Have I just killed a man?*

If so, it would be the first time. She attempted to identify any feelings that might have bubbled to the surface, but found that she couldn't. She had expected to be upset, maybe a little remorseful, or at the least a bit shocked. But she felt nothing. The emotions weren't there. What did that mean?

It means you're pissed off that you have to do this, she told herself. *You're having to clean up the ugly* mess *these misogynists have made.*

"Trey! Over here!"

She hurtled forward toward the sound. Locating the source, however, proved more difficult than she thought it would be. Annie decided to flick off the flashlight to avoid being seen by the caller, whom she presumed to be Makar. She thought she had detected an accent in the speech. Had he found Jason and Yana?

Annie pushed ahead, ignoring the scrapes and slashes of tree branches and brush. Five, ten minutes went by. She feared she had missed him, or he had moved on farther ahead.

The ground ahead was darker, some kind of hole. Annie turned on the flashlight and cast the beam over the terrain. There was a body in a shallow depression. She approached carefully, shined the light over the head and torso, and she winced. The man had been severely beaten with a blunt object. She squatted closer. It was indeed Makar Utkin.

Who did this? Trey? Not Jason! *No way . . .*

She couldn't imagine Jason Ward inflicting this kind of violence on another person. Had Trey gone off on one of his alleged anger spurts and murdered his best friend? Not likely. It couldn't have been his *father,* or could it? No, that wasn't rational. It had to be either Jason or . . . *the trafficking victim*. Of course. Yana Kravec, whether she was traveling with Jason or not, must have committed the deed. She would have possessed the hatred and need for vengeance.

Annie moved on, thinking that all of this had to end soon before others lost their lives.

39

Daylight was slowly streaming through the branches and leaves. Birdsong filled the air, replacing the drone of insects. The gray dawn brought a mist that hovered over the ground, reminding Jason of paintings that depicted fantasy scenarios—he had a wild incongruous thought that Little Red Riding Hood or Hansel and Gretel might show up. As long as the Big Bad Wolf stayed away, that'd be all right.

As he and Yana stumbled along, he kept thinking, *Where the hell is a road? The lake? Anything?*

The forest seemed endless. He had no idea how far they were from the cabin or his car or any sort of civilization. He was about ready to stop and veer toward the stream just to give them a better geographical landmark, but Yana's legs suddenly buckled. She collapsed and rolled on to her side, coughing and wheezing.

"Yana?" He halted and knelt beside her. She made a soft choking sound as she cleared her throat and spit dark phlegm.

"Sorry . . ." she said.

"That's okay." He wasn't doing so well, either. The gash on his leg wasn't deep, but it still bled. His trouser leg was soaked in dark redness, and he'd been tracking a little as he hiked.

"I can't go on . . ." There were tears in her eyes. "I can't . . ."

"We have to. There's *got* to be a road somewhere soon. Look, it's morning. There will be people out. We'll find someone to help us." She continued to breathe heavily, her eyes closed. Jason felt her forehead—she was burning up. "Damn, you have a fever."

He stood and took a good look at their surroundings. Nothing in sight but trees. Where could Trey be? It was only a matter of time before he tracked them down.

"All right, let's rest," he said. "For a little while."

He removed Makar's rifle from his back and set it on the ground, and he sat on a flat rock beside her. Examining the wound on his leg, Jason saw that it was dirty, black, and ugly. He imagined that all sorts of germs were having a grand time infecting it, and if he ever got back to the real world he'd end up losing the limb to gangrene.

Would be my luck . . .

Jason reached in his pocket and pulled out the cell phone. It was down to 18 percent of battery life, but he felt a burst of excitement when he saw that there was a single bar of service on the grid.

"Holy shit!" He punched "talk" and heard a dial tone. Jason immediately dialed 9-1-1. His heart picked up its rhythm when he heard ringing on the other end. The call answered—and a voice recording said, "All of our operators are busy. Please hold the line and someone will be with you as quickly as possible."

"*Really?*" He cursed aloud. "At 6 a.m. on a Saturday? They're *busy?*"

He waited as an elevator music arrangement of "Nights in White Satin" played in his ear. It made him want to throw up.

Then the connection filled with static. "Shit." He stood, his leg smarting as he did so. He'd been ignoring the pain up to that point, but there was nothing he could do about it as it worsened. He moved away from Yana, limping forward in an attempt to gain a better service signal. The line went in and out as the song selection switched to "Norwegian Wood (This Bird Has Flown)." Jason said aloud, "You've got to be fucking kidding me . . ."

He stopped and gasped, staring straight ahead.

Two black bear cubs stood watching him, positioned about twenty feet away. Their backs were around three feet high from the ground and their bodies were slender. Jason had read a little about bears when he was considering joining Mr. Paley on a hunting trip. Mother bears usually had their cubs in winter, so by August the little ones would be six or seven months old. Small enough to still look like cubs, but big enough to be dangerous. Because at that age, the cubs were still living with—

Jason immediately ended the call and froze.

—their mother.

The animals stood next to some kind of berry bush, where many of the small globules of fruit had fallen on the ground under it. Both bears made vocal noises not quite mature enough to be threatening growls as they stood their ground. Jason turned his head left and right, searching for other movement nearby. She had to be around. It was breakfast time; the mom and her teenagers were out looking for food. These bears were old enough to wander away from Mama, and they had found a treasure—but they wouldn't have roamed far. Mama bears *fiercely* protected their young at that age.

Shit, I left Makar's rifle on the ground next to Yana!

His next inclination was to run back to his companion, hoist her up, and hightail it toward the stream—but before he could do so, the bears abruptly turned away and concentrated on the berries, ignoring him. He was amazed they hadn't run away from *him*, the mysterious beast on two legs.

Jason thought his heart wouldn't stop pounding. He breathed deeply, grateful that nothing worse than a stare-down occurred.

Then she appeared. The mama bear came into view and approached the young ones as if to herd them along. She was huge. On all fours, she appeared to be close to five feet high. Her nose went to the ground to scarf up some berries, but then she lifted her head. The snout's nostrils were flexing, smelling something *strange* in the air. The beast lowered its head and looked directly at Jason.

He swiftly turned without thinking and quickly walked back the way he had come.

Don't look back, don't run, walk away, don't look back, go quick, don't run . . .

He looked back anyway. The spot with the berry bush wasn't visible anymore—it was just beyond a bend around a tree and some brush that now blocked his sightline. The bear wasn't chasing him.

Jason turned again and kept walking, now a little faster. Yana was just up ahead; he hadn't wandered very far from her . . .

He stopped. He was at the spot. He recognized the flat rock he'd sat on earlier, but Makar's rifle was gone. There was a depression in the dirt where Yana had been—but there was no Yana.

Fuck!

"Yana?"

"Where is she?" came the voice at his side.

Trey Paley stood next to a tree, fifteen feet away. He held his Win Mag .458 high, aimed at Jason.

"Trey!"

"Where is she, goddamn it! Before I blow your head off."

Jason held up his hands. "Don't shoot! Trey! For God's sake . . . !"

"You have three seconds to tell me where she is and then I'm drilling you. If you run, I'll shoot you in the back. I'm an Airborne Rangers marksman."

Jason didn't doubt him.

Think fast! Where is Yana?

"One . . ."

Jason couldn't speak. He tried to say something, anything, but his throat wouldn't function.

"Two . . ."

Jason pointed behind him, back toward the berry bush. "She's there," he managed to whisper. "She needed . . . she needed some privacy."

Trey walked forward, his eye still on the sight and the barrel pointed at his target. He got within ten feet and stopped. "Do you know what this gun will do to you at this range?"

"I . . . I think so."

Trey jerked his head in the direction Jason had pointed. "Lead on."

"You better go first."

"No, *you* take me to her."

Crap!

Jason kept his hands raised and started limping back to the berry bush. Trey assumed a position directly behind him, the gun still pointed straight ahead. Jason felt his presence, six or seven feet away, bringing up the rear.

He rounded the tree and saw the berry bush, twenty yards straight ahead. No bears. He continued to walk forward, his eyes darting left and right, hunting for the animals. Had they run away? Bears normally avoid people—unless they're threatened.

Within seconds, Jason reached the bush. Berries lay scattered on the ground. Trey stood a few feet away, the gun still raised. "Well?"

"She . . . uh, she was right here. I left her here."

"Call her."

Jason didn't know if that would attract the mama bear or send her fleeing. "Yana!"

They stood there a few seconds, but there was no return call. However, a rustling sound to the left was approaching—*fast*. Something large, heavy, and *full of power*.

Jason bolted and ran past Trey.

"Hey!" Trey shouted, but by then the bear was upon him. He screamed in terror as the beast rose on her hind legs, roared with the volume of a foghorn, and fell forward, its massive claws outstretched to knock the intruder down. Trey was unable to fire the rifle as the bear mauled him with a strong swipe of her paw.

Jason caught just a glimpse of the flurry of black fur, claws, and blood as he continued to run, past the spot where Yana had rested and into the woods that hopefully led to the stream. He kept going blindly, the fear overtaking him, knowing he was about to lose his life in the next few seconds—

"Jason!"

Yana appeared from behind a tree, with Makar's Win Mag in her hands.

"Run!" He shot past her.

"Jason! Wait!"

He managed to slow a little as she gathered the energy to join him.

"I saw the soldier!" she said.

Another cry from Trey knifed through the mist, and they heard a horrible roar from the beast.

"I know! There's a bear, too! Run!"

They did so for at least a full minute. There were no more screams behind them, but that didn't slow them down. Before they knew it, they had reached the clearing and the stream. Jason stopped Yana and put his hands on his knees, trying to catch his breath. He didn't believe the bear would chase them out in the open; and besides, the beast had already caught one of the interlopers in her domain.

"Did you say that was a *bear*?"

He nodded. "She got Trey. I don't know if he made it." He scanned the stream. "Come on, let's follow the flow. I don't think we have anything to worry about now." He eyed the rifle she was holding. "You want me to take that?"

She handed it over and he held it with both hands, ready to shoot at any threat.

Then, miraculously, a figure appeared from the woods on their side of the stream. A woman dressed in blue jeans. Dark hair . . . very familiar to Jason . . .

"*Annie?*"

"Jason! Oh my God!" She ran toward them.

Jason took Yana's arm. "Come on, she's a friend. She's works for the government."

Yana stiffened. "She will send me back to Russia."

"No she won't."

Annie reached them and Jason threw his arms around her in the tightest embrace he'd ever delivered. "My God, I'm glad to see you!"

"Me, too!" Annie laughed and held the hug. Then they separated and she looked at Jason's companion.

"Annie, this is Yana Kravec."

"I thought so." She held out a hand. "I'm Annie Marino. FBI. I've been looking for you."

Yana tentatively held out a hand and shook it.

Annie turned back to Jason. "I thought I heard someone scream."

Jason gave her a quick rundown of what had just transpired.

"Jesus," Annie said. "I think we better get to my car as soon as we can find it. I might know the way, now that it's morning." She saw his bloody trouser leg. "Oh, Christ, what happened?"

"Cut my leg on a log. I'll live, I think. Yana's pretty sick, though. I'm not sure what she's got."

Annie put an arm around her as they approached the water. "We have to cross the stream," she said. "Can you make it?"

Yana coughed and nodded. "I crossed an ocean. I can cross this," she said.

40

Jason and Annie helped Yana cross the stream again without incident. They followed it a ways on the opposite bank before Jason remembered his cell phone. "Hey, maybe we have service here, it's more open to the sky." He dug it out of his pocket.

Annie rolled her eyes and cursed herself for not thinking of that. She did the same and found several bars of signal "I got it," she said. She dialed 9-1-1, identified herself to an operator, and explained the situation. When it came to providing their location, she was at a loss. "Jason, pull up a map on your phone and use the GPS to find out where the hell we are."

He did so. They were very close to the small lake that abutted the Paley property. Apparently, they had been in national forest land, having roamed into it by crossing the stream the first time. Over the phone, Annie did her best to describe the condition of the road leading to the cabin—that it was blocked with vehicles approximately two miles away from the building. The operator promised that police, EMTs, and a couple of tow trucks would be at the site in thirty minutes.

"You know," Jason said to Annie, "I have your number in my phone. I might have called you last night if I'd had service at the cabin."

"Don't think I would've been much help," she answered, thinking about her own adventure.

The trio eventually worked their way to the edge of the body of water shown on the map. "This is a pond, not a lake," Jason muttered. There were no people in sight. Nevertheless, Annie was able to navigate their path and approximate where the cabin probably stood in relation to the water. She pointed to the woods on that side.

"We have to go through there. It shouldn't be too far. I don't see any trails; do you?"

Jason held a hand over his brow. The sun was already in full view, blocking his vision. "No."

Annie looked at Yana, who was very pale and wheezing loudly. She stood with her head down, weak and ready to collapse. "Can you make it, Yana?"

The woman nodded.

"Okay, let's go."

They found the cabin sooner than they expected, but law enforcement authorities had not yet arrived. Annie held the other two back as she scanned the clearing around the structure. There was no movement or sound.

"Wait here," she whispered. Drawing the Glock, Annie sprinted to the side of the cabin and flattened her back against the log wall. She inched around to the front door, held the weapon with both hands, and kicked. The door swung open and she swept the room with the pistol outstretched. The living area was empty. She quickly checked both bedrooms and the bathroom. Greg Paley wasn't there.

She went back outside and signaled for Jason and Yana to come on in. The first thing Jason did was go to the refrigerator and look for food. He found sandwich meat and cheese, but no bread. It would do. Annie told Yana to lie down on the sofa, then she turned to Jason and said she'd be right back. She left the cabin, went around to the back, followed the path to the shed, and found the padlock on the door of the shed as she'd left it. She dug out the keys and unlocked the door.

"Let me out of here!" Baines hollered. He lay on the bed, battered and blue.

"Not yet," she answered. "Just making sure you were still with us." She closed the door and replaced the padlock. The next order of business was to get to her Bucar.

Back at the cabin, she consumed several bites of the lunch meat and cheese that Jason had prepared for them. As her eyes rested on him, Annie felt satisfaction in trusting her instincts on Jason. He *was* one of the good guys. He was a goddamned hero. "You're really something, Jason," she said between bites.

"What?"

"What you did."

He shook his head. "Anybody would have done it." He shrugged, somewhat sheepishly.

Annie reflected on Jason's bravery. It was a testament to the human spirit that a brainy writer who normally sat with a laptop in Starbucks could have pulled off what he did.

After a few minutes, she felt strong enough to keep going. "Stay here," she said. "Keep your gun handy. Greg Paley is still at large"

"Greg Paley? He's here?"

Annie cocked her head. "Oh, that's right. You don't know, do you?"

"Know what?"

She nodded at Yana. "Your future father-in-law is responsible for all of this. He's the big boss."

Jason's jaw dropped. "No way!"

"Yes, way. Look after Yana. I'm going to check on our cars."

She went down the road toward Highway 82, her eyes darting in all directions as she moved. Paley could very well be hiding behind a tree, waiting for her to show up. The smart thing to do would probably have been to wait at the cabin for the authorities, but she was too restless.

The only sounds she heard were birds chirping in their natural habitat. The woods were truly beautiful—in the right context—but she had had enough of them. She longed to be back in her apartment in Chicago with the noise of the city invading her solace. That was more her speed. As she approached the cars, the unmistakable stench of skunk blanketed the area. Annie winced and kept going until she finally reached the site. What she found registered a bit of a shock.

Her Ford Fusion had been battered off the road and was crushed against the trees on one side. The Lincoln Continental was gone. Paley had rammed the Bucar repeatedly until he'd cleared enough space for himself to reverse past her car, turn around, and escape. In the process, he had encountered a skunk and shot it—its furry carcass lay on the road in the tire tracks.

Annie pulled out her cell phone to report that a suspect had fled in a rental car, most likely with a lot of damage to its rear end.

Then she heard the sirens approaching.

An all points bulletin went out nationwide for Greg Paley and the Continental, which they learned had originally been rented at the Detroit airport. Oddly, it was later found that afternoon parked behind the Lakeway police station. The back end was indeed crunched like an accordion, and the vehicle reeked of skunk. Greg Paley, however, was nowhere to be found. It was suspected that he had either stolen another car and fled, or that he was picked up by an accomplice. The APB still stood.

The Paley cabin became a beehive of activity for the rest of the day, which would most likely continue for most of the following week. Yana and Jason were taken to Spectrum Health Hospital in Big Rapids. Captain Mike Baines was arrested and also taken to the hospital for examination. He was released later in the day to the county sheriff and moved to a jail cell in White Cloud.

Louis Freund had miraculously survived by pressing his hand against the wound in his neck. He was arrested and also sent to the hospital. His loss of blood put him on the critical list, but he was a tough individual and was expected to live. The bodies of Trey Paley and Makar Utkin were recovered and transported to the county morgue after forensic detectives had thoroughly examined the crime scenes. Utkin's cause of death was blunt trauma. Paley had been mauled, his jugular vein slashed open. It was suspected that the bear had clawed him only once or twice and then fled, leaving the human to die.

Annie, exhausted and irritable, submitted to multiple interrogations. Eventually, she was able to reach SSA Gladden at home, and he immediately arranged for an FBI attorney to show up and represent the Special Agent at the county sheriff's office. Her Glock 22 was retrieved from the locked cubby in the Lakeway police station, and she handed over Captain Baines's weapon as evidence. The sheriff treated Annie to a full dinner, after which she learned that Jason had been patched up and released from the hospital. Yana, however, would remain for a while. She was diagnosed with pneumonia, as well as complications from physical and emotional abuse.

Jason repeatedly told his story to several different investigators during the day. He had wanted to say goodbye to Yana before leaving the hospital, but was informed that she had been sedated and was asleep. Several police officers told him that he was a "hero," and they treated him to a good meal, though Jason kept insisting that it was Special Agent Annie Marino who was the real hero. The police finally took him to retrieve his Elantra, which had been towed to White Cloud. The smart thing would have been to stay in a hotel that night, but he was anxious to get back to Chicago. He'd gotten a second wind after dinner, and he wanted the Michigan forest to be far behind him. When he asked if he could speak to Annie, he was told that she would be unavailable for some time. At close to nine o'clock that night, Jason hit the road.

There was one voice message on his phone from Natalia, asking him to call her back. When he returned it, she didn't answer. He tried several more times along his route back home, to no avail. Once he reached Chicago, he knew full well that she would have received his own message and seen the call records by now.

Nat obviously didn't want to talk to him.

By late Saturday night, Annie was allowed to go home. The problem was that she had no car. Annie decided to spend the night in Big Rapids so she could check on Yana in the morning; she had a lot of questions for the trafficking survivor. A sheriff's deputy gave her a ride to the Quality Inn & Suites on Highway 131, a no-frills motel chain with which the Bureau had a discount deal. It was after midnight by the time she checked in, and she had no toiletries or change of clothes. After spending the night in the forest, her clothes were dirty, odorous, and, as far as she was concerned, ready for the garbage bin. Her plan was to shower, sleep, and rent a car in the morning. She'd pick up some essential clothing at Walmart, put on fresh clothes, speak to Yana, and then drive back to Chicago. The investigation would continue for days, weeks, and possibly months. Gladden had told her she was still in charge of the case. He also said that the Bureau was "mighty proud" of what she had done, praise that made her smile involuntarily into the phone.

At the moment, though, all she wanted to do was get cleaned up and crawl into bed.

The clerk on duty at the motel informed her of a vending machine that contained items such toothbrushes, toothpaste, and other necessities, located with the ice dispenser in an alcove behind the office. She thanked him and practically sleepwalked to her room on the ground floor. She wanted to grab the ice bucket from the room first, so she could fill it as well as get supplies from the machines in one trip. Her room was clean, with a queen-sized bed, a TV, and a bathroom with a shower. Perfect. Annie didn't bother to remove her drop holster and weapon; it was a comfort to have her own gun back. She had felt even dirtier carrying around the Glock that belonged to the treacherous Baines.

Annie picked up the plastic ice container from the bathroom and left, allowing the door to remain ajar against the latch. She was too tired to think about having to use her key card again, and it was only fifty feet to the machines. As she approached the alcove, she glanced at the parking lot. It was a slow night—not many vehicles were at the motel; just a couple of SUVs, a Toyota Corolla, and two pickup trucks, one black and one red.

She filled up the bucket with ice and spent some money in the machine for a toothbrush, toothpaste, and a candy bar. There would be shampoo and soap in the room.

With her hands full, she walked back to her room. It was a pleasant August night—not hot or muggy but nice and cool, and the air was fresh with . . .

Her nostrils picked up an all-too familiar stench.

Jesus, they sure have a skunk problem in Michigan, don't they . . .

She came within three feet of her room door, which was still ajar, and stopped. Even with the fatigue that dragged her down, the instincts that her old Quantico instructor had told her to trust kicked in.

Skunk?

Annie turned and looked back at the parking lot.

The black pickup truck. It was the same one that had been parked behind the Lakeway police station when she'd first driven in on Friday night. Had Greg Paley dropped off the smashed-up Lincoln Continental and taken the black pickup? Did it belong to Louis Freund?

Quietly, she placed the ice bucket and toiletries on the sidewalk. She drew the Glock and flattened against the wall with the door to her left.

Can I do this? Should I call for backup? What if I'm wrong?

Again—the instincts. They told her to go for it. She'd never been in a situation like this, but she'd had the training.

Her adrenaline was pumping so hard that her exhaustion was no longer an issue.

Very slowly, she stretched out her left arm, placed the hand on the door—and pushed it open.

Gunfire erupted from inside the room, blasting the empty space in the doorway. As soon as the shooter realized there was no one standing there, the firing ceased. Annie dropped to the pavement on her right side, both hands on her weapon, and blindly fired six times into the room. It was only after she released her finger from the trigger that she was aware of the figure who had been standing in the room and was now lying on the carpet.

Greg Paley.

Annie bolted into the room and kicked his weapon—a Smith & Wesson M&P9—back toward the bathroom where he couldn't reach it. She then stooped to examine the damage. Paley was still dressed in the same clothes he'd been wearing the night before. The smell of skunk was almost overbearing.

He had been hit by three of the six rounds—in the chest, the abdomen, and the right leg. He was alive, gritting his teeth, and glaring at her. She was sure that with quick medical care, he would survive.

It had been stupid to leave the door ajar—she knew that now. He must have somehow kept tabs on her throughout the day, followed her to the motel, and waited for his opportunity.

Annie pulled out her cell phone, dialed 9-1-1, and asked for the police and an ambulance. When she hung up, she knelt beside him again. There were a hundred things she wanted to say to him, most of them not nice at all. Instead she told him what was an undeniable truth.

"You really *stink*, Mr. Paley . . . in more ways than one."

41

October

The indictments came down seven weeks after the weekend at the Michigan cabin. Annie attended a press conference in which Chicago Special Agent in Charge Michael Tilden announced the victory to the public. The investigation had been a joint operation between the FBI, ICE, local police and sheriff organizations in six states, and Russia's FSB. The Offices of United States Attorneys in the same number of states had a total of twenty-three prosecutors involved. It was one of the most complex cases of human trafficking that the government had processed.

Special Agent Annie Marino received a Director's Award for "Excellence in Criminal Investigation" for her work in tying together the pieces of the puzzle. The Bear Claws Case would become a textbook example of cooperation between numerous individuals and agencies.

Captain Mike Baines had flipped and provided plenty of evidence against Greg Paley and Louis Freund. He managed to secure a deal that would lessen his prison sentence if he pled guilty and testified for the prosecution. Freund had also attempted to make a deal but was denied. Paley faced multiple felony charges, including human trafficking, civil rights offenses, accessory to murder, attempted murder of a federal officer, money laundering, and racketeering. The evidence gathered was irrefutable. Investigators were also reopening David Paley's case of accidental death. Freund revealed to the police that he had witnessed Greg Paley shoot his own brother and created a cover-up in order to gain control of their father's company. Both Paley and Freund were going away for a long time, but their trials wouldn't commence for many more months. As for Palit Wool, Angela Paley had put the company up for sale. She was fortunate that her husband had wisely kept the legitimate business separate from his criminal activities.

Thanks to the information gained from Yana Kravec and other witnesses who were interviewed during the month of September, several arrests were made in New Jersey and Illinois. Robert "Bobby" Malik, Nadine Bartha, and Abram Tarr, the trio who ran the house in Newark where Yana had first been held captive after arriving in the US, were picked up by authorities before they could flee. Serbian immigrants Butch Janko and Fidel Loncar, who drove the van from New Jersey to Chicago, were also arrested. In Illinois, Ivan Polzin, Ludwig Vasiliev, Boris Modesky, and Sasha Treblinka were implicated and charged with lesser offenses—they, too, provided incriminating evidence against their employers. The Den, the Cat's Lounge, and Paradise strip clubs were permanently closed. Alexander Broughton and Freddie Smith, who operated the house in Chicago where Yana had been kept, were shot and killed during a police raid.

It was highly suspected that Greg Paley himself had been the disguised bag man in Milwaukee to whom Joseph Flanagan had paid money for Helena Nikolaev. Prosecutors were unable to prove this, but Annie was confident that Paley was the culprit. The salesman in that case, the man known as "Petyr," was never found. In any case, Eyepatch, LLC's money laundering mechanisms were uncovered, and the shell company was completely dismantled.

Forensics analysis on Trey Paley's weapons proved that he had indeed been the sniper who had killed Tiffany Vombrack and shot Harris Caruthers. Now back in Detroit, Caruthers was still recuperating from the shooting, on leave from the FBI for several months. While he was scheduled to appear as a witness in the upcoming trials, he had told Annie privately that he wasn't planning to return to the Bureau. She let him know that she considered this a mistake, but that she respected his decision. "Don't pull the plug for good until after you're well and the bad guys are convicted in court. You may change your mind then," she told him.

Much of the Russian connection did not escape the hands of justice. Evgeni Palit was arrested by the FSB and charged with a number of crimes associated with the trafficking operation. Palit Wool's St. Petersburg facility would be sold along with its US counterpart. A Russian container ship called the *Okulovka* was impounded in the Big Port of St. Petersburg. Several members of its crew, along with its captain, were taken into custody for conspiracy, international trafficking, and money laundering. Their fates would be decided by the Russian courts. ALAT Colin Clark and his undercover investigators provided enough evidence to send them away for a long time.

The only hitch in sewing up the network was locating and arresting Nikolai Babikov and any of his colleagues in the Novgorod mafia. Babikov had gone into hiding. Despite picking up various members of the organization and questioning them for days, no one would give up their chief. Such was the powerful hold the criminal outfit had on its men. Additionally, both Annie and the ALAT were convinced that government corruption in Russia protected Babikov. It was going to take a lot more than murder, kidnapping, trafficking, and racketeering to put a man like him behind bars. In that part of the world, this was an unfortunate truth.

Still, Annie was very pleased with the outcome. She had solved the case. She had done her job.

42

Yana Kravec announced her arrival and waited only a minute in the reception area of Safe Haven, the not-for-profit organization in Indianapolis, before Miranda Ward emerged from behind the door. Miranda smiled and held out her hand.

"Yana! How are you?"

Yana stood and shook Miranda's hand. "Okay. I am fine."

"Glad you could come. Come on back. Let's talk before we go to lunch."

The two women went down a hall past several offices until they reached the small office at the end, which Yana had been to before. Miranda had said that the human trafficking division consisted of just her for now, and that her office was the size of a "closet." It was indeed a little claustrophobic.

"Have a seat." Miranda gestured to the familiar chair in front of the desk. Yana removed her light jacket and sat. "So! You've completed all the forms and turned them in."

Yana nodded and smiled. "I have. That's all done."

"Good. I think I told you last time that it takes about six months for the naturalization process to complete."

"Yes."

"Okay. So we just have to wait, right?"

Yana nodded.

"How's the apartment?"

Yana smiled again and said, timidly, "I like it. It is nice."

It was really a space in a shelter and residence building owned by Safe Haven. It provided temporary residence for women and children who needed a place to stay, whether they were escaping abusive husbands or, like Yana, had been victims of other crimes against women. Yana didn't plan on staying there long.

Miranda sensed her hesitance. "Be honest, Yana, are you comfortable there?"

"Yes. It is fine for now."

"You said you had applied for a job?"

Yana held her hands in her lap and nodded. "It is for a barista position."

Miranda nodded, paused, and wrinkled her brow. "How are you feeling?" she asked more softly.

Yana was unable to look at her in the eyes. "I don't know. The nightmares won't go away."

"You've talked to the doctor about it?"

She nodded. The female psychiatrist she was referred to by Safe Haven was very warm and understanding, but Yana didn't consider herself a good patient. The shock of gaining freedom from such a horrid experience was a considerable emotional rollercoaster. First, she had struggled to get over the pneumonia and gain back her strength, which took nearly a month. While she'd been in the hospital in Michigan, Jason and his sister had come to visit, and it was Miranda's suggestion that Yana move to Indianapolis when she was able. The female FBI agent in Chicago and a federal attorney she had brought in had also been instrumental in arranging things legally for Yana after her ordeal. In short, her fear that the US "authorities" would deport her was unfounded. Nevertheless, she was still in pain. In the hush of the night, she continued to relive her experiences. Supposedly, the antidepressants would halt the daily tears, but her doctor had said that it could take at least a month for the pills to kick in. It had been longer than that, and she still didn't feel any better.

Miranda was gentle. "It takes time, Yana. It can take a *long* time, and it's possible there will always be bad . . . feelings. But you're doing the right things. You'll get through it."

She held a tissue box out for Yana, who took one to wipe her watering eyes. She nodded and said, "Yes, I know. Thank you."

"You're not convinced."

Yana smiled but shook her head.

"What have the other victims you met said?"

Two other women who had been trafficked were at the residence building. Yana hadn't known them before. "That it gets better."

"Yes. That's right."

"But I am so angry!" She spat it out, as if the pronouncement had been building in a pressure cooker. The tears came again. She took another tissue.

"Being angry is okay, Yana. You're right to be angry. And you're going to testify at the trials. That will empower you, Yana. Putting those men behind bars will go a long way toward giving you some kind of closure. Look, it will always be a memory, a part of you—but you will one day be able to live with it."

Yana managed to get hold of herself after a moment. "I am sorry."

"Don't be sorry. It's okay, you can tell me anything, it's why I'm here. You getting hungry? I promised I'd take you to lunch today."

"That would be very nice," Yana said.

"Okay, let's go. There's a good sandwich shop down the block. We'll walk, is that all right?"

"Yes."

"One other thing." She handed Yana an envelope. "It's a letter from your parents."

Yana's eyes bulged. "For . . . for me?"

"Yes."

She started to open it, but stopped. "I will read later. It will make me cry, I think."

"That's all right. Take it with you."

Yana Kravec followed Miranda out of the building and into the coolness of fall. Safe Haven was located a few blocks from the public library on busy Pennsylvania Street. She liked Indianapolis so far. It was nothing like St. Petersburg, but she wasn't interested anymore in the kind of excitement for which she had run away from home. While it could be very much a "city," Indianapolis was much more subdued. That suited her for now.

In her mind, she knew that Miranda was right. Healing *would* take time. Yana was smart enough to see herself objectively. She was aware that she was hurting, but she also had the fortitude and courage to move on. As the man who rescued her—Jason—had told her at the end of that long, wretched night, "You're Wonder Woman, Yana. Don't forget that."

Yes, it was going to take time . . . but things *would* be better in America.

Annie parked the new 2013 Ford Fusion—she had asked for an upgrade and managed to get only five years' worth—at the Cakewell Apartments lot, got out, and stretched. It was Thursday, nearly eight o'clock in the evening, and she was just getting home from the office. Her work had actually increased since August, and there were still plenty of loose ends to chase in the Bear Claws Case. The investigation was by no means finished—it would rumble on until the dates of the individual trials.

For fifteen minutes, she'd been a celebrity at the FO, but she knew not to let it go to her head. Many agents received their own fifteen minutes, sometimes more than once. More often than not, though, agents worked their asses off to solve cases behind the scenes, invisibly, only to have the resolutions credited to local law enforcement or other agencies. It was the nature of the FBI.

Although she was beat from a long day, Annie was more dedicated than ever to the job, and particularly to her area of the Bureau. After experiencing firsthand the horror of what had happened to women like Yana Kravec, she knew there were never enough hours.

The tap dancing would continue to suffer. She had told Derek that if she showed up for a lesson—great. If not—tough. He understood and insisted that she not worry about it.

The increasing time at work also meant, of course, that Annie still had no one with whom to share her personal life outside of the office. That might have been nice. Certainly not with a man like Eric, though. She knew she was over him when he had left a message on her voicemail to congratulate her, and she never bothered to call him back. It wasn't a priority. Having someone to date wasn't a necessity by any means, but still, it would be . . . nice.

Before heading to the Cakewell building, a sixth sense somehow directed her to the Starbucks across the street. She followed her intuition and, sure enough, he was sitting at the table in front of his laptop.

"There she is," Jason Ward said. "Are you stalking me?"

Annie grinned as she sat across from him. "Back at it, are you?"

"Not really. Pretending to. Class didn't let out until five-thirty, and then I went to hear an author friend speak at a book-signing, and after that I walked home. I picked up my mail—" he indicated a small stack of envelopes on the table—"and changed my mind. I turned around and ended up here. Not sure why. I even brought my mail with me. And here I am."

"Mm. So should I ask how you're doing?"

He shrugged. "Oh, I'm good. You?"

"Just busy. It's nuts."

"I can imagine."

"Everything going okay with the attorney?"

"Yep. Nothing to do right now. We'll have some more talks before the trial."

There was an awkward pause, and Annie started to get up to leave. Jason said, "Did I tell you that Nat and I are officially kaput?"

"You'd said the engagement was off."

"Yeah, well, we won't be seeing each other at all anymore."

Annie pursed her lips. "I'm sorry."

He shook his head. "No, don't be sorry. It's best that way. She won't denounce her father and brother. I guess I can sort of understand since they're *family* members and all, but still . . ." He sighed. "I think she kind of blames *me* for Trey's death."

Annie reached out and touched his hand. "She's wrong. You know that, right?"

"Yeah."

"But you're doing okay?"

"I am. I was dumbfounded by it all at first, you know? And then I was angry. And then I was just sad. I think Nat realized her brother was sick and twisted, but she was in denial. What she suspected or knew about her father I'll never know." He shook his head and glanced at the mail on the table. "Hey. Look here."

He pulled out an envelope addressed to him. Printed on the return label was *MAXIM PALEY* and the Highland Park address.

"Oh my. What's in it?"

He showed her. Inside was a small slip of paper from the notepad the old man kept in his lap. It read: *Sorry that my son and grandson are assholes. You, however, are not. Good luck to you.*

She raised her eyebrows. "How about that," she said.

"I can't imagine how *he* feels about everything." He shook his head again and tried to give Annie a smile. "Whatever."

"You sure you're okay, Jason?"

"Yeah. I'm just beginning to look ahead again. Going back to school for the teaching certificate helps. I'm focused. I don't dwell on it like I had been."

"Glad to hear it." She gave his hand a little squeeze and let go. She stood. "Well, see you later, neighbor."

"Hey."

"What?" She stopped and turned toward him again.

"Did you ever wonder about *me*? If I was involved with Trey and what he was doing? Wasn't it weird to you that there was this incredible *coincidence* here? The two of us being friends? Living so close to each other?"

She smiled. "I did wonder about that. It was just a coincidence. That's all it was. And don't worry . . . I trusted you. You were never a suspect in my book." It wasn't a lie. She might have had some early doubts, but her instincts about his character informed her otherwise.

"What might be coincidence for one person is destiny for someone else."

"Who said that?"

"I did."

She cocked her head at him. "Well, you're the writer."

He nodded. "Okay. See you." She started toward the door again. "Oh, hey."

She grinned again and turned back. "What now?"

"What are you doing this evening? I have a great bottle of cab I was going to open, and I was going to order a pizza. Would you like to come over and join me?"

Annie smiled. "Oh, that would be nice . . . but, not tonight, I'm just too bushed."

Are you really, Annie? she asked herself.

"Okay. Another time, then."

She left and walked the block to her building. Once upstairs and in her apartment with the door closed, she divested of all of her things from the day—weapon, purse, shoes—and smiled at the thought that Jason still found her attractive. And he wasn't so bad either, even if he was a few years younger than she.

Stop it. Jason was a material witness in a case.

Aloysius sauntered into the room and gave her a meow. "But it wouldn't be so wrong *after* the trials, would it?" she asked the cat. The animal rubbed against her leg and meowed again. "Think how convenient it would be. He lives right down the street. We could keep our own apartments. It'd be ideal." The cat meowed. "You don't know what the fuck I'm talking about, do you? Well, neither do I. Come on, let's get some grub."

She opened the fridge as the thought continued to linger in the back of her mind.

Another time.

Annie fed the purring animal, paused, and stuck her feet into her wedge heels.

"How the hell did that routine go? Oh, yeah . . ." She started to dance, reciting the moves in her head.

Right paradiddle, Left paradiddle
Right para para, Right paradiddle
Left paradiddle, Right paradiddle
Left para para, Left paradiddle
Right paradiddle, Left step
Left paradiddle, Right STOMP!

The FBI Civil Rights Unit provides these tips for identifying human trafficking violations:

For labor trafficking, look for any of the following being used to compel a person to provide labor or services: force or threat of force against *any* person; threat of serious harm to *any* person; threatened abuse of the legal system; and/or a scheme to place a person in fear of serious harm.

For sex trafficking, look for the following: a commercial sex act that was induced through force, fraud, or coercion, *or* a commercial sex act involving a person who is under the age of eighteen. Sex trafficking requires evidence of affecting interstate commerce.

More information can be found at www.fbi.gov.

ABOUT THE AUTHOR

Raymond Benson is the author of over thirty-five books and is primarily known for the five novels in his bestselling serial, *The Black Stiletto*, as well as for being the third—and first American—author of continuation James Bond novels between 1996 and 2002, penning six worldwide bestselling original 007 thrillers and three film novelizations. Raymond's other novels include *The Secrets on Chicory Lane*, *Sweetie's Diamonds*, *Evil Hours*, and *Dark Side of the Morgue* (Shamus Award nominee for Best Paperback Original), as well as several media tie-in works.

The author has taught courses in film history in New York and Illinois, and currently presents lectures about movies with *Daily Herald* film critic Dann Gire. Raymond is an active member of International Thriller Writers Inc., Mystery Writers of America, the International Association of Media Tie-In Writers, and a full member of ASCAP, and he served on the Board of Directors of the Ian Fleming Foundation for sixteen years. Raymond also happens to be a gigging musician and often performs around his base in the Chicago area.

www.raymondbenson.com
www.theblackstiletto.net